FABER AND FABER
has published children's
books since 1929. Some of
our very first publications
included *Old Possum's
Book of Practical Cats* by
T.S. Eliot starring the now
world-famous Macavity,
and *The Iron Man* by Ted
Hughes. Our catalogue
at the time said that 'it
is by reading such books
that children learn the
difference between the
shoddy and the genuine'.
We still believe in the
power of reading to
transform children's lives.

ABOUT THE AUTHOR

Lucy Boston was born in 1892 in Southport, Lancashire, one of six children. She went to a Quaker school in Surrey, and was married in 1917. She later moved to a beautiful manor house near Cambridge which provided the setting for her Green Knowe stories. She started writing at the age of sixty and won the Carnegie Medal for *A Stranger of Green Knowe* in 1961. Her books are illustrated by her son, Peter. Lucy Boston died in 1990.

VISIT THE GREEN KNOWE HOUSE

Lucy Boston wrote the Green Knowe stories about her own house and garden. It is a very old house built nearly 900 years ago, so it was easy for her to imagine all the different children living in the house in the past. She used to enjoy showing people the garden and the house. She particularly enjoyed showing people who had read the books, because they could then recognise some of the things they had read about in the stories.

To find out more about the house today, go to: www.greenknowe.co.uk

The Children of Green Knowe

and

The River at Green Knowe

LUCY M. BOSTON

ILLUSTRATED BY PETER BOSTON

faber and faber

The Children of Green Knowe was first published in 1954 and
The River at Green Knowe was first published in 1959
This bind-up edition first published in 2013
by Faber and Faber Limited
Bloomsbury House
74–77 Great Russell Street
London WC1B 3DA

Designed and typeset by Crow Books
Printed and bound by CPI Group (UK) Ltd, Croydon, CR0 4YY

A CIP record for this book is available from the British Library
ISBN 978–0–571–30347–2

FSC
www.fsc.org
MIX
Paper from
responsible sources
FSC® C101712

2 4 6 8 10 9 7 5 3 1

The Children of
Green Knowe

TO MY SON

A LITTLE BOY WAS SITTING IN the corner of a railway carriage looking out at the rain, which was splashing against the windows and blotching downward in an ugly, dirty way. He was not the only person in the carriage, but the others were strangers to him. He was alone as usual. There were two women opposite him, a fat one and a thin one, and they talked without stopping, smacking their lips in between sentences and seeming to enjoy what they said as much as if it were something to eat. They were knitting all the time, and whenever the train stopped the click-clack of their needles was loud and clear like two clocks. It was a stopping train – more stop than go – and it had been crawling along through flat flooded country for a long time. Everywhere there was water – not sea or rivers or lakes, but just senseless flood water with

3

the rain splashing into it. Sometimes the railway lines were covered by it, and then the train-noise was quite different, softer than a boat.

'I wish it was *the* Flood,' thought the boy, 'and that I was going to the Ark. That would be fun! Like the circus. Perhaps Noah had a whip and made all the animals go round and round for exercise. What a noise there would be, with the lions roaring, elephants trumpeting, pigs squealing, donkeys braying, horses whinnying, bulls bellowing, and cocks and hens always thinking they were going to be trodden on but unable to fly up on to the roof where all the other birds were singing, screaming, twittering, squawking and cooing. What must it have sounded like, coming along on the tide? And did Mrs Noah just knit, knit and take no notice?'

The two women opposite him were getting ready for the next station. They packed up their knitting and collected their parcels and then sat staring at the little boy. He had a thin face and very large eyes; he looked patient and rather sad. They seemed to notice him for the first time.

'What's your name, son?' asked the fat woman suddenly. 'I've never seen you on this train before.'

This was always a question he dreaded. Was he to say his unexpected real name or his silly pet names?

'Toseland,' he said.

'Toseland! That's a real old-fashioned name in these parts. There's Fen Toseland, and Toseland St Agnes and Toseland Gunning. What's your Christian name?'

'That is it – Toseland.'

'Do your mum and dad live round here, son?'

'No, they live in Burma.'

'Fancy that now! That's a long way away. Where are you going, then?'

'I don't know. That is, I'm going to my great-grandmother Oldknow at Green Noah. The station is Penny Soaky.'

'That's the next station after this. We get out here. Don't forget – the next station. And make sure there's some dry land before you get out of the train. The floods are bad there. Bye-bye, cheerio.'

They got out, shouting and joking with the porters and kissing the people who had come to meet them. They started off into the hissing rain as if they loved it. Toseland heard the fat woman's loud voice saying, 'Oh, I don't mind this. I like it, it's our home-rain, not like that dirty London water.'

The train jogged on again and now Toseland was quite alone. He wished he had a family like other people – brothers and sisters, even if his father were away. His mother was dead. He had a stepmother but he hardly knew her and was miserably shy of her. He had been at a boarding-school, and for the last holidays he had been left behind to stay with the head mistress, Miss Spudd, and her old father. They meant to be kind to him, but they never spoke to him without saying 'dear'. It was 'Finish up your porridge, dear, we don't want you to get thin,' or 'Put on your coat, dear, we don't want you to catch cold,' or 'Get ready for church, dear, we don't want you to grow up a heathen.' And every day after breakfast, 'Run along to your room, dear, we want to read the papers.'

But now his great-grandmother Oldknow had written that he was to come and live with her. He had never seen her, but she was his own great-grandmother, and that was something. Of course she would be very old. He thought of some old people he had seen who were so old that it frightened him. He wondered if she would be frighteningly old. He began to feel afraid already, and to shake it off he thought about Green Noah and

6

Penny Soaky. What queer names! Green Noah was pure mystery, but Penny Soaky was friendly like a joke.

Suddenly the train stopped, and the porters were shouting 'Penny Soaky! Penny Soaky!' Toseland had no sooner got the door open than a man wearing a taxi-driver's hat came along calling:

'Anybody here for Green Noah? Are you Master Toseland for Green Noah?'

'Oh yes, please. It's me.'

'This your luggage? Two more in the van? You stand here out of the rain while I get it.'

There were a few houses to be seen on one side of the line, and on the other nothing but flooded fields with hedges standing in the water.

'Come along,' said the taxi-man. 'I've put all your luggage in the car. It'll be dark before we get there and we've got to go through a lot of water.'

'Is it deep?'

'Not so deep, I hope, that we can't get through.'

'If it rains forty days and forty nights will it be a real flood?'

'Sure enough it would.'

Toseland sat by the driver and they set off. The windscreen wipers made two clear fans on the windscreen through which he could see the road half covered with water, with ditches brimming on either side. When they came near the bridge that crossed the river, the road disappeared under water altogether and they seemed to drive into the side of the river with a great splash that flew up against the windows; but it was only a few inches deep and then they reached the humpbacked bridge and went up and over it, and down again into deeper water on the other side. This time they drove very carefully like bathers walking out into cold water. The car crept along making wide ripples.

'We don't want to stick here,' said the driver, 'this car don't float.'

They came safely through that side too, and now the headlights were turned on, for it was growing dark, and Toseland could see nothing but rain and dazzle.

'Is it far?' he asked.

'Not very, but we have to go a long way round to get past the floods. Green Noah stands almost in the middle of it now, because the river runs alongside the garden. Once you get there you won't be able to get out again till the flood goes down.'

'How will I get in, then?'

'Can you swim?'

'Yes, I did twenty strokes last summer. Will that be enough?'

'You'll have to do better than that. Perhaps if you felt yourself sinking you could manage a few more?'

'But it's quite dark. How will I know where to swim to?'

The driver laughed. 'Don't you worry. Mrs Oldknow will never let you drown. She'll see you get there all right. Now here we are. At least, I can't go any further.' Toseland pushed the car door open and looked out. It had stopped raining. The car was standing in a lane of shallow water that stretched out into the dark in front and behind. The driver was wearing Wellington boots, and he got out and paddled round the car. Toseland was afraid that he would be left now to go on as best he could by himself. He did not like to show that he was afraid, so he tried another way of finding out.

'If I am going to swim,' he said, 'what will you do with my luggage?'

'You haven't got no gum boots, have you?' said the driver. 'Come on, get on my shoulders and we'll have a look round to see if anyone's coming to meet you.' Toseland climbed on to his shoulders and they set off, but almost at once they heard the sound of oars, and a lantern came round the corner of the lane rocking on the bows of a rowing boat. A man called out, 'Is that Master Toseland?' The driver shouted back, 'Is that Mr Boggis?' but Toseland was speechless with relief and delight.

'Good evening, Master Toseland,' said Mr Boggis, holding up the lantern to look at him, while Toseland looked too, and saw a nice old cherry-red face with bright blue eyes. 'Pleased to meet you. I knew your mother when she was your size. I bet you were wondering how you were going to get home?' It was nice to hear somebody talking about 'home' in that way. Toseland felt much happier, and now he knew that the driver had been teasing him, so he grinned and said: 'I was going to swim.'

The boat was moored to somebody's garden gate while the two men put the trunk and tuck-box into it.

'You'll be all right now,' said the taxi-man. 'Good night to you both.'

'Good night, and thank you,' said Toseland.

Mr Boggis handed him the lantern and told him to kneel up in the bows with it and shout if they were likely to bump into anything. They rowed round two corners in the road and then in at a big white gate.

Toseland waved the lantern about and saw trees and bushes standing in the water, and presently the boat was rocked by quite a strong current and the reflection of the lantern streamed away in elastic jigsaw shapes and made gold rings round the tree trunks. At last they came to a still pool reaching to the steps of the house, and the keel of the boat grated on gravel. The windows were all lit up, but it was too dark to see what kind of a house it was, only that it was high and narrow like a tower.

'Come along in,' said Mr Boggis. 'I'll show you in. I'd like to see Mrs Oldknow's face when she sees you.'

The entrance hall was a strange place. As they stepped in, a similar door opened at the far end of the house and another man and boy entered there. Then Toseland saw that it was only themselves in a big mirror. The walls round him were partly rough stone and partly plaster, but hung all over with mirrors and pictures and china. There were three big old mirrors all reflecting each other so that at first Toseland was puzzled to find what was real, and which door one could go through straight, the way one wanted to, not sideways somewhere else. He almost wondered which was really himself.

There were vases everywhere filled with queer flowers – branches of dry winter twigs out of which little tassels and rosettes of flower petals were bursting, some yellow, some white, some purple. They had an exciting smell, almost like something to eat, and they looked as if they had been produced by magic, as if someone had said 'Abracadabra! Let these sticks burst into flower.' 'What if my great-grandmother is a witch!' he thought. Above the vases, wherever there was a beam or an odd corner or a door-post out of which they could, as it were, grow, there were children carved in dark oak, leaning out over the flowers. Most of them had wings, one had a real bird's nest on its head, and all of them had such round polished cheeks they seemed to be laughing and welcoming him.

While he was looking round him, Boggis had taken his coat and cap from him and hung them up. 'Your great-grandmother will be in here,' he said, and led him to a little old stone doorway such as you might find in a belfry. He knocked on the door. 'Come in,' said a clear voice. Boggis gave Toseland a shove, and he found himself inside.

The room seemed to be the ground floor of a castle, much like the ruined castles that he had explored on school picnics, only this was not a ruin. It looked as if it never possibly could be. Its thick stone walls were strong, warm and lively. It was furnished with comfortable polished old-fashioned things as though living in castles was quite ordinary. Toseland stood just inside the door and felt it must be a dream.

His great-grandmother was sitting by a huge open fireplace where logs and peat were burning. The room smelled of woods and wood-smoke. He forgot about her being frighteningly old. She had short silver curls and her face had so many wrinkles it looked as if

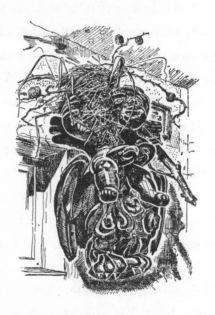

someone had been trying to draw her for a very long time and every line put in had made the face more like her. She was wearing a soft dress of folded velvet that was as black as a hole in darkness. The room was full of candles in glass candlesticks, and there was candlelight in her ring when she held out her hand to him.

'So you've come back!' she said, smiling, as he came forward, and he found himself leaning against her shoulder as if he knew her quite well.

'Why do you say "come back"?' he asked, not at all shy.

'I wondered whose face it would be of all the faces I knew,' she said. 'They always come back. You are like another Toseland, your grandfather. What a good thing you have the right name, because I should always be calling you Tolly anyway. I used to call him Tolly. Have you got a pet name? I'm sure they don't call you Toseland at school.'

'No, I get called Towser.'

'And at home?'

'My stepmother calls me Toto, but I hate it. It's worse than Towser.'

'I think I agree with you. Here we are all used to Toseland, it's the family name and doesn't seem queer to us. So you shan't be Toto here. Do you mind Tolly?'

'I like it. It's what my mother used to call me. What shall I call you?'

'Granny,' she said. 'What does one generation more or less matter? I'm glad you have come. It will seem lovely to me. How many years of you have I wasted?'

'Seven,' said Tolly, watching the flames tugging loose from the logs and leaping up the black chimney. They reminded him of bonfire flames wrestling and tearing and whistling in the sky on the fifth of November. Those had been frightening, but these were wonderful.

'Are these our flames?' he asked. 'I mean, are they our own?'

'The blue ones are yours and the orange ones are mine.'

'And the candle-flames?'

'All yours.'

Tolly hesitated, then asked in a very little voice because he hardly dared, 'Is it my house – I mean, partly?'

'Of course it is – partly, as you say. Well, now that you are here what shall we do first? Are you hungry?'

She rose and, standing, looked much older. Her figure was bent and shrunken, her face no higher than Tolly's own. The folds of her dress seemed both to weigh her down and hold her up. She brought a tray that was laid ready for him on the sideboard, and put it on a low table in front of the fire. There were egg sandwiches and chicken sandwiches and iced orange cake and jelly and chocolate finger biscuits. Toseland ate happily and tried not to make crumbs.

'I came in a boat with a lantern,' he said. 'I played the house was Noah's Ark.'

'Oh, the Ark! So you played it was the Ark.'

'Yes. Do you think Noah had a whip like a circus man and made the animals run round and round for exercise?'

'Yes. And Ham juggled with clubs and plates to pass the time away, and Shem and Japhet were clowns and tried to make Mrs Noah laugh. But she never did, because if she had done, all her buttons would have burst off. She was done up very tight.'

At that moment the fire went *pop*! and shot a piece of wood out into the room. *Pop*! again.

'Buttons! Who said buttons? Poor Mrs Noah.' Tolly chased the sparks and trod on them to put them out.

'Why do you live in a castle?' he said, looking round.

'Why not? Castles were meant to live in.'

'I thought that was only in fairy-tales. Is it a real castle?'

17

'Of course.'

'I mean, do things happen in it, like the castles in books?'

'Oh, yes, things happen in it.'

'What sort of things?'

'Wait and see! I'm waiting too, to see what happens now that you are here. Something will, I'm sure. Tomorrow you can explore the inside of the house up and down, and learn your way about and to feel at home in it, because you won't be able to go outside until the floods go down. And now you must come and see your own room, and you must go to bed early tonight.'

She led him up winding stairs and through a high, arched room like a knight's hall, that she called the Music Room, and up more stairs to the very top of the house. Here there was a room under the roof, with a ceiling the shape of the roof and all the beams showing. It was a long room with a triangle of wall at each end and no walls at the sides, because the sloping ceiling came down to the floor, like a tent. There were windows on three sides, and a little low wooden bed in the middle covered with a patchwork quilt, as unlike a school bed as anything could be. There was a low table, a chest of drawers and lots of smooth, polished, empty floor. At one side there was a beautiful old rocking-horse – not a 'safety' rocking-horse hanging on iron swings from a centre shaft, but a horse whose legs were stretched to full gallop, fixed to long rockers so that it could, if you rode it violently, both rear and kick. On the other side was a doll's house. By the bed was a wooden box painted vermilion with bright patterns all over it, and next to it all Tolly's luggage piled up, making the room look really his. A wicker bird-cage hung from one of the beams. On the only side that had no window there hung a big mirror reflecting all the rest – the rafters, the wicker cage, the rocking-horse, the doll's house, the painted box, the bed.

'In this house,' said Tolly, 'everything is twice!' He tried the lid of the painted box, but could not open it.

'The key is lost,' said Mrs Oldknow. 'I don't know what's in it. It used to be the children's toy-box.'

He put his hand on the rocking-horse's mane, which was real horse-hair. Its tail was real hair too, black and soft and long. He started it rocking. It made a nice creaky sound, like a rocking-chair. He opened the front of the doll's house. 'Why, it's this house!' he said. 'Look, here's the Knight's Hall, and here's the stairs, and here's my room! Here's the rocking-horse and here's the red box, and here's the tiny bird-cage! But it's got four beds in it. Are there sometimes other children here?'

Mrs Oldknow looked at him as if she would like to know everything about him before she answered.

'Yes,' she said, 'sometimes.'

'Who are they?'

'You'll see when they come, if they come.'

'When do they come?'

'When they like. Now let's unpack. Here are your pyjamas. Is there anything you want to have in bed with you – any books or photos that you put under your pillow?'

On the chest of drawers Tolly had seen two curly white china dogs, an old clock, and an ebony mouse, life-sized with shiny black eyes. It was so cleverly carved that you could see every hair, and it felt like fur to stroke. As he pulled the sheets up to his nose he said, 'Can I have the mouse in bed?'

Mrs Oldknow smiled. 'You want Toby's Japanese mouse? Here it is.'

'Who's Toby?'

'Well, really another Toseland. Toby for short. Now sleep well. I'll light the night-light for you. Oh, the clock's not going.'

She picked up
the old clock,
which had a sun
and moon painted
on its face, and
started it ticking. It
had a very slow tick-

tock, comforting and sleepy. 'There,' she said. 'Now, good night. My room is underneath yours – you can knock on the floor if you want me.'

She went away, and Tolly lay happily looking at the surprising shadows made by the little night-light – the beams, the big shadow of the rocking-horse, the low one of the doll's house on the floor, the elongated wandering criss-crosses of the bird-cage on the ceiling. The mirror repeated it all in the opposite direction, distant and slightly tilted. How could such a little light do it all? Never in his life had he lain in such a room, yet it did not feel strange. He felt with all his heart that he was at home. He held the mouse in his hand under the pillow and soon fell asleep.

H<small>E SLEPT LONG AND WELL</small>. In his dreams he was swimming towards the house in the dark when he heard the creak of oars coming to meet him. He tried to shout, but it was too difficult to do while swimming. In the effort he woke up. The funny thing was, that lying there with his eyes closed he could still hear the creak-croak. No, it couldn't be oars, it must be the rocking-horse. He sat up in bed, and it seemed to him that the horse had just that minute stopped rocking. The only sound he could hear now was the slow tick-tock of the old clock. The room was in dim half-light because the curtains were still drawn. Tolly jumped out of bed. First he put his precious mouse back between the two china dogs, then he went to the rocking-horse just to stroke its real silky mane, and to pretend to see if it was out of breath. Then he ran to the window and knelt on the window-seat behind the curtain to look out at the view he had not yet seen. When, just at that moment, Mrs Oldknow came into the room, all she could see of him was the soles of his pink feet. As she pulled back the curtain, he turned a happy excited face to her. 'Oh look! Oh look!' he said.

It was a brilliant, sunny morning, and all the view was sparkling blue water, right away to the low hills in the distance. From this high window he could see where the course of the river should be, because of the pollard willows sticking out along each side of the bank, and because there the water was whirlpooled and creased and very brown and swift, while all the miles of overflow were just like blue silk.

'It really is like being in the Ark,' said Tolly.

'Yes, all the children used to call it the Ark. Your grandfather did, and he learnt it from his father, who learnt it from his, and so on right away back. But you called it that by yourself.'

Tolly sat in his pyjamas on the rocking-horse, making it go creak-croak, creak-croak.

'Do you know,' he said, 'when I was lying in bed with my eyes shut I could hear the horse go creak-croak just like this? But when I opened my eyes it was quite still.'

'And did the mouse squeak under your pillow, and did the china dogs bark?'

'No,' said Tolly. 'Do they?'

Mrs Oldknow laughed. 'You seem ready for anything, that's something,' she said. 'Now get dressed and come down to breakfast.'

Tolly found his own way down the winding staircase,

through the Music Room that was like a knight's hall, down the winding stairs again and across the entrance hall with its polished wooden children and queer sticks of flowers, and into the room where he had first met his great-grandmother the night before.

Breakfast was on the table, but she was standing by an open door throwing crumbs on to the doorstep for the birds. There were so many of them that they seemed to drop from the branches of the trees like ripe chestnuts when the tree is shaken, and as many were going up again with a piece of bread in their beaks as were coming down to get it. A few yards beyond the doorstep the garden was under water.

'The birds are very hungry. You see, they can't get worms, or seed, or ants' eggs until the floods go. Would you like to be introduced to them?'

'Yes please,' said Tolly.

'Come here, then,' said Mrs Oldknow; and although her back was rather bent and her face was wrinkled, when she looked at him so mischievously he could almost imagine she was a boy to play with. 'They love margarine better than anything,' she said. 'Hold out your hands.'

She spread his fingers and palms with margarine

carefully all over, even between the fingers, then told him to go to the door and stand still, holding out both hands with the fingers open. She stood beside him and whistled. In a minute tits and robins and chaffinches and hedge-sparrows were fluttering round him till at last one ventured to perch on his thumb. After that the others were soon jostling to find room on his hands, fixing him with their bright eyes and opening their wings and cocking their tails to keep their balance. They pecked at the margarine on his palm and between his fingers. They tickled dreadfully, and Tolly wriggled and squealed so that they all flew away, but in a minute they were back.

'You must keep still and be quiet,' said Mrs Oldknow, laughing at him.

Tolly tried hard to obey her, but their beaks and little wiry clutching hands felt so queer that he had to shut his eyes and screw up his face to keep still. The tits hung on underneath and tickled in unexpected places.

While he was standing there pulling faces he heard a laugh so like a boy's that he could not believe his great-grandmother had made it, and opened his eyes to see who was there. There was no one else. Mrs Oldknow's eyes were fixed on his. The blackbirds were scolding in the branches because they were afraid to come on to his hands and could see the margarine was nearly finished. Then with a squabbling noise, like a crowd of rude people off a football bus, a flock of starlings arrived, snatching and pushing and behaving badly in every way.

'That will do,' said Mrs Oldknow. 'Starlings don't wait to be introduced to anybody. I'll give them some bread, and you can wipe your hands on these crusts and throw them to the blackbirds. Then run and wash your hands.'

She shut the door and sat down to breakfast. Tolly came quickly and sat down where a place was laid for him opposite the fireplace.

While he was eating he was looking round again at the room which was so different by daylight, though just as unusual, with all its big windows looking out on to water. Suddenly he saw something he had not noticed at all the night before, when the room had been full of firelight and shadows. Over the fireplace hung a large oil painting of a family, three children and two ladies. There were two handsome boys, wearing lace collars and dark green silk suits. They had long hair but looked anything but girlish. The elder of the two, who might be fourteen years old, was wearing a sword, and it looked so natural to him that Tolly was filled with hero-worship. He had his hand on the collar of a tame deer. The younger brother had a book under his arm and a flute in his hand. The little girl had a smile of irrepressible high spirits that seemed to defy the painter to do a serious portrait of her. She was holding a chaffinch, and beside her on the ground was an open wicker cage. One of the two ladies was young and beautiful. At her feet was a little curly white dog with a black face; on her arm a basket of roses. The other lady was old and dressed in black. They all had large dark eyes and all their eyes seemed fixed on Tolly. If he moved to one side all the eyes moved after him.

'Granny, they are all looking at me.'

'I'm not surprised. You have only just come. They must be tired of looking at me.'

'Who are they?'

'They are Oldknows. Your family. The boy with the deer is Toby, the other with the flute is Alexander, and the little girl is Linnet. She is six years old. That is their mother in the blue dress.'

'My mother was called Linnet,' said Tolly. 'And that's you behind them!'

'It's their grandmother, Mrs Oldknow.'

'Is this their house?'

'Yes, they lived here.'

'When did they live here?'

'Oh, a long time ago,' said Mrs Oldknow, fidgeting and being suddenly very busy about the breakfast table. But Tolly was only seven, and to him a long time ago meant more than seven years. Five lively pairs of eyes were challenging him to ignore them. Linnet was laughing straight into his. Even the dog looked as if it would play.

'Has Toby got a real sword?' he asked.

'Yes, of course.'

'Why?'

'Because he's going to be a soldier. His father gave it to him when he was thirteen.'

'Is Alexander going to be a musician?'

'He will go to the University. He wants to be a poet.'

'And Linnet?'

'My little Linnet –'

'Oh,' said Tolly, interrupting, 'that's the bird-cage in my room. It's the bird-cage in my room! It made such funny shadows on the ceiling when you put the night-light under it. Is the doll's house Linnet's?'

'No, the doll's house was mine when I was a little girl. I was brought up here by my uncle because I was an orphan.'

'Did you have brothers and sisters?'

'No; but I played that I had. I was lonely. That's why I put four beds in the doll's house.'

'Did you play that they were your brothers and sister?' said Tolly, pointing to the picture. Mrs Oldknow looked hard at him.

'Yes, my dear. How did you know?'

'Because I think that is what I shall play. Do you want to read the newspapers now?'

'Good gracious no, child. What should I do that for? The world doesn't alter every day. As far as I can see, it's always the same. But I have plenty to do, so you must amuse yourself. Can you?'

'Oh, yes. I would like to go up to the rocking-horse and the mouse. Can I play with the cage if I can reach it?'

'You can play with anything you like if you are careful. Don't fall out of the window.' Tolly took two lumps of sugar from the bowl. 'For the horse,' he said. 'Can I?' He ran upstairs to his room as happy as a little boy could be.

29

First he pulled a chair under the wicker cage so that he could reach up to it. He opened the door, which made a little bird-like squeak as it turned on its hinges. He had nothing else to put in it, so he put the mouse inside and closed the door. He pretended to feed the horse with the sugar and put what was left over of it for the mouse. Then he groomed the horse all over with his hairbrush, particularly its mane and tail, and passed his hands down its legs as he had seen men do in stables, and talked to it all the time. He mounted it and started a long ride, creak, croak, pretending that Toby and Alexander and Linnet had invited him to visit them. 'Horses always know the way,' he said aloud. 'I expect it will take hours and hours.'

He was cheerfully rocking along, singing at the top of his voice a song his mother used to sing to him, before she died and the stepmother came.

What is your one oh?
Green grow the rushes oh
What is your one oh?
One is one and all alone
And ever more shall be so.
What are your two oh?

Green grow the rushes oh
What are your two oh?
Two, two, the lily white boys
Clothed all in green oh
One is one and all alone
And ever more shall be so.

Presently he heard tip-tap at one of the windows, and while he looked in that direction, tap-tap at the window behind him. It was a chaffinch knocking on the glass, for all the world as if it wanted to come in. Toseland dismounted and went over to see. Still it did not fly away, but held on to the cross-bars and tried first one pane and then another.

'Do you want to come in?' said Tolly, opening the window. At once the bird flew in and perched on the cage. It hopped from one wicker strand to another, giving little excited calls until it found the door, which was shut. 'Cheep, cheep, cheep,' it scolded, and fluttered round the room, making a little sound of bird footsteps on the wooden floor when it hopped. Toseland opened the cage door, and the chaffinch flew straight across the room and into the cage. There it turned round and gave a little song, tried all the perches, hopping round to face both ways on each, swung in the swing, pecked at the sugar, and hopped out again on to Tolly's head. 'Don't,' said Tolly, shaking it. 'I don't like that. I can't see you.' The bird flew off on to the window-sill, looked round at him with a final chirp, and dived into a big tree near by, level with the window, where it perched and sang quietly to itself.

'Oh, come back, do come back, chaffinch! I wish I had some margarine. Perhaps sugar won't do. I wonder what Linnet used to put in the cage? Chaffinch! Chaffinch!'

The bird would not be coaxed, but when he had finished his song shot off across the water like an arrow and disappeared into a distant tree.

THE FLOODS HAD begun to go down. Already Tolly could see spikes of grass sticking up through the edge of the water. The shapes of lawns and flower-beds were showing through the ripples round the house. He longed for the water to go, so that he could explore the garden.

When he came downstairs for lunch, Boggis, in long

wading boots, was bringing in logs for the fire, making a big stack of them in a corner of the inglenook.

'Good morning, Mr Boggis,' said Tolly. 'Have you come in the boat? I forgot to look last night to see what it was called.'

'It's called the *Linnet*, Master Toseland, but I didn't come in it today. I came in my waders. The water's going down lovely.'

'The *Linnet*?' said Toseland, turning to his great-grandmother.

'Yes,' she said. 'There's always a boat called *Linnet* on the river.'

'That's right,' said Boggis. 'There's always a *Linnet*. This one's new – leastways not more than twenty years old – but I used to go out in the old *Linnet* when I was a boy, and my grandfather used to talk about fishing at night with torches from the *Linnet* when he was young. See, ma'am, I've managed to borrow these from my niece whose boy is in hospital.' He held out two Wellingtons. 'I reckon Master Toseland will need these. Isn't he the fair spit of his grandfather! Might be the same come back.'

'Yes, he seems to belong here,' said Mrs Oldknow. 'He has it all hidden in him somewhere. I like to see him finding his way about.'

'Shall I take him out with me into the barn this afternoon while I cut wood, to keep him out of your way?'

'He's not in my way at all, but I expect he would like to go.'

'Oh yes, please!'

'Very well, Boggis, you can keep him till tea-time. Goodbye, Toby.'

'You said "Toby",' said Tolly, pulling on his borrowed Wellingtons.

'Why, so I did! I was forgetting.'

Boggis and Toseland paddled off side by side across the drive and turned into a walled yard that was now a walled lake, though you could see the cobbles through the shallow water, all different colours like pebbles at the sea-side. Along three sides there were buildings or sheds, very old and tumbledown. The longest had a row of arches, and over them bits of broken stone carving stuck out of the wall. Inside it was divided up into little rooms with scrolled iron doorways opening on to a passage. Some were filled with straw, some with faggots or peat. One was empty, and one had a wall ladder with hand and foot holes instead of rungs. Up this Boggis went, and through a trap-door above.

Tolly followed, and found himself in a room rather like his bedroom but much larger, smelling of hay and sawdust, and rich with a soft, musty kind of darkness. There was only one small round window covered with cobwebs, so that the light that came through was dove-grey. Here and there a ray of white light came slanting through a broken roof tile, against which you could see the golden motes of dust in the air. It looked mysterious and enticing. The floor made hollow noises and had holes in it where the boards had rotted. Up here Boggis had a bench and saw, and as he finished a log he threw the pieces through the trap-door on to the floor below.

In one of the little rooms downstairs Tolly had seen a chair and table and a blue tea-pot and mug. 'Do you live here?' he asked. Boggis looked at him with teasing bright blue eyes. 'It all depends what you call living,' he said. 'When I'm awake I'm mostly here, but when I go home I mostly sleeps.'

'How long have you been here?'

'Fifty-five years. I came when I was twelve. But of course I knew it before that because my father worked here, same as me.'

'What are those little rooms downstairs with park gates instead of doors?'

'Stables,' said Boggis briefly, out of breath with sawing.

Tolly thought of the horses that had once lived in such grand rooms.

'Were they very special horses?'

'Oh aye, they were fine horses when I was a lad. Shining like the sun and dressed up like lords. I've never had an overcoat like they had! When they were led out, striking sparks out of the cobbles with their hooves and shaking their bridles, they were a proper eyeful. Your grandfather, Mr Toseland as was, he was a rare one with a horse. He could make them do anything by just breathing secrets into their ears.'

Boggis went on with his sawing, and Tolly roamed round, his eyes getting used to the patchy light. He found other trap-doors which he could not lift, a whole row of them all along one side. One was broken and lay off its hinges beside the square hole. Underneath on the stable wall was the iron basket to hold hay, into which he climbed. He crouched there trying to imagine that the stall was occupied by the warm silky body of a horse, feet stamping in straw, hindquarters fidgeting, tail swishing, and a great rolling black eye that could see backwards and forwards at the same time, half covered by mane and forelock. He tried so passionately to imagine it, to see, hear and smell it, that the wonder is that no horse was there.

'Hullo there! Master Toseland, where are you?'

'I'm here,' he answered, standing up so that his head stuck out of the hole.

'Trust you to get in the haunted stall! Were you looking for Mr Toby's horse by any chance? That stall's always kept empty in case he feels like spending a night there. Folk say you can hear him at night, whinnying for the young master.'

'Which young master?'

'Don't ask me! I bain't no good at history. One of the young masters, same as you.'

'Have you ever heard him whinnying?'

Boggis cocked a half-humorous, half-serious eye at him. 'I tells you, I sleeps at home. And that's where I dreams.'

Toseland climbed over the hayrack and let himself down into the manger.

'You haven't put any hay for him,' he said.

'Ghosts don't eat hay.'

'But they like to pretend.'

The manger was empty. It was as big as a bed and he

could lie full length in it. In that position, running his fingers along the cracks, he found a loose piece of wood wedged under the ledge of the manger at the back. Just for love of poking round, Toseland, with great difficulty, prized it out. On one side of it there was dirty paint. He rubbed it with his sleeve and saw that there were red and white patterns on it. He licked his handkerchief and rubbed harder. Some letters appeared, very queer spiky, spidery letters, not like print at all.

'Mr Boggis, look what I've found.'

Boggis came and peered through the trap-door.

'Now then, don't you take away nothing you finds here. We don't want no souvenir hunting here.'

Toseland put it down in the bottom of the manger. There ought to be hay, he thought. Of course they ought to put hay. Then he remembered that he still had a piece of sugar that he had taken for the rocking-horse. He put it carefully exactly in the middle of the painted board. Then he climbed down from the manger and ran up the ladder again to the loft. It was getting so dark that by now Boggis had lit his storm-lantern to finish his sawing. The loft looked even more exciting by lamplight, but in another quarter of an hour Boggis said it was tea-time – time to go in.

Toseland walked in front with the lantern, and they stepped from the stables into shallow water and waded slowly towards the house. As they went under the big yew trees the lantern lit up the underneath of the branches making them look like rafters in wild magic houses. The windows of Green Noah were all lit up again. Tolly felt as if he had lived here always instead of just one day.

Mrs Oldknow was sitting in front of a tea-tray by the fire, just as before, when Tolly came in all dirty with bits of straw in his hair.

'I can see where you've been,' she said. 'Go and wash yourself and get the straw out of your hair; then come and tell me all about it. I can see you are bursting with questions again.'

When he came back she said: 'Show me your hands. And now turn round and let me see if you have got

peat dust on the seat of your trousers. There! Now begin. Here's some hot buttered toast and honey.'

'Granny, what was the name of Toby's special horse?'

Mrs Oldknow put down her cup and saucer. 'Boggis has been telling you stories.'

'Yes, and I found something.'

'Toby's horse was called Feste. What did you find?'

'I found a funny board with patterns and writing on it. It looked like a name but I couldn't read it. It was funny writing.'

'It was a name. Feste. Good boy, you are doing well! I thought that board was lost – that someone had chopped it up by mistake, or on purpose. I haven't seen it since I was married. When the stables were built each horse had its name above the manger. Alexander had a white pony called Bucephalus. Poor little Linnet wasn't allowed a horse of her own. She rode in a pannier behind her mother or Boggis – I mean the Boggis there was then.'

'Granny, I do want to hear Feste neigh. Is my bedroom too far away to hear him – if he did, I mean?'

She smiled gently at him. 'No, I don't think it's too far away.'

'Did you hear him when you were little?'

'Oh, yes, I heard him. Generally at sundown. There were other horses then, of course, but I could always tell Feste's voice. It is quite individual.'

There was a long silence while Toseland imagined having a horse of his own, even a ghost horse.

'I did a silly thing,' he said at last. 'I put a lump of sugar for him.'

'That wasn't silly at all, darling,' she said.

'Granny, what did Linnet put in the bird-cage? The chaffinch didn't like sugar, He came, you know, but he wouldn't stay.'

'Linnet always left the door open. She didn't like to shut them in. She put crumbs of pastry and biscuit, and seeds that she gathered in the garden in the summer. The chaffinches came and went as they liked, but they always built their nest in the cage in spring. She put a forked branch of hawthorn for them. You can do that too. I am surprised they have remembered for so long; no one has used that room for years. I think they must tell stories to their nestlings.'

'Stories about Linnet, as you do to me?'

'Why not?'

'Tell me more about them, please. Why isn't their father there in the picture?'

'He was a ship's captain. There was an older boy too, Aubrey, who was a midshipman on his father's ship. Captain Oldknow sailed all over the world. He used to bring home presents for the family. From one journey he brought the mouse for Toby – your mouse – and that great silk Chinese lantern that hangs in the Music Room for his wife. It opens and shuts like an umbrella, but I never touch it now because the silk is so old and tender. Alexander and Linnet were not born then.'

'What else did he bring home?'

'From Holland he brought all that lovely lace that they are wearing, and the bird-cage; from Spain, Toby's sword; and from Germany, the book that Alexander's holding.'

'How could he read it if it was a German book?'

'It was in Latin and he could read it, and he loved it. From France he brought that little dog for Linnet and a lot of rose trees for his wife. Those are the flowers in her basket. Roses were almost a new discovery, very fashionable and exciting. Everybody wanted to have some. They are growing here in the garden still.'

'The same ones?'

'The same in a way, descended from them as you are from the captain.'

'I feel as though I had lived here always,' said Toseland. 'Why is it called Green Noah?'

Mrs Oldknow's face suddenly creased into rings of unhappy wrinkles.

'For someone who's lived here always, you ask a lot of questions,' she said.

'I know, Granny. But tell me, please.'

'It's not the real name,' she said. 'It used to be called Green Knowe, but it – got changed. A long time ago.' That was all she would say. But Tolly had more questions.

'You know,' he said, 'all those children's faces carved in wood in the entrance hall? They all seemed to be laughing when I came. Who put them there?'

This time Mrs Oldknow looked pleased. 'The grandmother in the picture found them in a builder's store. They came from the chapel of a monastery that had been pulled down. She bought them for the beams in the children's bedroom. She said they were guardian angels. Now, as you see, they are welcoming angels – though one was guardian to a chaffinch last year.'

'What colour was Feste?'

'He was chestnut with a white nose and four white

feet like a kitten, and he jumped like a cat. Toby and he loved each other more than anything on earth.'

'But the deer was Toby's too,' said Tolly, gazing at the picture. 'Isn't it beautiful! A deer seems more magic than a horse.'

'Very beautiful fairy-tale magic, but a horse that thinks the same thoughts that you do is like strong magic wine, a love philtre for boys.'

TOLLY LAY AWAKE in bed. There was so much to think about –the birds, the children, the floods, the stables where lovely Feste called for his master. It was a clear night with a full moon shining on miles of water and seeming twice as bright as usual. The bedroom was all silver and black with it as it poured through the window and flooded the floor with quicksilver. The flame of the night-light looked like a little golden pen-nib, giving less light than there was already around it. The moon shone in the rocking-horse's eye, and in the mouse's eye too when Tolly fetched it out from under his pillow to see. The clock went tick-tock, and in the stillness he thought he heard little bare feet running across the floor, then laughter and whispering, and a sound like the pages of a big book being turned over.

'It might be Alexander and Linnet looking at pictures by moonlight,' he thought, dreamily. 'But where are they?'

He sat up and stared all round the room. There was only his own bed and all his things just as he had left them, clearly seen in the moonlight, though there were black patches of shadow under the window where he could not see. Then there was all the room repeated in the looking-glass, more mysterious, the moonlit parts brighter, the dark more impenetrable. The whispering went on. If they were in the dark corners, he thought, they couldn't see the pictures.

'Linnet!' he called suddenly. 'Where are you? Come out into the moonlight.'

There was a laugh just where he wasn't looking, and when he turned that way, a patter of feet, and the whispering was where he had been looking a moment before.

'Are you just teasing me?' he asked, and was answered by such an infectious little laugh that he couldn't help laughing too. After that there was silence, but it was a companionable, happy one in which presently he smiled and settled himself to sleep. He dreamed that he was holding out his hands dripping with golden syrup, and that it was Feste who came with his soft white nose and pinky-grey lips and sucked it all off, while Linnet flew in the air like a bird and laughed from the branches of the trees.

WHEN HE WOKE Mrs Oldknow was standing by his bed smiling at him.

'It's time to get up. Look, the floods have all gone in the night. Come and see.' She opened the window to lean out. 'Tolly! Quick! Quick!'

Under the high window all the lawns were emerald green. Beyond them the river flowed obediently in its own course, and beyond that again were miles of green meadow. Right in front of the window where the last pool was draining away from a hollow in the grass, a large silvery thing was twisting and jumping violently in the sun.

'It's a great big fish.'

'It's one of Toby's carp from the moat. Silly thing – it got left behind when the water went away. Run, Tolly, put on your coat and your Wellingtons and throw it back into the moat.'

Tolly ran as fast as he could, slithering down the steep winding stairs in his socks and pulling on his Wellingtons by the front door. He reached the fish before anyone else, but it was nearly as big as himself, and flapped so wildly when he picked it up that he was afraid and let it fall again. Then it gasped horribly and lay still, and now he was afraid to touch it in case it was dying. Just then Boggis arrived with a wheelbarrow.

'Quick, quick, Mr Boggis! It's Toby's fish. It's dying! It's Toby's! Mr Boggis, quick!'

Boggis came without any hurry and bent his bright red face down to look.

'Ay, it's one of Master Toby's sure enough. What a size it have grown to! Must be hundreds of years old.'

He put the fish in his barrow and led Tolly to the moat, which was a ring of deep water all round the garden. There he tipped the barrow up and the fish plopped in and disappeared. They stood and looked at the place where it had fallen.

'Was it still alive?' asked Tolly. As he spoke, a fish face was poked above the surface, then there was a swirl of water, a flip of a tail, and it was gone.

'Sure enough it was!' said Boggis.

'It was a very ugly fish,' said Toseland.

'T'aint no beauty. No more will you be when you're a hundred years old! Master Toby used to feed it with bread.'

'It came when he called it,' added Mrs Oldknow, joining them. 'Its name is Neptune. Toby used to tell Linnet that it understood Latin. He always talked to it in Latin. She was very much impressed.'

'What did he say to it?'

'He said "*Veni Neptune. Panem dabo tibi et vermes*".'

'I don't know any Latin.'

'Neither did Linnet. It means "Come Neptune. I will give you bread and worms". In the garden you will find a platform over a pool where he fed them.'

They fed the birds together. Tolly wanted his hands to be buttered again, but was told that that was only for the introduction ceremony, not for every day.

'Do the birds understand Latin?'

'No, not Latin. Music. Alexander used to play the flute to them. They used to sing when he played, but all different tunes. Only the thrushes learnt his tune and the starlings who never sang it properly – they only made fun of it.'

48

'What tune did the thrushes sing?'

'"Greensleeves", for one.'

'Oh Granny, I know "Greensleeves". I do really. At school we had it on the wireless. I wish I had a flute.'

'Perhaps you'll get one for Christmas. That's quite soon, you know. Now finish your breakfast and then you can explore the garden.'

The garden had looked very desolate when the water was over it, but now even the trees looked different and every path seemed to lead just where it was most exciting to go. First he went round the east corner of the house that he had not yet seen. Broken stones stuck out all up the wall, as if there had once been a building there that had been pulled down. In fact there was still a high garden wall with arched slits in it that must once have been windows. Ferns and shrubs and ivy were growing out of the cracks between the stones and there was a lovely smell in the air. Quite suddenly he became aware of something so big that at first he had not seen it.

Against the side of the house, immensely tall and half covered with festoons of Old Man's Beard, was a stone figure. The first thing that attracted his attention to it was, close to the ground, some stone fishes swimming in what looked like stone water, as though the flood had left something behind. Then he saw that behind the fishes were two huge bare stone feet that seemed to be paddling with stone ripples round the ankles; above them, legs and folds of clothing. High above that, so that he had to step back to look up at it, among the twining strings of the creeper he saw the head of a giant stone man, carrying a child on his shoulders.

Tolly was astonished. He looked and looked at it and could not go away. He played round its feet for a long time, collecting coloured pebbles out of the gravel, and stones that were like different things, such as a peg-top, an egg, a calf's face, a hammer-head; and a real marble. Every now and then he would look up to see the statue again. Its surface was worn soft by rain and frost and wind, not shiny and hard like monuments in churches. It looked friendly and nearly alive. Tolly loved it.

At last curiosity led him away to see where the other paths would lead him. There were many big trees and wild places where there were only little paths like rabbit runs. As he went along the birds went with him. They whistled and chirped on every side and always flew out of the bushes just before he arrived there, to perch on others just ahead. He followed a track round the edge of the moat, shuffling his feet in the dead leaves and pine-needles and stooping under low branches. Here, in a little clearing between two huge trees he found his next great surprise.

Standing on the grass with its ears pricked up as if it had just heard him was a deer that was a bush. It was like Toby's deer in the picture, but cut out of live evergreen with brown bush-stalk legs growing out of the ground. Toseland stroked it; its neck felt soft. It seemed so much alive that it was queer that of course it couldn't have eyes. How wild it looks without eyes, he thought. How magic! It took his breath away. And then he saw, sitting under a big beech tree, a green yew squirrel with a high tail. That seemed to be listening too. Other living things beside the birds were rustling in the bushes, and he heard other calls, more like children than birds. Tolly ran, hoping to catch them. He found nothing but a live rabbit that bolted in long hops and shot down a hole. He ran on down the little path, past a yew peacock – that was comparatively ordinary. Further on there was a green hare sitting very erect by the water's edge; then the path suddenly turned and left the water, going by a bank of trees and dense undergrowth and brambles where it would be almost impossible to walk. It came out between a yew cock and hen, on to a large lawn.

Tolly wanted to get back to the water again, and by-and-by he found a flight of steps which led down towards it. Here the moat formed a deep pool overshadowed by trees, though now it was winter and the branches were bare except for the birds that had followed him and perched there. The water was brown with a blue gloss reflected on it from the sky, like a starling's back. The steps ended in a wooden platform. As Tolly stood and looked into the water he thought he saw, deep down, a great, shadowy fish swimming slowly. This, then, was Toby's platform.

Tolly tried to remember the Latin, but he knew it was hopeless. He would only make silly noises and the fish would know it was wrong. Just then something fell in the water. He couldn't see what it was because it sank and wobbled as it went down, but the old carp rose slowly to meet it and opened his mouth to suck it in. Then he sank again out of sight. What can that have been, thought Toseland. Perhaps a greedy blackbird took more breakfast than it could eat and threw its last crust away. And yet I don't believe that.

It couldn't have tut-tutted and called so much if its mouth was full.

He began to retrace his steps, and now in the wood path he was sure there were others beside himself. Of course, he thought suddenly. It's hide-and-seek! 'Cooee!' he called. 'The Green Deer is den!' He ran as fast as he could till he stopped, out of breath, with his arms round the Green Deer's neck. Then he heard unmistakable breathless laughter quite close to him and felt something on his head. He put his hand up and found a twig. It was not something that could have fallen off any of the trees round him. It was cut out of a reddish bush and made a perfect T.

When he got back to the house he turned for another look at the stone man. Mrs Oldknow was there with some garden scissors cutting branches off the shrubs, which he now noticed with a little disappointment were covered with the peculiar flowers he had first seen in the entrance hall.

'When I first came,' he said, 'I thought those were magic flowers in the hall.'

'So you were afraid I was a witch?'

'Yes, before I saw you.'

'Well, this flower *is* called Witchhazel. And this is

Winter Sweet, and that is Daphne. She was turned into a bush, you know.' Mrs Oldknow, who saw everything, was looking at the twig T in his hand. 'You found the Green Deer? And somebody's been teasing you, I see. When I was little I used to find a twig L in my lap. You see, my Christian name is Linnet.'

'Did they play hide-and-seek with you?'

'Yes.'

Toseland was looking at the stone man. 'Who is he?'

'He is our own St Christopher, and these ruins are where his chapel stood until some stupid wretch pulled it down. There is always a St Christopher by an old ford, and the ford across this river was at the end of the garden. You know the story? He carried the infant Jesus across in a storm, thinking it would be easy, but halfway across he began to feel the child as heavy as the sorrow of the whole world. Linnet loved St Christopher quite specially. She always liked to play here. I planted what you thought were magic flowers for winter incense. This is my favourite part of the garden too. Now, tell me where you've been this morning?'

'I've seen the Green Deer and all the other green things.'

'*All?* Which have you seen?'

'The deer and the squirrel and the peacock and the hare and the cock and the hen.'

Mrs Oldknow seemed relieved. 'And what else?'

'And I found Toby's steps by the water. And I saw the fish again. And *they* played hide-and-seek.'

Tolly was glad that Mrs Oldknow seemed not at all surprised by the hide-and-seek. He was not quite sure whether she thought that he and she were playing a game together pretending that there were other children, or whether she thought, as he did, that the children were really there.

In the afternoon he went back to the stables to look in Feste's manger. The sugar had gone! Toseland put another lump in its place and slipped away again so that it might be eaten quickly in private. Boggis had gone out on a message for Mrs Oldknow, and she herself was writing letters, so Tolly was alone again, but he had almost forgotten that it was sometimes dull. He went back to the Green Deer full of expectation, but all the birds seemed asleep and there was not a sound anywhere. The Green Deer did not seem magic now. It was not listening, its eyelessness was just stupid, not an added sense. The squirrel also was only a bush cut to shape. Tolly had come with an excited imagination. He collected beech nuts and put them before the squirrel, and handfuls of dry hay for the deer, but it turned out only a dull make-believe. Nothing moved, nothing happened. All his interest faded away. He could think of nothing to do alone and as the afternoon wore on he felt lonely and neglected. He went back to the stables, but they were only empty buildings. There was no echo, there was nothing, there was nobody. When it began to get dark he went indoors. Mrs Oldknow was getting the tea ready.

'Can I come in now?' he asked. She looked at him quickly and saw at once what was the matter.

'Yes, come in, darling. You've been alone quite long enough, and so have I. It's been one of those afternoons when nothing will come alive. I know them. Sit down there opposite your friends, and after tea we'll see what we can do together. Did you see your chaffinch today?'

'Oh!' said Toseland, very much ashamed, 'I forgot to put anything for him. Suppose he's been tapping and tapping at the window and nobody came. Will he come again, do you think?'

'Try shortbread crumbs and see if that pleases him tomorrow morning. He might have spent all afternoon with you if you hadn't forgotten him.'

Tolly felt in a better temper already. 'Who made all the green animals?' he asked.

'Boggis's grandfather. They were there when I was a child, and when I asked him about them he said the children wanted them for the Ark. There weren't any children living here then; my cousins were all much older than me. But at the time I thought I knew what he meant. He was very like our Boggis, but his face was redder and his eyes were bluer, and he dearly loved the bottle.'

'Did they have a tame squirrel?'

'They tamed everything. They seemed to understand animals. The hare used to come into the house, lolloping up and down stairs after Toby, or standing up to look out of the windows to see where he had gone. It was called Watt.'

When they had finished their tea Mrs Oldknow said: 'Make up a great blaze, Tolly, and then let's put the lights out and sit here, and I will tell you a story.' Tolly made a crackling fire, using the big leather bellows. There was a tear in one side, so that when they sucked in, the fire grew crimson and tried to follow the draught up the nozzle; when they blew out, the flames turned primrose and blue and sparks flew up as if from a catherine-wheel. Then he blew out all the candles and came and settled himself at her feet.

'What shall it be about?'

'Tell me a story about Feste, please.'

TOBY'S STORY

Once upon a time, when the floods were out and most of the country was under water, Linnet fell ill. Her mother would have liked to call in the doctor, but he lived many miles away on the other side of the river. There was no telephone in those days, so somebody would have to be sent to tell him.

'What shall I do?' said Linnet's mother. 'Boggis has broken his leg and he can't ride. The stable-boy is a young fool. I would never trust a horse to him alone on flooded roads.'

58

'Let me go,' said Toby. 'Feste and I would be quite trustworthy.'

'No, no,' said his mother. 'I should be more anxious about you than I am about Linnet. We will see if Grandmother's remedies will cure her.'

Their grandmother was very skilled in nursing, and kept a cupboard full of herbal medicines which she made herself, for every childish illness. Though she had done everything she could throughout the day, towards evening Linnet's fever was higher than ever. She lay with scarlet cheeks tossing in bed and talking as if she did not know what she said, so that the tears ran down her mother's face as she heard it.

'Mother, let me go for the doctor,' said Toby again.

'Dear boy,' said his mother, 'if I had let you go at first all might have been well. But now it is growing dark and who knows how the water is rising?'

'Feste can see in the dark, Mother. The dark does not frighten me, but it frightens me to see Linnet so ill.'

'He is right,' said the grandmother. 'Let him go. Feste will look after him.'

'You may ride to our neighbour the farmer, and tell him, I beg him to ride for the doctor at Potto Fen,' said his mother.

'The farmer may be away, or unable, or unwilling, and that would be so much time wasted, Mother. I will go quickly, and the doctor can be here this evening.'

Just then Linnet began to moan. She sat up in bed as if greatly distressed, and fell back on her pillow with her eyes open but seeing nothing. Her mother was distracted.

'Yes, Toby, go. Go quickly. But take care. Go the shortest way over the wooden bridge and up the hill. Tell him it is very urgent.'

Toby pulled on his long, loose-topped boots and took his thick cloak and ran down to the stables. He saddled Feste, and as he put on the bridle he talked to him, saying, 'Feste, we must get the doctor for Linnet.'

The horse, who had lowered his head to receive the bridle, nuzzled Toby's cheek and understood very well that he was troubled. He gave a little neigh, and as soon as Toby's leg was over the saddle he whisked round and started off. It was not dark yet, the sky was dim green like water, and shallow water was over the roads. As they cantered off the mud flew up like a dirty fountain round them. The lane took them for four miles and ended at the wooden bridge. The river looked very nasty in the half light. The current heaved and pushed and the middle of the river seemed higher than the sides, as if it had been squashed up. The bridge was still well above the water.

Toby pulled his horse to a walking pace lest the wood should be slippery, and expected that Feste would cross it as he had done hundreds of times before. But no; Feste, the obedient, would not cross it. He sidled and waltzed but he would not go on. Toby talked to him, coaxed him, scolded him, pulling his head round to face the bridge again and again, but all in vain. At last, for the first time in his life he lifted his switch and lashed him. Feste reared up and struck at the air with outstretched fore-feet so that it was all Toby could do to hang on in the saddle. When in this way Feste had exhibited his height and his strength and his angry pride, he came down from his prancing and without warning leapt the high hedge at the side of the lane. He slithered down the bank with his fore-feet stuck out before him, and after sidling some distance along the river bank he trumpeted a challenging neigh and, plunging into the cold ugly river, began to swim.

Toby could feel the powerful water buffeting and

shoving his leg on the upstream side, dragging and snatching at it on the other. It was as though the river were determined to separate him from Feste. Now and then a branch would hit him as a broken tree went past. Once they were tangled up in some floating straw from a rick. It nearly carried Toby out of the saddle, but he just managed to push it away. As they swam, they were swept gradually downstream towards the bridge. Toby, crouched over Feste's labouring shoulders, could feel that he was striking out for his life. His ears were straining forward and his eyes too, so that Toby could see the whites, and he snorted and grunted with his muzzle just above the water.

They reached the farther bank only a few yards upstream from the bridge, and scrambled up on the other side, Feste digging in with his toes while he gathered his hocks for the last great effort. At the top of the bank he stood with heaving sides and trembling shoulders shaking his heavy wet mane and hanging his head.

'Feste, you mad, crazy horse! Whatever possessed you to do that?' gasped Toby, twisting in the saddle to pull off his loose boots one by one to empty the water out of them. He was soaked to the neck and bitterly cold. His teeth chattered and his hands were blue. 'Stand, Feste, stand, you madman! The devil's in you!'

Feste was backing away from the bridge and flinging his head up and down so that Toby had to give up trying to wring water out of his cloak.

Suddenly there came a hair-raising scream, the scream of rending wood, sounding almost like an animal in panic. The wooden bridge twisted and cockled under his eyes and, with cracks like cannon fire, collapsed and was swept in a tangled mass downstream. Feste screamed too, and they were off together at full gallop up the hill in the fading light.

Feste chose his own way, jumping fences, jumping hedges, sloshing and slithering in the mud, but Toby did not interfere with him again. He gave him his head and was only concerned to stay with him. At last he recognized the outskirts of the village where the doctor lived. They rattled down the cobbled streets and it seemed to Toby that Feste stopped at the house of his own accord.

When the old doctor came to the door and saw the two of them standing dripping there, with their long hair plastered over their white faces, their coats covered with mud, he did not at first recognize them.

'What in Heaven's name!' he exclaimed. 'You're no bearer of good news. Martha! Bring the lantern. Why, here's young Master Oldknow in a fine state.'

The housekeeper came running with the lantern. 'Lord sakes, Master Toby, what brings you here like this?'

'Oh, sir, Linnet is ill of a high fever and cannot breathe. My mother begs you to make haste.'

'I can believe she's ill if your mother sends you through the floods for me. Martha, call the groom. Tell him to saddle the mare at once.'

'You must go round by Penny Soaky, sir,' said Toby, getting his breath again. 'The wooden bridge is down. Feste would not cross it, he chose to swim instead, and it crumpled up and went downstream just as we got to the other side. Feste knew. And the bridge screamed like demons.'

'Eh! Eh! What's this? You swam the river?' The jolly old doctor looked quite grey at the thought. Then he began to twinkle. 'So Feste chose to swim, did he? Do you let your horses choose, young man? I thought you knew more horsemanship than that.'

'He's never disobeyed me before, sir. And the worst of it is, I slashed him for it.'

'You go in, young man, and Martha will give you a hot grog and put you to bed while she dries your clothes. And as soon as I've gone, the groom shall see to Feste.'

'I'd like to see to Feste myself, sir. Nobody grooms him but me, and tonight especially I must, please.'

'Very well. But you can't stay in those clothes. You'll have to wear some of mine – or Martha's, which ever you please.'

Toby laughed, for both of them were as fat as barrels. 'I'll wear yours, thank you, sir.'

'As you please, young man. And then you go to bed and I'll tell your mother you'll be back tomorrow. I'll want to look at you myself before you go.'

The groom came round with the doctor's sedate mare, and Martha with hot grog for Toby.

'See that this young gentleman has everything he wants for his horse. And Martha, rig him up in anything of mine that he can stand up in. Good-bye, Toby, I'll see to your sister for you.'

It was no good trying to put the doctor's thick, voluminous clothes on Toby's slim body. He was so encumbered by the folds that it would have been impossible for him to do anything but trip over them. In the end he took a sleeveless jerkin that came down below his knees. He belted in its fantastic width like a kilt, and calling out: 'Way for Jamie Stuart, King of Scotland!' he ran barefooted out to Feste, who was tied up in a strange stable, whinnying for him again and again.

First he washed the four white feet in a bucket of warm water. Then he rubbed him hard with clean straw to get the mud off his coat and warm him by friction. Then he rubbed him with a cloth till he was dry all over, behind the ears, between his forelegs and round his fetlocks. He covered him with warm blankets and belted a coat round him.

All the while he talked to him, saying, 'Oh, my wonderful Feste, my golden eagle, my powerful otter, my wise horse.' As he combed the long mane, he sang as he had learned to do in church: '*Behold, thou art fair, my love, behold thou art fair. Thine eyes are as dove's eyes within thy locks. Thy neck is like the tower of David builded for an armoury, whereon there hang a thousand bucklers, all shields of mighty men.*'

When Feste was dry, shining and beautiful again,

he was given a hot bran mash. Toby could not bear to leave him, but sat against the wall watching with great satisfaction how Feste sucked up from the bucket and how the level in the bucket went down and down. When it was all gone, Feste gave the bucket a push with his nose and a knock with his hoof, and lifted up his dripping muzzle towards Toby.

'Feste, you're a messy eater,' he said, carefully wiping the horse's chin with one of the doctor's handkerchiefs. Feste gave a great sigh and began to bend his knees and his hocks to lie down. Down he went in his straw bed and curled himself up like a dog with his nose tucked into his legs.

Toby sat on, meaning just to watch him go to sleep. But he fell asleep himself. When the groom came in to see if everything was in order for the night, he found the young gentleman asleep with his head against the horse's neck. He approached to wake him up, to take him into the house, but Feste opened a rolling eye and put his ears back with a dangerous look, making it quite plain that no one was to disturb either of them.

The groom hesitated, then he went out and brought back two more blankets that he spread over Toby. Feste opened an eye, but did not move. When the groom had gone he sighed and shut it again. So there they slept together. The next thing that Toby knew was that Feste was blowing down his neck as if to say: 'That supper was splendid, but how about breakfast?'

TOLLY WOKE EARLY NEXT morning, still excited with the knowledge that the world into which he was born had once produced a Feste. He lay for a moment with his eyes shut, listening for any sound there might be in the room. The slow tick-tock came out of the silence, and then a soft whirring followed by the little tap of a bird perching, and lastly, sounding very loud because it was near his ear, a scratching of bird-claws on his sheet and the tiny bump of a bird's hop on his chest. When he opened his eyes he looked straight into the round black eye of the chaffinch.

It gave a loud chirp, as if it were making an important statement, something like 'I'm as good as you are', but with no boastfulness, only friendly confidence. Then it flew out of the window. In a moment it was back. 'I'm as good as you are' it said, and went into the cage for the last of the pastry crumbs.

It hopped round the room examining everything

with its head tipped sideways as if its eye were a spotlight. It tugged at Toseland's shoe-laces, picked up his Twig T that he had put carefully by his bed, tried to fly away with it, but found it too heavy and threw it away. In front of the big mirror it bowed to its own reflection, announced as usual 'I'm as good as you are' and seemed to wait for a reply. Getting none, it flew out of the window again.

'How quickly it makes up its mind about everything,' thought Toseland, getting out of bed and climbing on to the rocking-horse. He worked hard, making it rear high and higher until it stood right up on its hind-legs and he had to clutch it round the neck and lean forward to bring it down again. 'My golden eagle, my wise horse, my powerful otter,' he chanted as he rocked. Before he went down to breakfast he brushed its mane and tail and put two rugs over it, belting them round with the strap of his trunk.

He went to the bed to get his mouse from under the pillow. As his hand closed over it, it felt warm to his touch, and with surprise he saw pastry crumbs in the bed. Suddenly he remembered Mrs Oldknow's question: 'And did the mouse squeak and the dogs bark?'

'Mouse, mouse,' he said, looking into its shiny black eye, 'where have you been? This house is full of shiny black eyes, all looking at me.'

As he went down the winding wooden stairs he heard someone whistling in his bedroom behind him. A bird? He turned his head to listen, but what he heard was laughter in the Music Room below him. He pelted down the stairs, making a great noise with his shoes, but by then children's voices came from his great-grandmother's room beyond.

Mrs Oldknow was there, turning her head and bending down as if she were listening to a child that was clutching her skirts. She looked up with a queer smile as Tolly came in, rather as if she had been caught. 'What a hurry you are in for breakfast this morning! Pelting down your stairs as if you were chasing butterflies.' Toseland had a feeling that she was hiding something from him. The voices and laughter had vanished.

All that day it seemed that the children were determined to tease Tolly. In the house, in the garden, wherever he was not, they were. They sounded so happy, so full of games and high spirits that Tolly, in spite of all disappointments, still ran towards it when he heard 'coo-ee' in the garden, or stopped and crept stealthily round a corner when he heard whispering. But he found no one. While he was loitering round St Christopher's feet he was playfully pelted with beechnuts through the window-opening in the garden wall. When he visited the Green Deer he found twigs on the ground arranged like arrows pointing a trail. He followed these past the green squirrel, the green hare, the peacock, and the cock and hen, till he arrived at the fish platform. There all he found was more twigs arranged to form the letters T, A, L. He broke off two more and put another T underneath. There was a little dog barking somewhere, rather muffled as if someone were trying to keep it quiet.

He visited Feste's stall, walking in on tiptoe as some people do in church. The sugar was gone again! Joyfully he put another piece.

He felt very good-tempered all morning, but by the middle of the afternoon he had forgotten that yesterday he had been dull because there was no hide-and-seek. Now he was cross because there was too much of it.

'I hate hide-and-seek when you never find anybody,' he said to himself. 'It's a perfectly horrid game.' He

71

walked to the house kicking sticks and stones as he went. He even felt inclined to kick St Christopher, but stopped in time and was ashamed of having such a thought.

As he went along the entrance hall, past one of the big mirrors, something in it caught his eye. It looked like a pink hand. The glass reflected a dark doorway on the other side of the stairs. Behind the door-post, flattened against the wall on tiptoe to make themselves as thin as they could, their faces puckered with holding in their laughter, he saw Linnet and Alexander. It was Linnet's hand on the door-post. Their black eyes were fixed on him. There was no mistake, he knew them.

'I spy!' he shouted, whisking round to chase them, but they did not run away, they simply vanished.

He felt the wall where they had been; he looked all round. He ran out to the Green Deer, but the clearing was empty and quiet. Certainly the Green Deer looked magic enough, ready to spring away. The light was queer too, the sky was dark green, the wind dead. Tolly was half frightened. Something was going to happen.

As he looked up at St Christopher's face a snowflake drifted past it, then another, and suddenly it was snowing thickly. Like millions of tiny white birds circling home to roost, the flakes danced in the air. They filled the sky as far up as he could imagine. At the same time all the sounds in the world ceased. The snow was piling up on the branches, on the walls, on the ground, on St Christopher's face and shoulders, without any sound at all, softer than the thin spray of fountains, or falling leaves, or butterflies against a window, or wood ash dropping, or hair when the barber cuts it. Yet when a flake landed on his cheek it was heavy. He felt the splosh but could not hear it.

He went in plastered with snow, and here tea was ready, with Mrs Oldknow sitting by the fire waiting for him. In the fire the snow drifting down the chimney was making the only noise it ever can – a sound like the striking of fairy matches; though sometimes when the wind blows you can hear the snow like a gloved hand laid against the window.

Tolly made the toast and his great-grandmother spread it with honey. They talked about Christmas. Mrs Oldknow said Boggis was going to buy the tree the next day, unless they were snowed up. Tolly hoped they would be. He liked the idea of being snowed up in a castle. By the light of the candles he could see the flakes drifting past the windows.

'What will the birds do?' he asked.

'They do not mind the snow so long as we feed them. Is your window open enough for the chaffinch to get in? Take some shortbread and make him welcome.' Tolly did as she said. When he came down again the curtains were all drawn, and he settled down by the fire in hopes of another story.

'Granny, both my pieces of sugar have gone out of Feste's stall.'

'Perhaps Boggis takes them and puts them in his tea,' she said, laughing.

Tolly's face fell. He had never thought of anything so low-down, so common. He was shattered.

At that moment, while Mrs Oldknow was still laughing at him, outside the door that led into the garden someone began a Christmas carol. Children's voices, delicate and expert, were singing 'The Holly and the Ivy'. Tolly had never heard such beautiful singing. He listened entranced.

O the rising of the sun
The running of the deer
The playing of the merrie organ
Sweet singing in the choir.

'What will they sing next?' he asked in a whisper, and waited in silence. 'I saw three ships come sailing by' was the next, and then a carol Tolly did not know, which began, 'Tomorrow shall be my dancing day' and which ended:

Sing O my love, my love, my love, my love,
This have I done for my true love.

When that was finished there was a pause and a little girl's laugh – ah, he knew that laugh now! Mrs Oldknow's eyes were fixed on him and she saw him start.

'Shall we let them in?' she asked. Tolly nodded, unable to speak. In his mind he could see the three of them standing there in the snow with their lanterns, ready to come in. She opened the door. Cold white snow blew in out of the darkness, nothing else. Mrs Oldknow stood there smiling at nobody. Tolly flung himself face downwards into one of the big chairs, with angry tears.

'I want to be with them. I want to be with them. Why can't I be with them?' he cried. Mrs Oldknow came to comfort him.

'Don't cry, my dear. You'll find them soon. They're like shy animals. They don't come just at first till they are sure. You mustn't be impatient.' She stopped, then shook him. 'Toseland, listen! Listen! Do you hear what I hear?'

Tolly sat up and strained his ears. Did he? Mrs Oldknow opened the door again, and then he heard it. Faint and muffled by the falling snow a high insistent whinny came from the stables. Tolly listened with bright dry eyes, till the whinny ceased. Toby and Feste were together, and he, Tolly, was content that it should be so.

That night Mrs Oldknow, when she came to see him to bed, stayed longer than usual. The chaffinch was already there, fluffed up in his cage with his head under his wing, taking no notice of either of them. The night-light was lit, and Tolly was pleased to see on the ceiling in the patterned shadow of the cage, the shadow of a bird, as big as a football.

'See how much quicker the shadow-horse goes than the rocking-horse,' said Mrs Oldknow, giving it a forward push. The shadow-horse leaped ahead, stretching out a long neck and forward-pointing ears, as if it could leap out of the room at a bound.

'When I was little, I used to pretend the rocking-horse had got Feste's shadow instead of its own.'

'Who told you about Feste?'

'My grandfather first. But afterwards I used to hear them talking.'

Tolly had a very big question troubling him, that could not wait. He wriggled under the bed-clothes until only his eyes showed, and then in his smallest voice he asked: 'Granny, do you see them?'

'Not always,' she said, as if it were quite a simple thing to talk about.

'Did you see them tonight when you opened the door?'

'Yes, darling. They were all three there. At the very beginning I only saw them sometimes in mirrors.'

Tolly came out from under the bed-clothes. 'I do,' he said proudly. 'At least, only Alexander and Linnet, once.'

'Toby is always the rarest. You see, he is often with Feste.'

'Do you ever see Feste?'

'Never,' she said sadly. 'But my grandfather told me he did sometimes.'

Tolly breathed again. There was still hope.

'Was his name Toseland too?'

'Yes, my dear, it was.'

Tolly put the ebony mouse into his pyjama pocket, thinking to himself it would make it come warm more quickly. Mrs Oldknow watched him.

'Is the mouse behaving?'

He grinned happily. 'Not bad,' he said.

I N THE MORNING HE was woken up by the chaffinch scolding and tut-tutting, and the sound of its feet skidding on the polished floor. At first he thought it must be having a fight with another bird, in the far corner of the room behind some boxes. He got up to look. Outside it was still snowing hard. He could see nothing out of the window but passing flakes.

The chaffinch was tugging at a piece of string that went down between two floor-boards where the crack was rather large. His claws were spread to give him a better hold on the floor, but when he arched his back to pull and jerked his head, his claws slipped again, so that he was clearly cross.

Tolly gently moved him away and lay down to look into the crack. He pulled on the string, but the other end was fast to something. It looked to him like an iron ring. He could not move it however much he pulled or poked. At last he remembered an old silver button-hook that lay at the back of a drawer in the table. (The chaffinch by now had lost interest and was collecting fluff under the bed.) With the button-hook Tolly was able to give a tug on the ring and work it about. It proved to be something quite big, and when at last he was able to pull it out of the crack he saw that it was an old key.

His first thought was the right one. The toy-box! The key fitted and turned. Tolly put his hand to the lid, and then stopped. He would not open it without Mrs Oldknow. Down his narrow winding stairs he went helter-skelter, shouting for her at the top of his voice.

'Come and see what I've found. Come quickly, come and see.'

Mrs Oldknow was getting dressed. She came in a quilted black dressing-gown and without her teeth.

She looked so old that Tolly could easily believe she was as old as the house. He would not tell her what he had found till she had panted up the stairs and they were kneeling together before the toy-box.

'Shall we open it now?' she asked.

Tolly nodded and they each put out a hand and lifted the lid.

The box was full. Lying right on the top was a long, narrow, leather case decorated with gold patterns. Mrs Oldknow gave a long 'Oh!', as if for once she was really surprised. 'It's Alexander's flute! Oh Tolly, will you learn to play it?' She took it out of its box where it lay in a velvet slot, put it to her lips and began to play.

In almost no time there was a sound like wind, and outside the windows the air was as full of birds as of snow. Somewhere downstairs a little dog barked, and in his pyjama jacket Tolly was sure the mouse squeaked.

The old lady was trembling with excitement. She laid down the flute. Under the flute-case there were books, which her hands touched one after the other, as if she dared not take them out. Suddenly she shut the lid. 'Come, Tolly, let us go and feed the birds since we have called them. We'll look at the rest after breakfast.'

They hurried to finish their dressing and met again downstairs, both their faces so bright with excitement that for all the difference in their age they were very much alike.

Great flakes of snow blotted out all the distant view. The bushes in the garden were upholstered with fat snow cushions. The yew trees by the house were like huge tattered snow umbrellas. The branches were weighed down nearly to the ground and shielded it from the snow. Underneath them the birds had gathered to wait for their breakfast, shaking off the snow that had settled on their heads and backs during their flight round the upper windows.

'We'll have a bird party to celebrate finding the flute,' said Mrs Oldknow. 'Yes, I'll butter your hands again, and we will put plates of cake crumbs and grated cheese on the floor.'

When it was ready she opened the door wide. She had the flute in her hand and, as she played, the birds flew in – chaffinches, cole-tits, blue-tits, longtailed-tits, robins, wrens and hedge-sparrows were there immediately. They behaved as if quite at home: Tolly was nearly covered with them. The air was electric with the whirr of wings. The blackbirds stood off by the threshold at first, then one by one, as if in a tournament, they charged in long galloping hops into the room and out again with their loot. Close outside in the branches, the most exciting bird Tolly had ever seen was waiting to pick up what the blackbirds dropped.

'Is that a phoenix?' he asked, pulling Mrs Oldknow's arm. She still had her lips to the flute. She shook her head.

'Woodpecker,' she said, between two notes.

The little birds were well mannered. They gave the impression of talking and laughing and enjoying themselves very much. Tolly thought it was the gayest party he had ever been to. When everything was eaten the robin sang a little song, perching on top of a picture. The tits explored the room, perching right way up or upside down on chair backs, on curtains, on candlesticks and light shades, showing great curiosity and making little polite remarks. They seemed pleased to stay in out of the snow. The blackbirds fought like border raiders all over the garden for what they had taken away. The woodpecker had flown. Mrs Oldknow was just closing the door to keep out the snow when the starlings arrived, late and noisy as usual.

'I won't have them in the house,' she said, throwing out a plateful of crumbs and shutting the door.

She and Toseland took their breakfast and sat by the fire to eat it. Outside their castle walls all was silence again and falling snow, but inside they laughed to each other as happily as if they were bewitched. When they had finished she gave him his first lesson in playing the flute. It was difficult, but he made some sounds that he thought were lovely.

While she was showing him how to do it, his eyes wandered to the window, and there outside, sitting up in the snow with its ears pricked, was a hare. When Tolly ran to look, with shouts of joy, it lolloped away. Too late then he began to whisper, 'Toby's hare, Granny, Toby's hare!'

They went upstairs together to see what else was in the box. The chaffinch came too, hopping round hopefully as if there might be something for him inside. The books were very big, bound in leather, the pages spotted with brown marks. There were lots of pictures.

'Ah,' said Mrs Oldknow, 'here's the *Aeneid*. That's the book Alexander has in the picture, that his father brought with him from Germany. And here's

Aesop's Fables. That's Linnet's. She used to look at it in bed, and laugh! Especially at the Ass in the lion's skin. Here's *Merlin the Sorcerer* and Malory's *Morte d'Arthur*. Those are Toby's, but they all loved them. *The History of Troy*. That's Alexander's again.'

'What's this?' said Tolly, dragging out something like a big dog-collar, except that it was so beautiful, in blue enamelled leather with tiny jewels on it.

'You know what that is. Think! You've often seen it.'

'I know, I know! It's the deer's collar. It belonged to Toby, then. I'll put it on Toby's heap. Couldn't we clean it? It looks almost like a crown. Something for Linnet now – she's only got one book.'

Mrs Oldknow poked into the corner of the box and brought out a small painted wooden figure. Its skirts came down to the ground and there was a large shawl over its head and shoulders so that it was the shape of a round bottle and stood up by itself. The paint was rich and old and nearly worn off.

'It's a box,' she said. 'See if you can open it. The lid's at the bottom.'

The bottom came loose with a loud wooden squeak, and out fell another figure, exactly like the first but painted in different colours and just a little smaller.

'She's got a daughter!' said Tolly, opening the second to reveal a third, and a fourth, and a fifth, and so on, until the last one was shaken out, only as high as a pea. They made a family of ten.

'Those came from Russia, when Captain Oldknow went to the Black Sea. And this box from China,' Mrs Oldknow said, handing him a highly polished black box. Inside it were little jugs and bowls and plates, all cut out of ivory and so paper-thin that they were half transparent. The biggest was not as big as a thimble.

'Yes, yes,' said Tolly, as excited as if he were preparing presents under a Christmas tree. 'These are for Linnet's heap.'

He began to set the plates out as if he were laying the table.

'There are no tea-cups,' he said.

'They weren't invented when Linnet was little, only bowls and mugs. Nor were forks. They all ate with their fingers.'

'Do you mean that if they came to dinner with us they would eat with their fingers? Suppose it was stew?'

'They would sop it up with bread in their fingers.'

'Did you eat with your fingers?' asked Tolly, who

86

could never be sure she was not the old lady in the picture. 'And Toby too?'

'Toby, and his mother and his grandmother and his great-grandmother, all the way back to Adam. But they did it very nicely; you would hardly notice. And they had napkins. Aubrey Oldknow's wife (your great-great-great-great-grandmother) was the first lady in this country to use a fork. It was *very* grand. People were afraid to come to dinner in case they did it wrong. Old gentlemen were very annoyed and said they could not enjoy their food picking away at it with a silver prong. Captain Oldknow never would. He said it was fiddle-faddle.'

She handed Tolly a box of ivory and ebony dominoes.

'You can put them on any of the heaps. They all played with them.'

'I'll put it on Toby's because he is the oldest.'

'And your favourite.'

At the bottom of the box, lying from corner to corner, was a long bundle wrapped round in green cloth. Mrs Oldknow lifted it out and put it on the floor while she unwrapped it. At first they saw a tangle of belts, straps and tassels, and then Tolly gave a great cry.

'It's Toby's sword!'

If Toby had fallen a little from his high place in Tolly's admiration because he ate with his fingers, how high he rose now, when Tolly pulled the real sword out of its scabbard! It had a long, fine blade with an edge on each side. Tolly lunged forward to poke the bed with it. It went in about four inches.

'Stop putting swords through the bed-clothes,' said Mrs Oldknow in an ordinary voice.

'Did Toby use it?' asked Tolly solemnly.

'He never stuck it into anyone, if that is what you mean. But he learnt to fence, and he wore it on Sundays when he went to church with his mother.'

'Why doesn't he want it now?' Mrs Oldknow looked at him with an uneasy wrinkled face. Then she sighed.

'Because he's dead,' she said at last.

Tolly sat dumbfounded, with his big black eyes fixed on her. He must have known of course that the children could not have lived so many centuries without growing old, but he had never thought about it. To him they were so real, so near, they were his own family that he needed more than anything on earth. He felt the world had come to an end.

'Are they all dead?' he said at last.

'They all died together in the Great Plague. The farm bailiff, Boggis, had been to London on business and he brought the infection back with him. Toby and Alexander and Linnet and their mother all died in one day, in a few hours. And little Boggis too. Only poor old grandmother was left, too unhappy to cry.'

Tolly sat cross-legged with his head hanging, trying not to show his face.

Mrs Oldknow got up and walked to the door where she could look down the staircase into what Tolly called the Knight's Hall, as if she were looking for someone.

'After all,' she said, 'it sounds very sad to say they all died, but it didn't really make so much difference. I expect the old grandmother soon found out they were still here.'

Tolly was watching something travelling across the floor towards him. It was a marble, a glass one with coloured spirals in the middle. It stopped by his listless fingers. He picked it up. It was warm.

He glanced round the room but saw nothing, except that the dust of which the old box and its contents were full was hanging in the air as if newly disturbed. Then under his eyes the dominoes began of their own accord to stand themselves on end one by one, till they made a long regular curving line, each an inch behind the other. When they were all standing, an unseen finger pushed the last one, which fell over and knocked down the one in front of it. With a soft purr which startled the inquisitive chaffinch up into the air, each domino in turn fell forward till all were lying flat on their white faces, showing a long ribbon of black backs.

Tolly laughed suddenly and loudly. Mrs Oldknow looked round.

'Ah,' she said, smiling, 'their grandmother taught them that game. Wouldn't she be surprised when she saw it happen all by itself? That's Alexander. Linnet never could do it right.'

'Aren't they teases?' said Tolly, quite comforted. 'I'm going to look at their books.'

Mrs Oldknow looked at him with loving approval.

'All right,' she said. 'Dust the books first and then wash your hands. The books are very valuable.' She went away.

Tolly did as she said. 'I'll clean Toby's sword for him afterwards,' he thought, settling himself down with the book of *Aesop's Fables* open on the floor. The print was difficult, but he knew the stories and enjoyed the pictures. After a while, he came to the page that had the Ass in the lion's skin, Linnet's favourite. He bent down to have a closer look, but as he did so two hands were pressed over his eyes from behind and he could feel breathing beside his ear. He put his hands up and felt two very little ones and some curls, soft little cobwebs.

'Linnet!' he said at once, trying to catch hold of the fingers, but they melted away and there was nobody.

'All right,' he said, 'you tease – I can tease too. If you won't let me look at your book, I won't let you look at it either.'

He shut *Aesop* up and sat on it, listening and looking on every side. He heard nothing and saw nothing, but underneath him the book began to move, as if someone were tugging at it. Suddenly he was frightened and jumped up and ran away downstairs to his great-grandmother's reassuring company.

'It did feel horrid,' he thought, to excuse himself as he caught hold of her dress and followed her round. She asked no questions and they sat down together for lunch.

Tolly had almost forgotten the snow, but it was still snowing hard. The garden was getting stranger and stranger. The bushes were just hummocks, little hills in the smooth snow. Even the big yews had lowered their branches to the ground under the weight of it and were getting tied down under the drifts. The snow lay thick round the doors and windows, stopping all draughts, so that the room was warm and rosy with firelight.

'This will be a night for telling stories,' said Mrs Oldknow. Tolly was happy.

'And this afternoon I want to clean Toby's sword,' he said.

They spent the afternoon cleaning it together. Tolly did the blade with paraffin and glass-paper. He was very careful and did not cut himself. Mrs Oldknow did the scabbard, which was covered with velvet. Boggis, coming in out of the snow, very skilfully and lovingly undid the belt and straps.

'I was once a cavalry officer's servant,' he told Tolly.

'These straps want soaking in oil for a week before they are touched.'

'Where shall we put it?' said Mrs Oldknow when the sword was ready, all but the belt which Boggis had taken away. 'We must hang it up somewhere. Would you like it in your room? It would make a lovely shadow at night.' They hung it beside the mirror opposite Tolly's bed.

T HIS WAS THE TALE that Mrs Oldknow told him by the fire that evening.

THE STORY OF BLACK FERDIE

A long time ago, when Boggis's grandfather was the gardener here, my grandfather Sir Toseland Oldknow was the owner. He had three grown-up sons who kept many beautiful horses. In particular the youngest, Alexander, my father, had a black mare which was famous as the fastest racer in the country. They thought of nothing but horses and could have done with much more stable room. Nevertheless, as you know, one stall was always left empty.

Now it happened in the year when my grandfather was made a Judge that some gypsy caravans passing through this country camped for a while on a common outside Greatchurch. In one of the caravans lived an old gypsy woman called Petronella and her son, who was called Black Ferdie.

Black Ferdie was tall and slim and very handsome. There was no girl who would say 'No' to him when he smiled. He was without an equal as a horse-breaker or as a rider. He was afraid of no horse on earth, but all horses were afraid of him because he sat them like the Devil, relentlessly. He was famous among the gypsies and the pride of his mother. He was in fact a horse thief.

Black Ferdie soon heard of my father's mare and made up his mind to steal her. He began to watch the house, hiring himself out to farmers as a hedge-cutter in order not to attract attention, and he cut off his long gypsy hair and even washed his face.

There was a girl called Ivy who worked for my grandmother as a linen-maid, and she went every day to hang the washing on the hedge to dry. She was a pretty, good-natured girl who loved to talk and laugh. Black Ferdie knew as soon as he saw her that his work would be easy.

He spoke to her every day, and he was so handsome, so amusing and so flattering that very soon he was her best friend. She could think of nothing else and often brought in the washing before it was dry because she could not wait any longer to see him again. Wet days were an agony to her because she could not go out to him but had to sit darning.

One day Black Ferdie, who called himself Tom, asked her if there was no place at the Hall for him, because if he could work there he could see her all the time.

'It is true,' she said, 'they want an under-gardener, but everybody who works here is a son or nephew of someone who has always been here. Judge Oldknow would never take you.'

'But they took you just because you were so pretty,' said Black Ferdie.

'No indeed. I am the daughter of Mr Alexander's sergeant who saved his life in the Low Country.'

'Well, my beauty, you only have to say that I am your cousin, who has served in the Navy and now wants to settle down. My name is the same as yours, you know.'

'Is it really?'

'Well, what is yours?'

'Ivy Softly.'

'Just what I said. Mine is Softly too, Tom Softly.'

'Oh, Tom! Isn't that strange? I may call you Tom if you are my cousin. But I never knew I had any.'

'Everyone has cousins they never hear of,' said Black Ferdie, and he told her a wonderful tale about a mutiny in the Far East in which he had saved the captain's life, only afterwards discovering that they were cousins too.

Poor Ivy believed all he told her, though she was not absolutely convinced he was her cousin. It was not difficult to persuade her to ask my grandmother to recommend Tom to the Judge. She thought that if it was not true about his being her cousin, it was only a very little lie, and if he became her husband he would be in the family then if he was not before.

So Black Ferdie became under-gardener. He was exceedingly civil and industrious and made a good impression. As luck would have it, the first job he was given was to weed the cobbled yard. As he knelt there all day, picking out the grass and mosses, he saw the horses being led out and in, and admired the black mare that he had come to steal. He noticed where the stable key was hung.

That evening Judge Oldknow was entertaining one of the neighbouring squires to dinner. While this was in progress, Black Ferdie sat in the kitchen with his arm round Ivy, telling breath-taking stories about the Navy to the other servants.

Most of it was quite impossible, because he had never been to sea, but neither had the other servants, so they believed everything, with the exception of old Boggis, who every now and then gave a most irritating sniff when Tom's conduct (in the story) was more than usually admirable.

When he could hear that the gentlemen in the diningroom were growing merry and noisy, Black Ferdie made an excuse and slipped out into the yard. Stealing round in the shadow of the buildings he entered the stables.

Earlier in the evening he had given young Boggis, who was to watch the horses, a bottle of wine to pass the time away in case the gentlemen drank late. He found him now, as he expected, asleep in the harness-room with his head sunk on the table. The lantern hanging from a nail in the wall only lit a corner of the stable corridor. Outside, the rising moon was hidden from the earth by mist and trees, but high-sailing clouds caught its light and with their silver-gilt brightness reflected a glimmer through the stable windows that was enough for a thief's trained eyes.

Black Ferdie took a bridle and moved quietly along the stalls. Most of the horses were lying down, dim shapes that stirred and blew, shaking their manes. Ferdie passed them one by one, accustoming his eyes to the gloom. The neighbour's horse was standing, being in a strange stable. It was a staid old hack of no interest to him.

The black mare was also standing, because she was a fidget. As she sensed his presence her head flew up as high as the halter would let it, and she snorted and sidled into her corner.

The moon must have cleared the trees, for just then the light grew stronger and Ferdie saw in the stall beyond hers a horse that had not been led past him during the day. He had counted them, and his eye, used to rounding up horses at night, could recognize them more certainly than you or I could by day. This horse was a chestnut with four white feet, with an arch to its neck and a spring in the movement of its haunches, a nervous delicacy in the lifting of its feet that put all thought of the black mare out of Ferdie's head.

'Now, there's a horse for a man to ride!' he thought, and turned into the chestnut's stall with the bridle in his hand.

As he approached, whistling softly, the horse turned its head towards him, putting back its ears and showing its teeth and the white half-moons of its eyes.

There was no rattling of the halter ring to which it should have been tied. Black Ferdie saw that it was as free and relentless as he was, and that there was a quality of moonlight in its eyes and teeth that his nerves could not endure.

He ran in sheer terror, but the horse reared round after him, wheeling through the narrow openings and out at the main door.

It caught him halfway across the cobbled yard, snatching the back of his belted breeches in its teeth. It swung him dreadfully in the air and tossed him away. He crashed on to the cobbles and broke his knee.

The chestnut stood and lifted its head to give a prolonged, penetrating neigh, so that the cheerful gentlemen indoors put down their glasses to listen with white faces. All the other horses then joined in the clamour, stamping and kicking in their stalls.

'Horse thieves!' shouted Alexander, and they snatched up their pistols and ran out.

They found Black Ferdie lying helpless with his broken knee, his teeth chattering and his face grey and damp with sweat. However, he did his best to make up a story.

'The thieves have got away with the chestnut,' he said. 'I saw the stable door open and I came to see if anything was wrong. They were just coming out with the chestnut, two of them, and when I tried to stop them they rode me down. They haven't taken the black mare.'

The judge and his guests stood by him with their pistols while the two elder sons did what they could to ease his knee. Alexander, with the servants, went to search the stables. The eldest son, while he was trying to arrange the injured man so that he could lie more easily, pulled a pair of pistols out of his great-coat pocket, while Ferdie swore with rage.

'Look, sir,' said the son, 'he was armed!' Alexander came back then.

'Everything's all right, sir,' he reported, 'except that Harry Boggis is asleep beside a bottle of wine. It takes more than a bottle to put him under the table, so I guess it was drugged. One of our bridles was lying in the black mare's stall.'

'Come here, Alexander,' said his father, 'and be a witness to what this man says. Now Tom, which horse was stolen?'

'The chestnut with four white feet,' said Black Ferdie with his teeth chattering. 'In the stall next to the black mare. It rode me down and broke my knee. Hurry, sir, you may overtake them yet. There were two up.'

'The chestnut in the stall next to the black mare,' repeated the Judge.

Nobody spoke, and Ferdie's hair began to stand on end. The Judge's guest, who had not yet spoken, now took a lantern and held it to Tom's face.

'I know this man,' he said. 'He is a gypsy known as Black Ferdie. He sold me a horse last Michaelmas at Norwich fair.'

'Take him up,' said the Judge, 'and lock him up safely for the night. In the morning we will send him to the prison hospital.'

Poor Ivy cried bitterly when she confessed that she had told a lie about his being her cousin. The Judge would have sent her home in disgrace, but my grandmother pleaded for her, because, she said, Linnet loved her so much. They all thought she meant me – I was only a baby and I had no mother – but sometimes now I wonder.

'What happened to Black Ferdie?'

'He was tried and found guilty and sent to Botany Bay in Australia.'

'What did his old mother do then?'

'No more questions,' said Mrs Oldknow, suddenly in a hurry. 'Old Petronella was as bad as he. Worse. Now off you go to bed.'

THERE WERE MANY things waiting for him in his bedroom now. The chaffinch was curled up and fluffed out on its perch. The not-quite-ordinary mouse was there to be put under his pillow. There were all the quivering shadows thrown by the night-light, and now there was a new one. Behind Toby's sword was another larger, fiercer, man-sized sword hanging on the same nail. The books were on the table. They made mountainous steps on the sloping ceiling.

Tolly took the Russian doll and placed that on the table too, beside the night-light. At once its shadow stood in the room, nearly as big as St Christopher. There seemed hardly any space left for Tolly himself, so he pushed the doll a little further away from the light till the shadow grew smaller. 'I don't want it any bigger than Linnet,' he thought. 'Linnet wrapped up in a shawl.' When the room was comfortably full of shadow doubles of things he liked, and his own shadow had sat up in bed and stretched a long arm to touch the outstretched nose of the shadow rocking-horse, he blew out the candle by his bed and curled up to sleep.

Outside the wind was singing, and soft noises came from the windows which would have been rattling if they had not been cushioned up with snow. Tolly slept, and his dreams were most wonderful, but when he opened his eyes in the morning he could not remember at all what they had been. The window-panes were covered thickly with frost-patterns of forest ferns – he could not see the real world at all. The chaffinch was pecking at the glass on the inside, but the window was frozen shut.

'Come, chaffie,' said Tolly, holding out a finger. 'I'll let you out downstairs.'

The chaffinch flew to him as if it understood, and

they went downstairs together. The other birds were
feeding at the open door where Mrs Oldknow stood.

Outside, the world was most magical. It had stopped
snowing. The garden looked like the back of a giant
swan curled up to sleep. There was nothing but white
slopes, white curves, white rounded softnesses with
bright blue shadows. Nothing had been scraped aside
or trodden on. The only footmarks were the birds'
round the door. The yew trees had disappeared. In
their place were white hills with folds and creases in
their sides. Tolly picked up a handful of snow and
found it was made up of tiny violet stars. He could
hardly eat his breakfast for excitement.

'Can I go out in it? I won't be able to walk without making marks.'

Mrs Oldknow hesitated. Then she smiled.

'I won't allow Boggis to sweep or walk round here,' she said. 'I love it so much quite untouched. But you have never really met deep snow before. You must learn what it is. You can go, darling. You are just the right age.'

'I won't mess it just here,' he said. 'I'll go round by the wall and keep out of sight.'

He set off, taking huge strides, sinking in to the top of his legs at every step, so that the snow was needle-cold on his bare knees and thighs. St Christopher was a snow-buttress stuck on the side of the house, up to his armpits in a drift. Tolly made slow progress, so slow that with everything unrecognizable it was quite hard to know where he was. He looked backwards and saw his own dragging footprints, like wounds in the snow. In front of him the world was an unbroken dazzling cloud of crystal stars, except for the moat, which looked like a strip of night that had somehow sinned and had no stars in it. The water was blue-bottle black with slabs of green ice floating just beneath the surface. Thick snow banks overhung the edge. Tolly could see them at the far side with snow caves underneath, so he was careful to keep away from the near edge lest he should go through.

Where was anything he knew? Was that hump the position of the Green Deer, or was it only an ivy bush? Which of these strange shrouded trees had the green squirrel sitting in the drift against its trunk? And what was that in the pathless garden that looked like a giant snowman eyeless among the slender tree-trunks and the soft hills that might cover anything?

The smell of the snow made him feel a little dizzy, and the deep silence and the absence of any footprints but his own rather frightened him. He felt like turning back and running for home, but who can run when up to his waist in snow? It was then that he noticed some other footprints beside his own.

Along the top of the snow, as if their owner had almost no weight, pointed feet were printed, a little animal that went in long bounds. It had gone towards the snow tent of a yew tree. The footprints disappeared inside the folds of the thick curtain. Tolly followed the trail, feeling ashamed that he could not help leaving such big ugly marks behind him. He bent down to go in under the tree without shaking the snow off the branches. As he crouched at the entrance, he heard the enchanting notes of a flute near at hand.

Inside was a high, tent-shaped room with branches for beams and rafters, lit with a shadowless opal light through the snow walls. In the centre, leaning against the bole of the tree, were Toby and Alexander, with Linnet sitting on the dry yew-needle carpet at their feet. It was Alexander of course who was playing, while a red squirrel ran up and down him, searching in his pockets for nuts. Toby was feeding the deer, the real deer, the beautiful dappled deer with black ears and a white breast. It wagged its tail like a lamb as it ate from his hand. Linnet was playing with the lanky hare, making it stand up and dance to the music. With its long ears raised it was taller than she as she knelt. Her little dog danced on its hind legs more vigorously than the hare to attract her attention.

Tolly was afraid to breathe or move lest they should vanish, but their eyes were all on him, and they smiled. He sat down just where he was, by the snow wall, and said nothing.

All kinds of animals were round the children. There

was a shallow bowl of milk on the ground from which a hedgehog was drinking. Beside it, a rabbit that had just finished was sitting up wiping its whiskers. Alexander took the flute from his lips just long enough to say, 'Keep an eye on the fox. I don't want him to hurt the rabbit.'

Tolly looked round, and there next to him, sitting up like a dog with the sharpest of sharp looks, was the fox.

'He's not so bad,' said Toby, 'and he has had a piece of meat. But he needs watching.'

Up in the branches were hosts of birds. A thrush was learning the tune. Whenever Alexander stopped, it tried a solo. Then he would play the notes it wanted and the bird would repeat them. Robins and tits, of course, were everywhere, and field mice running backwards and forwards taking crumbs to their larders. High up in the shadows, looking very haughty, sat the woodpecker. Every now and then it tapped the tree in time to the music but twice as fast. Toby poured some more milk into the bowl. The hedgehog was contentedly moving off, but a mole was putting its nose to the milk.

'That's Truepenny,' said Linnet. 'Poor Truepenny, he's blind. Let me have the squirrel, Alexander. I'm tired of Watt. He's too dreamy.'

'Funny Watt! He reminds me of a poor scholar at Cambridge. He is very intelligent, you know.'

'He's too well-behaved,' said Linnet. 'He's all Sunday go-to-meeting. He's one of Cromwell's preachies.'

'Nonsense,' said Toby. 'Watt is lovely magic. Haven't you ever seen him dancing with his bride in the twilight? He is cousin to the leprechaun and a distant relation of Feste.'

Just then there was a harsh noise at the door, like a badly cracked bugle, and a silly face wearing a crown was thrust in, followed by a long thin neck that never seemed to end. It closed its eyes and opened its beak to repeat the horrid shriek, advancing to draw behind it a gorgeous body and a tail like a coronation cloak. They all laughed.

'There's your high society for you, Linnet; the confounded peacock. No more music now, nothing but shrieks and posturing. We might just as well go.'

They were gone, like a magic lantern picture when the slide is taken out. A shower of loose snow came down from the branches as all the animals disappeared. Tolly had a feeling as if he had been dropped into the snow out of the sky. He did not know where he had been, nor for how long. He gazed round, noticing again the terrible silence of the snow. There was no sound, his ears ached with silence. After so much life there was suddenly nothing, no one but himself. Then he saw there was one other – Truepenny, who was blind and moved uncertainly. He looked bewildered too. Tolly picked him up. He was soft, velvety and helpless, with pink hands and feet.

'Poor Truepenny! I wonder where you came from? Can you hear flutes from your tunnel under the grass? You'd better go home again – it's all over.'

He put the mole down and waited to see it shuffle away into a heap of dead leaves that perhaps hid its hole. He sat for a while looking at the empty, glimmering, magical tent. Had he been dreaming? When at last he crept out again between the snow curtains, the sun was shining and above the snow the sky was blue. Somewhere in the garden a thrush was trying to whistle Alexander's tune.

Tolly followed his own footsteps now. 'Without them,' he thought, 'I feel as if I could get lost.' On the way, he looked again at the hump that might perhaps be over the Green Deer. It had a slightly rumpled look, like a bed when someone is pretending never to have been out of it. Through a thin place in the snow he recognized the bent brown stem that was the deer's back leg. Tolly tripped and fell full length in the snow. He got up and slipped again and the snow went into his mouth. He began to feel dreadfully tired, as if this bit of garden had been a great journey.

He was glad when he reached the house. Mrs Oldknow was waiting for him by the door. When she saw his eyes shining like big lamps she was very gentle.

'Sit down,' she said. 'I'll help you to get rid of some of this snow. I expect your Wellingtons are quite full. Pull! And all up inside your sleeves and your trousers – you are packed in snow!'

Tolly said nothing, but leant against her, and it felt nice. She was real, certain, and understanding. They ate their lunch without talking; it was chicken and Tolly was very hungry so they both enjoyed it. Afterwards he came and leant up against her again because he wanted to talk privately.

'Granny,' he said, 'isn't it queer?'

'You've seen them all three, then, today?'

'Yes, under the tree.'

'That's because of the deer. It always goes there

111

when the snow is deep.' Tolly did not like to mention the stem leg that he had seen afterwards sticking out of the snow eiderdown. It puzzled him too much.

'It's a wonderful snow house,' he said. 'It's like being in heaven and playing in the clouds. And then the confounded peacock came and spoiled everything.'

'It's the silliest thing that ever lived,' she said. 'And stuck up! Was it wearing its crown?'

'Yes, on its stupid little head.'

'On the end of a long, long neck like a hosepipe.'

'All the better for seeing round corners!' They both began to laugh, as people do when a silly mood takes them.

'It can't decide whether it has hands or feet.'

'When it walks it lifts up its toes like the hands of grand ladies, as if it wore rings and was looking for its handbag.'

'Then it scratches its ear with them.'

'It's deaf. It ought to have an ear-trumpet.'

'Then it and its wife could shriek at each other in turn.'

'What would happen if you trod on its tail?'

'I think it would hiccough.'

When they had finished making sillies of themselves

and Mrs Oldknow had wiped the laughter tears from her eyes, she suggested a lesson on the flute. Tolly was willing. 'But,' he said, 'Alexander has got it. How can there be two of it?'

'The one he has now is part of him. This is the one he used to have. It is like a snake-skin when the snake sloughs it off.' Tolly was displeased with this idea.

'No, Granny. This is Alexander's flute. It's the real one. I know it is not a flute-skin.'

He put it to his lips, curling them under in a funny smile as she had taught him. And though it was he who blew and moved his fingers it felt to him as though the stops pulled his fingers to them and the flute took his breath and played itself. A phrase of rippling notes came out. Tolly was ravished.

'That's what Alexander was playing to the birds,' he said.

He put it to his lips again, and the flute played it all through. Mrs Oldknow listened: for once she was completely astonished.

'I think Alexander has given you his flute,' she said. 'I'll teach you all the tunes he played. We will have some music every day, and you shall sing too.'

Before tea Tolly plodded out in Boggis's footsteps

to the stable. He looked everywhere for prints of horses' hooves, but he saw none. He left a lump of sugar, being careful that Boggis should not see, for he could not forget Mrs Oldknow's suggestion that it went into the blue tin tea-mug. What could I ever do, he wondered, to make Feste come for me? That of course was his highest ambition, but he almost despaired of it.

After tea there was another story by the fire. 'It is about Linnet this time,' Mrs Oldknow began. 'All the stories cannot be about Feste. It is about the river again, because the river is a very lively inhabitant here, always to be reckoned with, and there are many stories about it.'

LINNET'S STORY

It was Christmas Eve. There had been snow, then a dripping thaw that had filled the river, followed by a sudden hard frost. The trees dangled with icicles that tinkled like Japanese bells. The eaves were jagged with ice daggers. The ground was hard like glazed rock, the moat frozen. Toby and Alexander, with their mother, had gone on foot to Midnight Mass at the big church in Penny Soaky across the river. The little church in this village belonged to what Linnet called the preachies, who did not celebrate Midnight Mass. The family had gone on foot because the road was too slippery for horses, the ruts too hard for a coach. Linnet could not walk so far, so she was put to bed and the grandmother sat downstairs alone. Linnet took Orlando, her little black and white curly dog, to bed with her.

She had a little spruce tree in her bedroom – it was her own idea – for the birds. On such a cold night her tame birds had come in to sleep in its branches. They were curled up with their heads under their wings. The tits were balls of blue, or primrose-green; the robins red; the chaffinches pink. Linnet had put a crystal star on top. It glittered among the shadows in the candlelight.

As she lay in bed she heard the wind singing through the icicles outside. It was an eerie sound that made her think of the enormous silence of the country across which it blew. Every now and then an icicle broke off with a sharp crack.

Linnet lay and listened, thinking of her mother and her two brothers walking along the field paths in the brilliant moonlight with their black shadows following under their feet. If she listened for the outside noises she could hear the water going through the water gates and over the weir. There was no flood, but a deep, strong current. She could hear occasionally the owls and the desolate herons. Once she heard a fox bark. Inside her room perhaps one of the birds shifted and chirped softly in its sleep. She could hear Orlando breathing into his own fur. She could hear the candle flame fluttering like a little flag. It was all so very quiet.

Presently she heard something else, something very strange. Outside on the ice-hard ground there were footsteps that could be nothing and nobody that she knew, not Boggis's hobnailed boots, not her grandmother nor the quick young maid, not a horse! She was not frightened, she was simply certain that it did not belong to the everyday world. Orlando woke up and listened. Linnet could feel his tail softly beating against her ribs.

She got out of bed, wrapping herself in the cover so that she looked like the Russian doll, then she opened the window and leant out. Orlando stood beside her with his paws on the window-sill. She could distinctly

116

hear the steps, heavy but soft, coming along the side of the house. The wind was like a knife against her cheek and all the stars twinkled with cold. Orlando's reassuring tail was wagging against her.

Out into the moonlight came St Christopher himself, huge and gentle and with his head among the stars, taking the stone Child on his shoulders to Midnight Mass. As they went past, Orlando lifted his chin and gave a little cry, and from the stables came a quiet whinny. All the birds in the spruce tree woke up and flew out of the window, circling round St Christopher with excited calls. The stone giant strode across the lawns with his bare feet and soon came to the river. At the edge there was thin, loose ice that shivered like a window-pane as he stepped in. The water rushed round his legs and the reflection of the moon was torn to wet ribbons. The stream crept up to his waist and, as he still went on, to his armpits. When it looked as if he could go no farther Linnet heard a child's voice singing gaily. The sound was torn and scattered by the wind as the moon's reflection had been by the water, but she recognized the song as it came in snatches.

Tomorrow shall be my dancing day
I would my true love did so chance
To see the legend of my play
To call my true love to the dance.
Sing O my love, O my love, my love, my love,
This have I done for my true love.

As the Child sang, it clutched St Christopher by the hair to hold him firmly.

St Christopher felt his way carefully, foot by foot, through the deepest part and came out safely on the other side. Linnet saw him striding away across the meadows. The birds returned, coming in one by one past her head at the open window and chattering as they settled down again on the tree.

When St Christopher was out of sight Linnet realized that it was cold. She also remembered that she had got into bed without saying her prayers. She said them now, and Orlando lay on her feet and kept them warm till she had finished. Then she got into bed again and before long the bells rang out for midnight, and it was Christmas morning. When the boys came back she told them what she had seen. Alexander said he too had seen

St Christopher kneeling among the tombstones outside the church in the shadow of a big cypress tree. He thought nobody else had noticed.

Of course they rushed out first thing in the morning to look, and found St Christopher in his place as usual with icicles all over him, but the sun was falling on the stone Child and the hand that it held up looked almost pink.

TOLLY WENT UP TO BED, taking some crumbs for the chaffinch to eat in the morning. And who knows, perhaps the mouse too. When he reached his room at the top of the stairs, he was delighted to find a pair of tits there as well. 'Perhaps I'll have a Christmas tree with a star on top. That will make another lovely shadow.' There were the two china dogs on the chest of drawers staring him in the face. 'What can I do to have an Orlando? I can't put those icy cold things in my bed. Besides, they might fall out and break. I'll have to make do with the mouse.' When he was in bed he stroked it in his pyjama pocket and said, 'Mouse, mouse, come alive. Mouse, mouse, be magicked.' The mouse gave a twist in his pocket and squeaked, and climbed out and ran across his neck and squeezed past his ear, and flipped his cheek with its tail. But Tolly was already asleep.

The next morning, to Tolly's immense relief, the snow was still lying thick and sparkling, its surface touched only by the light feet of birds. There had been a fresh fall in the night that had half-filled Tolly's steps of the day before, so that they only showed as deep dimples. He could hardly wait to go out – much too anxious, lest he should find no children in the tree house, to be able to eat his breakfast. He stood by the door into the garden and fluted for all the birds and animals to hear, as a sign that he was coming as soon as he could.

He set off after breakfast round the corner past St Christopher, who was still warmly blanketed up by drifts of snow and wore a cowl of snow that wrapped his head and the stone Child's together. He tried to follow his own tracks but soon lost them. The wind had blown the drifts into different shapes. It was a new journey, as lonely and difficult as the last, but this time he knew what he wanted to find. He could see the pyramid of snow that was the yew tree. He would find the opening if he had to struggle through snow up to his neck. All the while he looked right and left for the springing trail of the squirrel, but it was Watt's ears he saw at last, sticking up from behind a hummock. Watt lolloped slowly along as if to show him the way, till Tolly, with his heart thumping with suspense, crawled after him through the low opening.

They were all there. Toby's handsome head was bent over a piece of rope that he was splicing. The deer was munching hay and oats out of a wooden bucket beside him. It looked round as Tolly came in, scratching behind its ear with a hind hoof. Linnet and Alexander were putting Linnet's little gold bracelet round the squirrel's neck. It fitted beautifully. They looked up together, meeting Tolly's eyes as so often in the picture. Tolly had bottled up so many questions inside him that they had to come out.

'Where is your mother?' he said.

'Why, in heaven of course, Ignoranty.' (Linnet said 'Ignoranty' as if it were a pet name.) 'But she doesn't mind our coming here.'

'Was the Great Plague awful?'

Alexander looked up smiling. 'No,' he said. 'It only lasted a few hours. I'd forgotten all about it.'

'I don't remember it at all,' said Linnet. 'What was it, Alexander?'

'Who's Ignoranty now?' said Toby.

'I am. I don't know anything about your stupid Plague,' said Linnet, laughing and rolling over, with her curls all mixed up with yew needles and ivy leaves. It seemed that anything was funny enough to make Linnet laugh. She couldn't help it.

'If you rolled about in the snow outside you would be a Linnet-snow-sausage.'

'Mind the milk! Truepenny hasn't been yet.'

'I did flute for him,' said Tolly, 'in case you hadn't got your flute with you.'

'I've given it to you,' said Alexander.

'Oh, oh! I've rolled on Hedge-prickles!' said Linnet, sitting up and rubbing her arm as the hedgehog hurried away.

Orlando came to comfort her.

'Did you make that enormous snowman with no eyes?' Tolly asked Toby. There was a silence.

'Over there, I mean,' said Tolly, pointing through the wall to where he thought it was, 'among the trees, as big as St Christopher.'

'Oh, Ignoranty! He means Green Noah,' said Linnet.

'Keep away from him,' said Toby.

'I'm not afraid of him,' said Linnet. 'He can't hurt me. I'm dead.'

'I didn't mean you, little Flipperty-gibbert – I mean him,' said Toby, nodding towards Tolly.

'Don't go near him,' said Alexander. 'He is eyeless and horrid.'

But Linnet was dancing round Toby in mock solemnity with turns and curtseys.

'I made up a rhyme to tease him,' she said, quite irrepressible. 'I dance round him and I sing, like this:

> *Green Noah*
> *Demon Tree*
> *Evil Fingers*
> *Can't catch me!'*

Toby made a grab at her, and while they tussled and laughed together Alexander said, 'The only thing the confounded Peacock is good for, is that it always gives warning if Green Noah moves.'

'Where is the Peacock?'

'I expect it's sulking because you and Granny laughed at it so much.'

'Why, where were you when we were laughing?'

'Sitting in the inglenook. Toby was in the other.'

'Yesterday? Why couldn't I see him?'

'Well, you were sitting in the same place, so how could you? It's as if you were both in the same person.'

Tolly sat breaking twigs between his fingers as he tried to work out this new problem. But it made no sense to him – it was too hard. He looked up again to grin at Alexander, but found he was alone. They had all gone.

Never was a little boy more desolate than Tolly. He wanted them so much, every minute of every day, and he had no sooner found them than they vanished. With hot, salty tears he scattered the heap of broken twigs under his hands, and there lay an old bracelet, bent and black, a tiny one that would fit a squirrel's neck. 'They always leave something where they have been,' he thought, comforted, as he brushed the soil off it. He spent some time trying to get his own narrow hand through it, and at last he succeeded. He plodded back to the house, marching up to Mrs Oldknow with his hands behind his back.

'Guess what I've found.'

Mrs Oldknow took hold of his hands and pulled them to her. He held them out with tightly clenched fists, and she wasted much time trying to open his fingers. At last she felt something under her own fingers round his wrist. She knew at once. Her wrinkles creased up in a boyish, excited smile.

'My own dear little Linnet! You've found her bracelet! Tell me where it was?'

'She put it round the squirrel's neck. It looked marvellous there, all glittery in the fur.'

'She would, of course! I might have thought of that. But she might just as easily have put it on Truepenny, who would have taken it down to wear in the dark of his tunnels. It was a present from her Granny on her sixth birthday. Let's clean it up. Look, she is wearing it in the picture.' They took it in turns to rub it till it was bright gold again.

'Can I have it?' said Mrs Oldknow. 'I know you found it, but I would like to keep it.'

'Yes,' said Tolly, feeling very proud. 'You can keep it. I have the sword.'

'It will have to go to the jeweller's to be mended. Look, the seed-pearls have gone out of these little holes.'

Every few minutes there was a fizz from the fire, as drips came down the wide chimney, but they were too much interested in the bracelet to notice. Afterwards they had a music lesson, in the course of which Tolly called out, 'Granny, look! The snow's all melting.'

It was thawing fast, slipping off the trees in big, slushy drops, and turning to mud on the paths. Tolly

126

could hardly believe that all those powdery drifts could turn wet and nasty and sink away so quickly. By tea-time the tree house had nearly gone. The branches showed through, green and dripping.

'Unless it freezes hard tonight, we shall have another flood,' said Mrs Oldknow. 'If it does freeze, pity the poor birds! Their feet would be frozen on to the branches. We must leave your window open, but not enough for the owls to get in. They snatch little birds while they are asleep. Perhaps the tits and robins will follow the chaffinches in.'

'I've got an idea. May I go and ask Mr Boggis for something?' Toseland ran out. He found Boggis and asked him to cut some big branches of evergreen, as big as he could. Boggis cut some four-foot lengths of stout ivy, a large branch of bay, and the top of a laurustinus that was like a young tree. All these Tolly carried upstairs to his room. He fixed the branches upright, tying them to the backs of chairs; the ivy he laid along the beams. Then he opened the window, from which he seemed to look down on the sun setting in streaks of grey mist, and took up his flute. 'Help me please, Alexander,' he said, putting his lips to it, and the flute and he played together.

The birds heard. One by one they flew in and inspected their lodging. Two robins quarrelled over a bush, but in the end one of them went to bed in the doll's house instead, where he spent the night in the music room where the beams were just the right size for a perch. Tolly set the window just wide enough to let a late-comer in. He thought an inch and a half would do, but was not quite sure how thin an owl could make itself. Cats, he knew, could squeeze through very narrow gaps. After all this, he went downstairs again, very pleased with himself.

'You haven't ever told me a story about Alexander.'

'Very well, I will tell you one tonight.'

ALEXANDER'S STORY

All of the children, as you know, because you have heard them, had beautiful voices, but Alexander's was the best. Toby and he sang in the choir in the church in Penny Soaky, where they were very strictly trained. They also sang at home, for their mother played on the spinet and was a clever musician. It was a great treat when their father and elder brother were at home too, to add a bass and a tenor to their part-singing and to teach them sea shanties.

On one of Captain Oldknow's visits he took the whole family to Greatchurch to dine with some friends, and afterwards to see the sights, in particular the church famous for its music and its stained glass. This was at a distance of twelve miles. The Captain and his three sons rode. The two ladies and Linnet went by coach. It was Linnet's birthday. She had a new Dutch doll and was wearing her best dress, the one you know from the picture, and her mother too. In fact the picture was painted not very long afterwards, in honour of the events of which you are going to hear.

At the house of their friends there was much laughter and excitement, first for welcome and pleasure, but also because of the latest news – the proposed visit of the King to a neighbouring mansion. The conversation during dinner was all about it, for it was expected that some kind of entertainment would be provided for His Majesty in the evening, at which all the young people of the county had hopes of appearing, either as performers in the masques, or as members of the audience.

'There is no hope at all for you, my dear,' said Captain Oldknow to Linnet. 'We are quiet country people with no friends at court. No one will think of asking us.'

After dinner they walked to the church to admire the stained-glass windows that had escaped damage from the pikes and stones of Cromwell's soldiers, and so could show to the future the riches that almost everywhere else in the country had been wantonly smashed. The children followed their parents in, expecting to see a church like any other, but bigger and handsomer. It was, however, quite different. It was more like an empty banqueting hall, but so long and so high that, as they stepped inside, they felt themselves dwindle to the size of ninepins. The four walls seemed to be all stained glass, with only enough stone to hold them together, but the stone was decorated high and low with carved crowns, animals and flowers.

Linnet looked round in astonishment. 'Alexander!' she said. 'It's one of Merlin's palaces.'

Alexander could not speak. He was beside himself with delight at the building and the glass.

The afternoon was dull, so that the colours in the

windows were deep and rich like sunset seen through a wood, and the stone vaulting looked velvety. A verger was lighting candles two by two all round the walls. Alexander listened to his footfalls sounding like fingertaps on a kettle-drum under the high hollow of the roof. The whole place was vibrating and ecstatic. He felt as if he had fallen under an enchantment, as if he could do impossible things. 'But it's not Merlin's cheating castle,' he thought. 'Its name should be *Joyous Gard*.'

He strayed from his family the better to concentrate on the sensation of tingling emptiness and expectation in the building that he found so strange and so enthralling. If one of the other visitors, intent on looking up at the high windows, made a false step, the sound came to him remote and beautiful as if a pigeon with flapping wings had taken off in the roof. When Alexander was separated by the length of the building from the others, who were just going out by the west door, he heard the final syllable of Toby's voice slipping in a whisper down the wall from the roof at the east end, where he stood himself. It was queer to think of it travelling silently like a butterfly across the immense length of the honey-combed vaulting, to fold its wings and drop there in a half-breath of sound to his ear.

Alexander stayed on, making no sound that could remind them that he was left behind. How could they go so soon? But he was glad to be undisturbed. The verger had gone, and no one else had as yet come in. He stood alone in a magic world. The candles waved in the air that was as much in movement as if in a forest. Every now and then a spindle of wax breaking off a guttering candle fell into the brass holder with a bell-like note that seemed to go up and up and be received into Heaven. Alexander held his breath and listened. There was no sound except a low droning of wind passing along the distant vaulting, the kind of sound that is in a shell.

He had a sudden great desire to sing, to send his voice away up there and hear what nestling echoes it would brush off the roof, how it would be rounded and coloured as it came back. Standing by the choir-stalls he sang what first came into his head, part of a new song that his mother was teaching him. He tossed his notes up, like a juggler tossing balls, with careless pleasure. He could feel the building round him alive and trembling with sound.

I call, I call, I call, (he sang)
Gabriel! Gabriel! Gabriel!

He stopped to listen. It was as if the notes went up like rocket stars, hovered a second and burst into sparklets. The shivered echo multiplied itself by thousands. One would have thought every stone in the building stirred and murmured. He tried it again, louder.

Gabriel! Gabriel! Gabriel!

He could almost imagine the Archangel must hear, might come. He looked round, suddenly awe-struck. To his confusion he saw that he was not alone. Leaning out of the organ loft was a Jack-in-the-box of a man with a pointed red beard and a bald head like a marble.

'Boy! Boy!' he shouted, and all the echoes roared like lions. 'Boy! Boy! Stay there (*there*). On your life (*life*).'

Alexander thought he was wild with anger at his presumption in daring to sing. He decided that, considering he was in church, he had better stay and take his scolding.

The little man burst out of the organ-loft stairs, seized him by the arm and held him relentlessly. He had light eyes with very black pupils, like a parrot's, and his beard was raised like a weapon every time he shut his mouth.

'What's your name, boy? Where do you come from? Who is your father? Your father is just outside? Come along, take me to him.'

He dragged Alexander with him, still holding him as if he were a wild animal that might escape.

'There he is, with my mother and my brother and sister.'

'Sir! Sir! (What did you say your name was, boy? Oldknow?) Captain Oldknow! Sir!'

All this commotion attracted the attention of the passersby as well as of the Captain whose son was being dragged towards him as if for fearful punishment.

'Oh my dear sir! Dear lady! What a voice, the most astonishing voice! I can't take a refusal. This boy must sing. He must sing before the King. It's a miracle. Calling me by name! Gabriel! Gabriel! (He sang this in a squeaky falsetto.) Admit it was startling.'

Captain Oldknow interrupted the stream of words with an amused gesture. 'What is all this about, sir?

And why are you dragging my son as if he were a malefactor?'

The wild man clutched Alexander all the more desperately.

'No malefactor, sir – an angel. The voice of an angel. I cannot let him go.'

'Alexander,' said his father, 'can you explain all this to me? How did you meet this gentleman?'

'Gabrieli McTavish, at your service, sir,' interrupted the old man.

Alexander, feeling very foolish, explained as best he could, and all his family laughed with him.

'Now, dear sir,' said the Captain, 'I begin to see what this is all about. My son has been experimenting with echoes and has raised one where he least expected it. It seems that his few notes were approved of. Is that all?'

'All, sir! Sir, it falls to me to arrange the musical diversion for His Gracious Majesty next month, but my best boy's voice is breaking. I dare not trust it, and the second best boy is sick. I was in despair, I was like to be disgraced. But now we have only to come to an arrangement.'

The gist of the matter was that the organist, Gabrieli McTavish, was to produce the masque Cupid and

Death before his Majesty, and by a series of mischances there was no boy available who could sing the part of Cupid. If Alexander were to stay and be trained for the part, all the family could have seats for the show.

'Oh!' gasped Linnet and her mother together, with such feeling that it was probably from a wish to give them pleasure that Captain Oldknow decided to allow Alexander to live with their friends, if they would take him, until the royal visit, and be trained by his new singing master.

On the great night, the Oldknow family coach joined the procession of other more elegant coaches driving to the magnificent house where the King was being entertained. The drive in itself was an extraordinary excitement, for they saw the arrival of all the nobility of the district; and among them the court beauties and their escorts. More amusing to Toby was the running hither and thither of liveried servants with lights; the haughty grooms with handsome horses drawing their empty coaches out of the way and shouting at their rivals when wheels became interlocked or ill-guided horses sidled into theirs.

Seats had been found for Alexander's family in the musicians' gallery, from which they had an excellent view of the King's party and the masque. The story that was to be acted and sung was this: Cupid and Death had put up at the same inn, and while they were sleeping, the arrows in their quivers were changed over, so that afterwards whoever was shot by Death, instead of dying, fell in love, while whoever was shot by Cupid, instead of falling in love, died. This was all very amusing, because Death shot the old people, who as lovers were ridiculous; and laughing Cupid was vexed and perplexed when all his young lovers died. On the whole Death had the most fun, but he took it gloomily.

If Alexander was nervous of appearing before such a grand audience he did not show it. He was a wonderfully mischievous Cupid and sang with confidence. His voice was the success of the evening, though Linnet shared his popularity when she hung over the balcony at the close of the play and shouted 'Bravo, Cupid!' in the silence when everyone was waiting for the King to rise.

The King turned to look, and smiled to see Linnet blushing, with her hand clapped over her mouth. He talked awhile with the ladies who were with him, the younger of whom seemed gently to urge him to send one of the gentlemen in waiting on an errand. This gentleman found Alexander in the actors' room and told him that His Majesty did him the honour of sending for him. Alexander followed him through the jostling, staring crowd, feeling very naked, as indeed he was, having nothing on but a wreath of flowers, a white Grecian kilt and his wings and sandals. In front of the royal dais he dropped on to one knee. The King, who had a long sarcastic face and melancholy eyes, looked at him mockingly but with pleasure.

'Take his bow from him,' he said to a gentleman standing near. 'I cannot risk any more trouble. My hands are quite full already. Master Cupid, these ladies desire to know you better. Your arrows may be sham, but your voice, it would seem, strikes home. You have given us and our companions pleasure and we should wish to give you some token of it. In your present nakedness it is impossible to guess what you might lack. Have you any boy's wish that your King might supply?'

'Your Majesty,' said Alexander simply, 'I would like a flute.'

'You shall have it. Addio, Master Cupid. It was well sung.'

So that was how Alexander got his flute.

MRS OLDKNOW'S FEARS were justified. It did freeze that night. The air sang with frost as Toseland lay in bed, and the birds roosted in his hospitable branches. The owls hooted outside. Their sound seemed to echo from a glassy, frost-hard sky. Tolly could literally hear how wide the meadows were.

He was dropping off to sleep and already his waking thoughts were mixed with dreams of an echoing palace inhabited by a man with eyes like a parrot, when a direful shriek startled him and he huddled in bed, wide awake. An owl had come close to the window, perching on the gutter with his ogre claws. His voice sounded almost in the room. The birds twittered with fright, the mouse squeaked and so – if truth must be told – did Tolly, pulling the bedclothes up to cover his ears. It was with an effort of courage that he dared to look towards the window to see if the owl could possibly get in. His night-light had guttered out in the draught and he had to strain his eyes for the movement of shadowy forms against the dim window.

There was something outlined against the panes. It was the back of a curly head, and two little fists hammering on the glass inside scared the owl away.

He heard a scamper of bare feet, and Linnet's voice saying, 'Ugh! My feet are cold. It's a punishment because I said my prayers in bed tonight. I hope the owl doesn't come back.'

'I'll go next time,' said Tolly.

'*Matthew, Mark, Luke and John, Bless the bed that I lie on,*' said Linnet.

'You're saying them in bed again,' said Alexander.

'I know, but he's going to be punished for me next time. He said he would.'

Tolly and Alexander laughed and there was peace and company in the dark room. If the owl came back, they were all asleep.

Next morning there was a fringe of icicles all round the roof, as if the house needed its hair cutting. The trees twinkled with needles of ice. The garden was an ice switchback. At breakfast Mrs Oldknow said: 'I must really get ready for Christmas. There are only a few days left.'

'Can we give *them* a present?' said Tolly.

'What would you suggest?'

'*The first day of Christmas my true love gave to me,*
A partridge in a pear tree.'

Tolly was thinking aloud.

'I think that would be perfect, but a little difficult. Not absolutely impossible. It would be difficult to get a live partridge and harder to make it stay in the tree. It ought really to be a tame one.'

'It could be in a cage, and we could tame it afterwards.'

'I'm sure they never had a partridge. Linnet would

love it, with all its brood running after it like tortoise-shell thimbles with legs. Let's try, Tolly. It's a perfect idea. We'll advertise: 'Wanted, live hen partridge, preferably tame.' And I'll write to a gamekeeper I know in Scotland. Bring me my writing paper, I'll do it at once.'

Tolly and she enjoyed themselves writing what seemed ridiculous letters. They also chose out of a catalogue a pear tree described as having 'juicy melting flesh, delicious flavour'.

While they were writing, Boggis brought in some magazines and a note from a neighbour, who offered to drive Mrs Oldknow in to Greatchurch if she had anything to do there, and also to take her to a concert.

'That means I can't take you, Tolly. What a shame. But we will go together another time. Boggis will have to look after you. Please thank her, Boggis, and say I will be ready at eleven. What are those papers?'

'Something about the house, m'm, that she thought might interest you.'

Mrs Oldknow with her baskets for the Christmas shopping went off in her friend's car. Tolly went out into the garden. The snow, first melted and then frozen over, looked messy, lifeless and uninviting. There was thin ice on the moat, not strong enough to bear his weight. He went to the fish platform and broke the ice there, clearing a pool and throwing bread in. Neptune's ugly snout with whiskers made of flesh like sea-anemones came and sucked it in. But Tolly could not love Neptune. Mrs Oldknow said that when he was young he was almost as pretty as a goldfish. Tolly fed him for Toby's sake, but thought he was horrid.

Turning away from the pool he looked around for the tree that during the snow had been like a snowman, the tree called Green Noah. He was startled to find himself so near it. In the tangle of briars, saplings and brushwood which the wood path, that he had so often followed, skirted at a careful distance, stood a tall yew column, roughly shaped like Noah with his usual square shoulders and fantastic flat bowler hat. It was not surprising that Tolly had not noticed it before, because it was so long since it had been trimmed that it had grown wild and hairy, its outline almost lost. Most shocking of all, two long, undisciplined arms had grown out from shoulder height with open fingers and hanging sleeves. Tolly was seized with panic and ran as fast as he could over the icy slopes to find Boggis.

Boggis was whitewashing the little saddle-room where he kept his blue tea-pot and mug and his primus stove. Today he had a little fire in the grate. His face looked redder and his eyes bluer than ever, and the whitewash had a comforting, homely smell.

'Can't do nothing outside today,' he said. 'I made a fire so we could have our dinner cosy-like, seeing that you're alone.'

At each side of the grate old horse-shoes were hanging, arranged in overlapping rows to make a sort of frame for it. They were all different, as if one had been kept from each horse that had lived there. Boggis had whitewashed the wall and had hung them all back on their nails. Tolly studied them with interest. How they varied! Some were obviously cart-horses' and some ponies', but in between were the carriage horses' and the hunters', the thoroughbreds'. One perhaps was Feste's. Is there among horse-shoes one that stands out for its delicate curve, suggesting the perfect hoof, the sure and dancing step? Tolly thought so. He chose out one shoe for his love, and when Boggis was not looking he wrote in the clean circle of wall behind it, 'Feste'.

'Boggis,' he asked presently, 'have you got a grandson?'

'I had, but he was killed in the last war.'

'Well, have you got a son?'

'I had, two. But they were killed in the first war.'

Tolly was upset by this news. How would anything go on if there wasn't a Boggis? Then he remembered that he was only there himself as if it were sideways, through his mother.

'Well, haven't you a grand-daughter, then?'

'Yes, I have. And she's got a son.'

'But he won't be called Boggis.'

'Yes, he will that.'

'Oh, then that's all right.'

'No, it isn't all right. It's all wrong, because she isn't married.'

'But there must be a Boggis, mustn't there?'

'Well, Master Toseland, I shouldn't say so, least of all to you, but I do like to think he'll have the name. The child just missed being called Liquorice, and what sort of a name is that!' Boggis guffawed, rocking on his heels. 'Percy Liquorice! That's what he'd have been. And his mother's a good girl barring accidents.'

Boggis spread newspapers on the table for a cloth and sent Tolly to fill the kettle and to fetch the sandwiches that Mrs Oldknow had put ready for him. They sat down one each side of the blue teapot. Boggis hung his cap on the point of a horseshoe. His bald scalp was as white as a hard-boiled egg above his scarlet face. He made the tea, taking the tea-leaves from his waistcoat pocket. The sugar was in the pocket on the other side. He slipped the spoon straight into it. So it was unlikely he had taken the lump sugar put out for Feste.

Tolly thought his own sandwiches were so much nicer that it was embarrassing. His were ham, and then cheese and lettuce, and afterwards banana. Boggis had slabs of bread and mustard-coloured pickle. He refused any exchange with scorn.

'I like something you can taste,' he said. 'These pickled onions eat lovely.'

'Did you know my grandfather?' said Tolly as they munched.

'That I did. He was a limb of mischief, he and his brothers. There were six of them. I remember

146

one day they were all in that field at the back here, looking for mushrooms. The bull had been put out with the cows and the boys hadn't noticed, till all of a sudden he was well-nigh snorting in their pants. I seed them all run for the river and pop in one after the other, swimming with all their clothes on like so many frogs. I couldn't help but laugh. My son was batman to your grandfather in the first war. They were killed together. In the second war it was my grandson as was the sergeant and your father was his corporal. He carried my grandson across an open bridge when his legs were shot off. That's how he came here and met your mother, Miss Linnet. He came to see me and bring my grandson's things and tell us about him.'

'Tell me about my mother.'

'She was a proper caution too. Many a time she made me laugh, she did say such things. I remember once when she was only a little thing she said to me, "Boggis," she said, "are you as red all over as your face is?" She did! Are you as red all over as your face! "No, Miss Linnet," I said, "I'm as white all over as my head is," and I pulled my cap off to show her. How I did laugh!'

147

Boggis's tales were not nearly as good as Mrs Oldknow's. The queer thing was, that the nearer to the present time they were, the more remote they seemed. Tolly was far more interested in Toby than he was in his father as the corporal.

After lunch he wandered back to the house. It seemed very empty without Mrs Oldknow, as though not only she had gone, but all the possibilities of the house had gone with her. Even the picture looked different, and Tolly was almost surprised to see that the children's grandmother was still there.

On the table lay the two magazines that had been brought in by Boggis. Tolly looked at them. One was called *Here and There*. There was a red pencil mark under the title 'Homes the Crusaders Left Behind Them'. It was a long article, too full of historic references for Tolly to read, but it was illustrated with photographs of such houses as still existed from which crusaders were known to have gone. Green Knowe was one of them, and there was a photograph of St Christopher and an imaginary drawing of the Chapel.

The other magazine was called *Adam's Seed*. It was all about gardening, and the sender had marked with red pencil 'Some Unusual Topiary'. There were photographs of different things that had been cut out of yew and holly – yew eagles, a yew ship, yew chessmen, crowns, armchairs, a holly horse, a yew lady in a bath in a willow summerhouse plaited like a basket out of living wands. Turning the page he came upon the green deer, the squirrel, the hare, the cock and hen – and Green Noah, a photograph taken a long time ago, because it showed Noah smaller and closely trimmed. Tolly began to read in earnest.

'Perhaps the most unusual and romantic of these examples is that of the Green Noah which now gives its name to the estate on which it stands, though the original name was Green Knowe. The story about it is widespread. It has been told me in much the same form in different "locals" all over the county, and also still further afield, by old men who remembered hearing it in their childhood. It seems that an old gardener called Boggis first shaped the various animals and later added a figure of Noah. He was much addicted to drink and suffered from delusions, but no one can deny his skill, and his employer appears to have allowed him a free hand. When Noah was a few years old and growing nicely, it happened that a famous horse-thief was caught red-handed in the stables of Green Knowe, as it was still called. He came up before the owner, Judge Oldknow, for trial. He was condemned, and after lying in Newgate prison for some years, he was deported to Botany Bay. His mother, Old Petronella, a gypsy and a notorious witch, is said to have revenged herself by breaking into the gardens during an eclipse of the moon and there with horrible dancing and laughter that was heard in the house (though no one knew what it was that so chilled their blood) she laid a curse on the Green Noah. The traditional version is:

> *Snippet snappet*
> *Shapen yew*
> *Devil's image*
> *Take on you.*
>
> *Evil grow,*
> *Evil be,*
> *Green Noah*
> *Demon Tree.*

'As the tree grew, a series of unexplained accidents overtook the men of the family, in every case due to shying or bolting horses. According to the villagers, the horses panicked because of a blind figure that prowled by night. Some say that Old Petronella herself was caught by him in the end. Before long the name Green Knowe was forgotten, the people insisting on calling it Green Noah. The photograph that is reproduced here is at least thirty years old, as for a long time nobody has been willing to trim the Old Gentleman. It is to be hoped that in the end he will lose all resemblance and the curse will lapse.'

As Tolly finished reading the story, he suddenly realized that not only was Mrs Oldknow still away, but Boggis had finished his work and gone home. It was nearly dark, and he was alone. For some reason he felt convinced that until his great-grandmother returned, not so much as a marble would move in the house. He felt no such assurance about the garden. He lit all the candles, made up the fire, laid out the tea, and sat down to wait in the inglenook where once Toby had sat. He played sad little tunes on his flute with many wrong notes, and he wished with all his heart that she would come back.

When at last he heard a car he hurried to meet her.

'I thought you were never coming!' he said.

Mrs Oldknow had masses of parcels and was laughing with pleasure. 'Tolly, my dear, I've had a lovely day. I've brought back the Christmas tree – Boggis has taken it into the stables. And I've done some lucky shopping. Let's have tea at once and I'll tell you all about it. Oh, darling, you've put everything ready!'

She seemed as pleased to be with him again as he was to be with her. They laughed as they ate: they found everything funny. They made silly remarks for the sake of laughing at them. She told him about an old friend whom she had met for lunch who had grown a little queer in the head. 'She wore two hats and two wrist-watches, neither of which would go: but she knows a lot of sporting people. And I *believe* I've got a partridge. I must ring up an address she gave me tonight. If it's all right we'll go together and choose a pear tree at the nursery gardens. The old nurseryman who has sold me garden things all his life will think I have gone mad at last, when I say I want a four-year-old pear tree and it must have branches strong enough to bear a partridge cage and partridge. You say it, Toby. It won't matter so much if you seem mad.'

'You called me Toby,' said Tolly, putting his arms round her neck from behind.

'Well, how can I tell which of you it is when you are behind me?'

'Well, it's Tolly, unless Toby's in the same place as me, like Alexander said.'

'Well, if it's Tolly, you can tell me what you did all day.'

'I had a picnic with Boggis. He keeps his tea in one waistcoat pocket and his sugar in the other. He just puts the spoon straight in.'

'Very convenient. My Boggis had an old tail-coat with pockets in the tails. He had a bottle of beer in each and he kept his sandwiches in his hat.'

'Boggis's were horrible yellow ones.'

'Pickled onions, I expect, like his grandfather's. They would taste better with beer than with tea, but Boggis's grandfather drank so much beer that it has frightened his descendants ever since. They have all been teetotallers.'

There was a silence.

'And what else, my dear?'

Tolly noticed, when they were not talking, that the silence now had not that dead and frightening quality that it had when Mrs Oldknow was away. He could not quite say whether he heard or only felt, that the house was alive. Perhaps it was only the wind, but there seemed to be movement. A great deal was going on out of sight. He turned, comforted, to his great-grandmother.

'And what else, my dear?' she repeated.

'These,' said Tolly, handing her the magazines *Here and There* and *Adam's Seed*. 'I read these.'

Mrs Oldknow turned over the pages and soon came to the story of Green Noah. She read it quickly while Tolly watched her face.

'Yes,' she said, 'that's the end of the story of Black Ferdie. I didn't want to tell you lest you should be frightened. But we leave Green Noah alone and take no notice of him. He is growing into quite an ordinary tree. The curse is very old and I suppose it doesn't last forever. Old Petronella and Black Ferdie died ages ago, and they don't care any more.'

'I only saw it this morning. I never noticed it before, it's so wild and uncut. Only it made a snow man.'

'I know.'

'I thought it hadn't eyes because no one could reach to put cinders in.' Tolly couldn't help a shudder.

'Don't think about him. St Christopher is much more lasting.'

'Linnet's not afraid of anything,' said Tolly, whose thoughts moved quickly from St Christopher to Linnet and from Linnet to the owl. Perhaps Mrs Oldknow's thoughts went the same way.

'How were the birds last night?' she asked.

'They made an *awful* mess. Don't they know?'

'It is surprising from such well-mannered little things. They don't know and they can't learn! You'll have to spread newspapers. It thawed this afternoon, but it is freezing again now. How the owls screamed last night!'

Tolly laughed, partly because he had been so frightened, partly with pleasure because the little birds had been safe. 'I hope they screamed with rage,' he said boldly.

THEY WENT UPSTAIRS TOGETHER. As they entered Tolly's room there was a sound of rustling leaves. The birds were there already. The candles made tree shadows covering all the others. Mrs Oldknow tucked him up and said good night, and very soon he was asleep.

He dreamed that he was sleeping in the doll's

house with Toby, Alexander and Linnet in the three other beds. Toby was telling them all a wonderful story. Tolly could not have said what it was about, but it was wonderful – when suddenly he broke off with 'Hush! Keep silent!' and cupped his hands round the night-light to cover the light. Tolly heard shuffling, leafy steps as something came into the real bedroom, fumbling round as if it were dark, though the nightlight was burning. Tolly in his doll's-house bed could see everything. The Thing found its way to his own empty bed and suddenly pounced on it. It gave a silent yell like a gale in a tree, and threw the bedclothes right and left. Then it went fumbling round the room, feeling in the corners and on the saddle of the rocking-horse, but it never thought of the doll's house. At last Tolly saw that it had turned into an owl. It stood in the middle of the room doing a kind of war dance, lifting first one claw and then the other and swaying its head. Its shadow was huge. Then Toby got out of his bed in the doll's house and took his night-light and set it under the owl's tail feathers. There was a loud spluttering and commotion. Tolly woke up to find an unfortunate moth in the wax of the night-light. He was in his own bed.

One or two birds shifted and called as if in their sleep. Had they been dreaming of owls too? He thought he could hear gentle breathing in the room, and then suddenly, as if it had only just begun after being asleep itself, the slow tick-tock of the clock came to his ears, almost as loud as a hammer.

T HE NEXT DAY MRS OLDKNOW and Tolly set out by bus to visit the nurseries where they were to choose the pear tree. Tolly's mind had been busy. He had notions of his own about a present for his great-grandmother, an idea that had come when he was turning over the pages of *Adam's Seed*. It suited him very well to go to the nursery garden.

They were met by the old foreman. He looked like a field-mouse, if a field-mouse could be as big as a small man and wear an old grey hat and gaiters. His eyes twinkled and his movements were quick and sudden. Mrs Oldknow could never get to the end of a sentence before he answered, 'Yeslady', or 'Nolady', as the case might be, speaking rapidly as if he were nibbling. Tolly thought it was a pity he had no whiskers to wiggle as he said it. He said 'Yessir, Nosir' to Tolly who had never been called Sir before. While Mrs Oldknow was wandering up and down the lines of young pear trees to pick a strong one, Tolly put a private question.

'Have you a rose in a tiny pot that only grows three inches high?'

'Yessir. Rosa minimissimasir. Threeandsixpencesir.'

'Does it smell?'

'Yessir, they saysosir; if your noseissmallenoughsir.'

Tolly had some money which his father had sent him, so he paid and put the tiny parcel in his pocket. Then he joined Mrs Oldknow. The pear tree was a little disappointing because of course it had no leaves.

'The one in the illustration to the song was in full blossom, not just sticks. I suppose they did it by magic,' said Tolly sadly.

'Mustavedonesir, suresir,' said the foreman.

It was thawing slowly, but they spent the rest of the day in the town, where they forgot all about the snow which, in any case, had been shovelled up there and carted away. When they came home again at tea-time it was to find the garden green and brown and sodden.

Tolly's thoughts were full of Christmas, for there

were now only three days to go. He received a letter from Burma, from his father. The envelope and stamps were exciting, but the letter made him feel further away than ever. There was a P.S. in an oversized scrawly writing: 'Mother sends love to Toto.' Toseland put the letter in the fire but kept the envelope.

At night he dreamt of Christmas. He found the field-mouse foreman decorating the Christmas tree. This time he had long wiggling whiskers. He was busy hanging up coconuts, and strings of peanuts, pears hung on skewers and bags of silver net full of almonds and raisins. His eyes were brimming with twinkle and his cheek was full of nuts. He hung up a small round red cheese. Presently, out of his bulging pockets from which hung a tail of raffia, he pulled a parcel wrapped in paper on which were printed coloured maps. It was covered all over with foreign postmarks. He looked at this, wiggled his whiskers, and dropped it at Tolly's feet.

Tolly unwrapped it, as full of anticipation as if he expected Aladdin's lamp. Inside, in cotton wool, were two plastic big toes such as you might buy from the joke counter in toyshops to fit over your socks. There was also a card saying 'For little Toe-Toe.'

Tolly was in a rage. He stamped and shook the Christmas tree furiously. The field-mouse foreman stopped, staring at him, and suddenly with frightened eyes dwindled to a real field-mouse and, with his tail held up, whisked away and disappeared.

Tolly woke up quietly. 'Mouse?' he said into his pillow, and thought he felt a wriggle under it. He laughed softly to himself. At breakfast, grinning over the top of his cup at Mrs Oldknow, he said, 'I've thought of a present for Boggis.'

'Clever boy. Boggis is always so difficult. What is it?'

'Two plastic big toes to fit over his socks to frighten his wife with!'

'Where have you seen those?'

'I haven't. I invented them last night in bed. But somebody else may have invented them too. Conjurors have pretend thumbs with long iron nails sticking through them to frighten people. Who decorates the Christmas tree?'

'You and I do. We'll do it tomorrow.'

'Shall we hang presents for the birds – I mean coconuts, peanuts and things?'

'We will, outside on the yew tree for Christmas day. And hazel nuts for the squirrels and woodpecker.

And biscuits on the ground for the robins and blackbirds.'

'I dreamt all that,' said Tolly proudly.

'You're a good dreamer. What else?'

'Well, there's Truepenny and Hedge-prickles, and there ought to be an invitation to field-mice.'

'Truepenny and Hedge-prickles could have some truffles for a great treat. I've a little jar that was given me that I don't think I shall ever use. And field-mice love bird-seed. You shall make trails from different parts of the garden, leading to the tree.'

'It will be *their* tree, of course.'

'Of course! Which else? You wouldn't want to hang everything on Green Noah to make a Christmas tree of him, would you?'

Tolly only grinned. He was in high spirits and had more grins than he knew what to do with. So much so, that when he was larking round the garden by himself, not looking for the others but just taking it for granted they were there, he had a sudden inspiration to show off for their benefit. Dancing along the path that circled Green Noah, which was as near as he could come because of the brambles, he chanted Linnet's song at the top of his voice.

Green Noah
Demon Tree!
Evil fingers
Can't catch me!

Then he did a kind of war dance, such as the owl had done in his dream. He was so pleased with it that he capered off across the lawn, getting wilder and wilder, stamping, whirling and pointing till he bumped into Boggis.

'Anyone would think you had been drinking, acting so silly,' said Boggis severely. 'Mrs Oldknow is waiting for you to decorate the tree in the music room.'

Off ran Tolly, still full of joy.

'We must do it today,' said Mrs Oldknow. 'There will be so much to do tomorrow – look, Boggis has brought in the holly and the ivy and the mistletoe. We will put that up first.'

When they had finished decorating it, the old room looked more like the Knight's Hall than ever. Against the stone walls, on top of the stone chimney-piece, the dark green leaves themselves looked mediaeval. It was an ancient castle prepared for an ancient feast. When Tolly was handing up great bunches to Mrs

Oldknow on the steps, it often seemed to him not so heavy as he expected, as if someone were helping him. 'Did *they* do this?' he asked.

'Yes, they always decorated the house, but they didn't have a Christmas tree. Christmas trees began much later, in England at any rate. They had their feast in our dining-room, which their father had altered and improved. It was he who had our big fireplace put in, and the big windows on to the garden. And it was their mother who first used this as a music room. She used to teach them some of the songs that I teach you.'

It was late afternoon before they finished the Christmas tree, and it was growing dark. They lit the old red Chinese lantern and many candles so that they could see to work. There were no glaring electric bulbs on this tree. Mrs Oldknow had boxes of coloured glass ornaments, each wrapped separately in tissue paper and put carefully away from year to year. Some were very old and precious indeed. There were glass balls, stars, fir-cones, acorns and bells in all colours and all sizes. There were also silver medallions of angels. Of course the most beautiful star was fixed at the very top, with gold and silver suns and stars beneath and around it. Each glass treasure, as light as an eggshell and as

163

brittle, was hung on a loop of black cotton that had to be coaxed over the prickly fingers of the tree. Tolly took them carefully out of their tissue paper and Mrs Oldknow hung them up. The tiny glass bell-clappers tinkled when a branch was touched. When it was all finished, there were no lights on the tree itself, but the candles in the room were reflected in each glass bauble on it, and seemed in those soft deep colours to be shining from an immense distance away, as if the tree were a cloudy night sky full of stars. They sat down together to look at their work. Tolly thought it so beautiful he could say nothing, he could hardly believe his eyes.

As they rested there, tired and dreamy and content, he thought he heard the rocking-horse gently moving, but the sound came from Mrs Oldknow's room, which opened out of the music room. A woman's voice began to sing very softly a cradle song that Tolly had learnt and dearly loved:

> *Lully Lulla, Thou little tiny child*
> *By by, Lully Lullay.*
> *O sisters too, how may we do*
> *For to preserve this day*

This poor youngling
For whom we sing
   By by, Lully Lullay.

'Who is it?' he whispered.

'It's the grandmother rocking the cradle,' said Mrs Oldknow, and her eyes were full of tears.

'Why are you crying, Granny? It's lovely.'

'It is lovely, only it is such a long time ago. I don't know why that should be sad, but it sometimes seems so.'

The singing began again.

'Granny,' whispered Tolly again with his arm through hers, 'whose cradle is it? Linnet is as big as I am.'

'My darling, this voice is much older than that. I hardly know whose it is. I heard it once before at Christmas.'

It was queer to hear the baby's sleepy whimper only in the next room, now, and so long ago. 'Come, we'll sing it too,' said Mrs Oldknow, going to the spinet. She played, but it was Tolly who sang alone, while, four hundred years ago, a baby went to sleep.

THEY WENT DOWN then for their tea, which they needed badly, for they had worked long and hard, as well as hearing strange things. Tolly was very good at lighting candles. He did not spill wax or drop red-hot matches. He helped to get the tea ready and made excellent toast. He could hardly believe he was the same boy who had spent miserable holidays alone in an empty school.

'I shall take you to Midnight Mass tomorrow, if you would like to come – and if the weather is possible. It is a long walk. Do you know, I thought I heard thunder a minute ago? Who ever heard of thunder at Christmas?'

Tolly was far too excited to think of going to bed. His head was in a whirl, thinking of the Christmas tree, of the live partridge that should arrive tomorrow, of his present for his great-grandmother, of the probability that there would be some sort of a present for him, of the cradle song in Mrs Oldknow's room, of the children, of the loveliness of everything. The only thing he never thought of was something he had done himself that morning. Now he was trying to contrive ways of staying up longer. Asking questions seemed the easiest way.

'Shall we go to Midnight Mass if it snows?'

'I believe it is thunder,' said Mrs Oldknow. 'Open the door, Tolly, and listen.' Tolly opened the door into the garden. It was a dark evening with tattered clouds in front of a slatey sky. He heard no thunder. It was even unnaturally quiet. Perhaps it only seemed unnatural because he himself was brimming with excitement. He heard the weir pounding at the end of the garden. It only made the quietness quieter. It was rather like a heart that is only heard when it beats too loud. Tolly wondered how loud Feste's heart would sound if you put your head against his ribs after a gallop.

'Granny,' he said. 'I haven't put any sugar for Feste. Can I take the flashlight and go out with some before I go to bed?'

'Yes,' she said. 'Your name should be Hopeful. Shut the door, it's cold.'

He let the heavy curtain fall behind him and went out, shutting the door. He was surprised to see how short were the stretches of garden that the flashlight lit up in front, and it lit nothing at all at the side. It was difficult to find the familiar paths, but he was childish enough to play that he was on a motor bicycle. Instead of going the nearest way to the stable he set off along the lawn, following his tiny beam, intending to go all round the garden side of the stables and in at the far corner. He had just discovered that whichever way he turned it, the beam lit up nothing at all but grass, so that he was not even sure of his direction, when he was startled nearly out of his skin by a long-drawn screech from the peacock. For a minute he thought it was a terrifying bugle. Tolly stood stock-still.

Then came thunder like a rattle of drums. The effect was like the opening of a Punch and Judy show on a monstrous scale, a Punch and Judy show that wasn't for fun. He looked all round. There were no stars. For once the curtains were all drawn in the house and no lights shone. He could see the point of the roof against a patch of sky, but the walls were muffled with darkness, as if it were something real that he would have to struggle through to get back. The garden was not pitch-black, but it seemed covered over with a mass of shadow. There were so many overlapping shadows that he couldn't tell what anything was. He couldn't tell a tree wasn't a shadow till he bumped his face on a branch.

He was alone, and the garden seemed no longer his.

He felt like a trespasser as he moved along it. The thought reminded him of Black Ferdie. He wished he had gone straight to Feste's protective stall. His flashlight was growing weaker and weaker. It was only a little pin of light. He shook it. It died out altogether. At that moment he remembered what he had done in the morning. He remembered how he had danced and pointed, and pulled faces. He heard again Toby's voice saying. 'Don't go near him,' and Alexander's saying, 'He is eyeless and horrid,' and 'the only thing the confounded peacock is good for . . .'

The peacock gave a screech that seemed unending. Tolly could imagine how it would stretch out its neck, long and thin, in the effort, with curved open beak and wagging tongue. When it stopped, there was a sound of dragging, of brushing and snapping twigs. The other birds woke and flew out of their roosting places with a panicky twittering. In the dark Tolly could hear them moving from tree to tree across the garden in agitated bands, as if they were escaping from a forest fire.

He himself remained rooted to the ground. He did not know which way to run, where there would not be entangling branches or the edge of a path to trip him up. How could one hide from the blind? They would not even know you were hiding. The fumbling fingers were just as likely to hit on you behind a bush as in the open.

Then there came a flash of lightning in which the whole scene was clearer than the sharpest thought. By its terrible flicker Tolly saw in the middle of the lawn a tree where no tree should be – a tree shaped roughly like a stooping man, that waved its arms before it and clutched the air with its long fingers. In the clap of thunder which followed, Tolly, frozen with terror, raised his thin child's voice in screams of 'Linnet! Linnet!'

Perhaps he had no need to call, for as the thunder died away in distant precipices of sky, Linnet's voice like an anxious bird was beating the air, calling: 'St Christopher, St Christopher, come quickly, St Christopher!'

Other voices joined hers, Toby's and Alexander's, piercing and boyish, and other unknown children's.

Suddenly their cries ceased. Did that mean it was already too late, that in the darkness any moment he would be pounced upon and feel the tightening of the leafy fingers? Or had St Christopher heard? Was

he already stirring the creepers and moving out from
the house?

Moaning winds were rushing and leaping round
the circle of the garden, leaving a silence in the centre
where something dreadful was certainly taking place. It
felt like the pressure of opposing thunderstorms before

they break. The air was prickly and the suspense so great that Tolly could not breathe, could hardly stand, his heart nearly choked him. At last a great forked lightning zig-zagged out of the sky, so bright that Tolly could not see anything else, with instantaneous thunder crashing and rolling, enough for ten lightnings. The air was full of a smell of burning.

'Ah!' said Linnet, Toby and Alexander from the shadows.

'Ah!' said lots of other happy voices. 'Green Noah's gone.'

As Tolly reached the house, not knowing if he walked or ran, the door opened with a flood of warm light and Mrs Oldknow came out to look for him.

'Tolly, Tolly! Are you all right? What's happened? Has anything been struck?'

'Green Noah's gone,' said Tolly, falling in a dead faint in her arms.

'Shall I carry him in, ma'am?' said Boggis, appearing with his lantern. 'I came up to see if you were all right.'

He carried Tolly in and laid him in a big armchair. Then he fetched a jug of cold water and Mrs Oldknow splashed some on Tolly's face.

'He's had a fright, that's what it is,' said Boggis. 'A rare fright by the look of it. I'll go out and see if I can find anything burning, or anyone about. You'll be all right till I come back.'

When Tolly opened his eyes again, the first person they rested on was Toby, who was standing with Alexander by the fireplace.

'Feste's calling you,' said Tolly faintly.

'I know,' said Toby. 'He trumpeted his loudest when old Noah was struck. I was just waiting for you to come to yourself again. I'll go now.'

'I wish I could see Feste,' said Tolly, turning a tired head on his cushion. Toby gave him his most brilliant smile.

'Perhaps Christmas Day is your lucky day,' he said.

'You should try wearing his clothes,' said Alexander.

Linnet and Mrs Oldknow were kneeling by the arm of his chair. He smiled happily at them; then he remembered how silly he had been and his smile went crooked and funny. Linnet pulled what she thought was a terrifying face and wiggled her fingers at him, and they both laughed. Toby went out, passing Boggis in the doorway, who came in without appearing to see him, or Alexander or Linnet. Tolly was sitting up looking nearly himself again, but Boggis was looking very queer.

'Sit down, Boggis,' said Mrs Oldknow. 'You look upset. What is the matter? I hope there's nothing serious?'

Boggis wiped his bald head with a coloured handkerchief.

'There's nothing burning now,' he said with an effort at calmness, 'but there's been a tree struck. There's a charred stump lying on the edge of the lawn – can't think where it fell from. And there's things moving.'

'What things, Boggis?'

'I wouldn't like to say, ma'am. Things as didn't ought to.'

'Stone things,' said Linnet in a whisper to Tolly, laughing all over her face.

Mrs Oldknow poured out a brandy and gave it to Boggis. 'Drink that,' she said. 'I know you are a teetotaller, but it will do you good. Tolly's had some.'

Boggis poured it down his throat and smacked his lips.

'And I saw something queer too,' he said, beginning to twinkle again. 'I met someone in the garden, and

who do you think it was? Now who do you think?'
Mrs Oldknow and Tolly made no suggestions.

'Well, believe it or not, if I could believe my own
eyes I'd say it was my grandfather Boggis as died sixty
years ago. And as drunk he was! – as drunk as a lord
and singing hymns to God Almighty!'

This time it was Mrs Oldknow who laughed. Tolly
turned to share the joke with Alexander and Linnet,
but they had vanished.

'Dear old grandfather Boggis,' said Mrs Oldknow.
'I liked him very much when I was a child. He was so
funny when he was drunk! I was never frightened of
him. So he's celebrating tonight, is he?'

Soon Tolly was comfortably tucked up in bed and
felt at peace with everything. Old Noah was gone for
good and all. It even seemed almost a pity.

'What shall we do now?' he asked Mrs Oldknow.
'Will you change the name of the house back to
Green Knowe?'

'No, I've come to like Green Noah better. We'll
plant a new one. We will have Noah and Mrs Noah,
one each side of the flood-gate, and I'll get Father
Patrick to come and bless them.'

NEXT MORNING TOLLY helped Boggis to clear away what was left of Green Noah. He was sawn up and split and taken into the house for firewood. 'We'll burn it on Christmas day,' said Mrs Oldknow.

'I'd be scared to do it,' said Boggis. 'Too much like hell fire for me! Might burn the house down with his last breath.'

'I think his last breath has been singed out of him. There's no sap in the wood at all.'

When old Noah was neatly stacked in short logs in the corner of the fireplace, there was the pear tree to plant. Tolly wanted it somewhere near St Christopher. They planted it in front of one of the old chapel windows in the wall, because Mrs Oldknow said she would like to see the children's faces poking through the blossom when it came into flower. 'It always was a hide-and-seek window,' she said.

The delivery van arrived, and there was much secrecy and winking and running to and fro on the part of Boggis, but a basket had arrived labelled 'Live Birds. URGENT', which so excited Tolly that he noticed nothing else. It was found to contain two partridges, a cock and a hen, neat plump little creatures of great charm but rather nervous.

Tied to the basket was a card that said: 'I have sent a mate with her in case there are none in your district.' As there were two, they were put in a large coop at the foot of the tree. Tolly fed them and gave them water. He thought they were pretty and funny beyond belief and he was very proud of his present.

Before tea, when it was getting dark, he tied a label on the coop, on which he had printed as well as he could in different coloured crayons:

T   A   L

with much love

from

T

Then he covered the coop with a sack to keep the partridges warm for the night.

When Boggis came in to wish them good night and a Merry Christmas tomorrow, Mrs Oldknow and Tolly gave him a bulky parcel for his great-grandson Percy.

'What are you giving him, Boggis?' said Tolly.

Boggis's face was just a red, teasing twinkle.

'I always give him the same every year,' he said. 'A box of Liquorice Allsorts.'

'Boggis!' said Mrs Oldknow.

'Oh, he likes that, ma'am. He knows it's coming. He looks forward to that.'

Tolly did the animals' tree last of all. Mrs Oldknow had given him several triangles of cheese that he pierced with a wire and hung up on a branch. He had burnt holes in the coconut with a red-hot poker, and that was hung up too. He put the nuts and almonds and raisins in a hollow in the trunk; a mound of crumbs and grated cheese on the ground; another of ants' eggs and another of pine-kernels; the truffles in a saucer near the pile of twigs where once Truepenny had disappeared; a big cabbage for the rabbit and Watt; and some oats in a wooden bucket. Then he laid trails of birdseed from the four corners of the garden to the yew tree, scattered very sparingly so that the field-mice could not have had enough before they got as far as the party.

THAT NIGHT THERE was neither thunder nor snow, but a bright moon and keen frost. Before starting to walk to Midnight Mass with Mrs Oldknow, Tolly had been privately to look at St Christopher. The moon shone full on his weathered stone face. He looked as if he had not moved since the beginning of time. As they set off with their moon shadows playing on the path round their feet, Tolly wondered if Linnet was looking out of the top window.

His shadow had long legs that he was rather proud of.

'Granny,' he said, 'your shadow looks just like a partridge.'

'I've often thought you don't always know whose shadow comes out with you.'

They were going to the church where Toby and Alexander had sung in the choir, where St Christopher had knelt unseen among the cypresses and tombstones.

The footpath went along beside the river, through wide flat meadows. It was surrounded by miles and miles of silent moonlight. There was almost no view but sky. Tolly had not yet been to the church; he imagined it as the most beautiful and exciting end to a thrilling walk. In fact he was confusing it in his mind with that other church where Alexander had experimented with echoes and which he had called JOYOUS GARD. In the moonlight the frozen meadows looked like sheets of frosted glass and the river like gold, old gold full of black creases like Linnet's bracelet when they were cleaning it. The cold made an eerie humming in the telegraph wires, a sound that grew suddenly alarmingly loud if Tolly put his ear against the post. There were no lights showing from any cottage window, nor any living creature out in the countryside but themselves. It was a long walk: it took them an hour and felt like a pilgrimage, but they saw nobody else going the same way. Tolly began to feel that he and his great-grandmother were going secretly to meet Toby and Alexander and perhaps their father and mother; that it was to be a mysterious and delightful family affair.

When they came inside the church, the first impression that he received was the mixed smell of incense and clammy mould, with the mould predominating. There were a few other people there, dingy, unromantic townsfolk, no children at all. The church was battered and dank, festooned with cobwebs round the windows, carpeted like a kitchen with brown coconut matting and bleakly lit with electric light. It is true that on the altar there were candles and chrysanthemums, but he could not help feeling that it was ugly and disappointing. There was a huge picture hanging on the wall on his left that was so horrifying that he kept one hand up to the side of his face like a blinker in case he should see it by accident. When they stood up to sing, the organ wheezed out as if it were the funeral march for a cat. Tolly was afraid to hear his own voice above the faint caterwauling that dragged after it. He was tired and felt suddenly very sad. Finally he fell asleep against Mrs Oldknow's shoulder.

When he opened his eyes, the electric light was out and far more candles were burning. The church looked new. The stone, instead of being grey, stained with black damp, was a nice sandy colour. The pews had gone. The pillars rose out of the floor like tree-trunks, leaving the nave spacious and gay. Instead of the wheezy organ there was a sound of fiddles and trumpets. People came in walking freely as if to a party, and stood in groups here and there.

Tolly turned round at a clinking sound close behind him, and there was Toby walking in with his mother on his arm. He was wearing his sword. When he had placed his mother near Mrs Oldknow he bowed formally to them and went out again. His place was taken by someone who could only be a Boggis, who stood respectfully just behind young Mrs Oldknow. She smiled at the old lady and at Tolly, raising one eyebrow at him as if to say, 'You here too?'

When at last he could take his eyes off her and look towards the choir, the boys were just coming in. There were six of them in surplices with white frills round their necks. Two little boys came first. One was laughing and turned to look at them as he went by. Alexander and a stranger came next, and then Toby and another, and after them the men. But Tolly was looking at the first little boy who just could not be solemn, for he knew now that it was Linnet, dressed in boy's clothes, in church, in the choir. He looked anxiously at Mrs Oldknow, fearing to see a look of angry shame come over her face, but she was looking at her book and smiling. He nudged his great-grandmother but she only laid her fingers on her lips and put her hand through his arm.

The singing was beautiful. Tolly knew it was part-singing, but he could only hear all four notes when there was a pause and they all hung together on the air. It gave him pleasure almost painful. Sometimes Toby sang solo for a few minutes and sometimes Alexander. His voice flew up to the roof as easily as a bird. Tolly feared it would make him cry, but that passed off when he saw Linnet hitching up her trousers. They were probably Alexander's and too big for her.

Then, gazing round the church, he saw, or thought he saw, through the wavering candle shadows, leaning against the wall, as much a part of it and as little noticed as if he were at home, St Christopher himself. Linnet was almost opposite him. She made signs that Tolly did not understand until he craned up to see better. Then he saw, pressed against the stone ripples that washed St Christopher's feet, the little black-and-white dog Orlando, fixing obedient eyes on his mistress and thumping the floor with his tail. Tolly gave a little squeak of laughter, but it was luckily drowned in the peal of bells that broke out.

Mrs Oldknow said: 'Wake up, Tolly. A Happy Christmas to you! We are going back in my friend's car, so you will soon be in bed. Did you have nice dreams?'

Tolly looked quite bewildered. 'Yes, Granny,' he said. 'Were you asleep too?'

'Perhaps,' she said. 'I hardly know.'

TOLLY SLEPT ALL THE way home and must have put himself to bed sleep-walking, for he remembered nothing about it. The first thing that he knew was that he was awake in his bed and that it was Christmas morning. The room was still half dark, but right in front of his eyes something was hanging from the bottom of the bird-cage. This was his stocking, with a right-angled corner sticking out at the calf and an elongated toe. The chaffinch was already out, hanging on to the stocking and tugging at the label. It followed Tolly back to bed, and when he had lit the candle they unpacked the stocking together.

There was a flashlight refill from Boggis. A telescope from his father. In his bedroom he could only use the wrong end but it was almost better. He looked at the rocking-horse and it would have fitted into a matchbox. He found Toby's sword, the right size for a chaffinch. The chaffinch was hard to find, no bigger than a ladybird. In the looking-glass opposite his bed he saw himself as if across a wide valley, miles and miles away. And if the things in the room were small, their doubles in the doll's house had reached vanishing point.

The thing that stuck out of the calf of the stocking

was a tin box shaped like Noah's Ark, filled with biscuits, each of which was glazed with brown sugar and had on it a picture of an animal in white sugar. He found a hare, a squirrel, a fox, a deer, a dog, a hedgehog, a peacock, a fish, an owl and, of course, a horse. Tolly couldn't bear to eat any of them except the owl. He bit its head off in one bite, then held it out in his lips to the chaffinch, who pecked at it once or twice, then gave a sharp, determined tug and flew away with the piece.

After that they shared the fish, and then the peacock. Next came two boxes of Bengal matches, one green and one red. Tolly struck one, and saw the chaffinch cock a startled eye like a bright round emerald.

'Now I'll make you see red,' said Tolly, striking a red one.

But the chaffinch did not like that at all. He drew all his feathers tight round him in a fright and flew off to the cage.

The toe of the stocking had a banana, a tangerine and an apple. Last of all Tolly opened an envelope tied to the top. He expected – for no one can help expecting a little – that it would contain a postal order, perhaps for two-and-six or even five shillings.

It contained a Christmas card with a picture of two curly white china dogs with black faces.

Underneath was written in his great-grandmother's hand:

Their names are
Wait   and   See

Tolly laughed, but he felt sure it meant something more. He put his legs out of bed to start to get dressed, but at first he could not see his clothes. Someone had thrown what looked like an old curtain over them. Tolly snatched it off and was about to throw it on the floor when he stopped at the sight of silver buttons all down one side. The stuff was green silk, faded yellow in some places and stained black in others. He held it at arm's length, turning it about to see what it was. It was not a woman's blouse. It was some kind of coat with big skirt pockets outlined in tarnished cord. Tolly put it on and looked at himself in the mirror. His own black eyes looked straight back at him and immediately he knew what he was wearing. His heart felt as if it would jump out of his mouth. 'You should try wearing his clothes,' Alexander had said.

The coat was much too big for him, but he rolled up the sleeves, dropped the apple from his stocking into the deep pocket, and off in his bare feet he went, down the twisting wooden stairs that, with practice, had come to seem so easy and rapid, along the cold brick floor of the entrance hall, running as fast as he could across the hurting gravel drive, hardly noticing the strange morning twilight, only pausing outside the stable. Here he took a long breath and walked with what he hoped was Toby's step into the shadowy stall, closing his eyes for fear of disappointment.

There was a steaminess and a friendly, lived-in smell. Tolly stood there like someone in a trance with his hands over his face, and heard a stirring of feet in straw, then warm, velvety lips began to try to pull his fingers away from his eyes. With his eyes still closed he put his arms round a bending neck, just behind the ears, twining his fingers in the long mane that fell over them. Then he felt a prod on his thigh from the apple in his pocket, which was being nosed and pushed about. Tolly pushed the apple upwards from the bottom till he heard Feste's teeth crunch into it. 'Oh, why didn't I bring sugar?' he thought. 'Now he won't know who puts it there.' Just then the outer stable door swung wide open with a bang as Boggis tramped in wheeling his bicycle, whistling loudly. The dust raised by the slam must have gone into Tolly's nose. He sneezed and sneezed and sneezed again.

''Struth!' said Boggis, looking over into the empty stall where Tolly cut a peculiar figure in his old-fashioned ragged coat and bare feet, sneezing in the dust of centuries. 'What in heaven's name is going on here? I thought you were a gypsy. What's that you've got on?'

'Happy Christmas, Boggis,' said Tolly. 'These are my special Christmas clothes.'

He went pattering off towards the house, but skirted round the garden path, partly to avoid the painful gravel, partly because in imagination he was riding a high-spirited horse and needed room to gallop. As he came along the lawn he saw the children grouped near the tree. Linnet was holding one of the partridges in her lap and feeding the other with corn. The peacock was sharing it, looking for once very beautiful and gracious. Toby was coatless, wearing a shirt which had full sleeves like a bishop's with lace at the wrist. He looked slim and athletic, as if he had just come from a fencing lesson. He was holding and examining something which, as Tolly drew nearer, stuffing his hands into the pockets of Toby's coat with quiet swagger, he saw was Truepenny. The deer and Watt were browsing at Toby's heels. Alexander was standing by with a handful of nuts which he was cracking between his teeth and eating. The squirrel was on his sleeve helping itself out of his palm.

Toby looked up and smiled at Tolly, raising one eyebrow just as his mother had done in church. 'Come here, Linnet,' he was saying. 'Will you hold

Truepenny for me? Alexander's too busy eating the squirrel's nuts. Hold him upside down. I want to get a thorn out of his hand.' Linnet took the little velvet thing and held him carefully. He looked pathetic with his pink palms and soles kicking at the four corners of his body, for his limbs were so short he looked as if he had none. He opened and shut his mouth but no sound came. There was truffle on the end of his nose. One of Linnet's curls, falling forward as she bent her head, lay on his stomach like an eiderdown. Toby had neat skilful fingers and the thorn was soon out.

'Give him to me,' said Alexander. 'I'll put him back among the thruffles.' He said it with difficulty because his mouth was full of nutshell.

'Did they all come?' asked Tolly.

'Oh yes, it has been a splendid breakfast party. I wondered where you were,' said Toby, grinning at him. 'I had to tie Reynard up because the new partridges were too much for him. Even the badger came today. He ate all the raisins.'

Linnet looked round, all alive with fun. 'The partridges are sweet,' she said. 'I've got a pocket full of field-mice, too. Look!'

She put her hand into the pocket of her silk apron and brought out a bright-eyed handful. One of them she put on the ground. It ran towards Tolly, so he picked it up and tied it in his handkerchief and put it in his pocket.

'I think I'll keep that one and tame it,' he said. They all laughed.

'Yes, keep it and tame it,' echoed Linnet, laughing like a little mad thing.

Her laughter was drowned in a rushing sound almost like a passing aeroplane, but it was only the arrival of the starlings. They descended in a gabbling cloud, blotting out everything else for a moment, and when they had alighted, the ground was carpeted with their waddling shiny figures, pecking at top speed to right and left among the crumbs of the feast. They had the place to themselves.

Tolly had gained a new confidence, perhaps because he was wearing Toby's coat. He no longer feared that the children would disappear and leave him, and perhaps never come back. He felt that they were like brothers and sisters who come and go, but there is no need for worry: they are sure to come home again. He remembered with remorse that he had not yet wished his great-grandmother a happy Christmas. She was preparing breakfast and smiled when she saw him.

'Good morning, Barefeet. Happy Christmas!' she said. 'Do you like your toes blue with cold?'

'Do you know who I am this time?'

'Why, Toby, of course! That means you will want two eggs for breakfast. Dear me, that coat is getting shabby. It is worse than shabby – it is coming to pieces like tissue paper.'

'I'll take it off carefully and fold it up and put it in a drawer by itself,' said Tolly.

'I forgot to tell you,' she called after him, 'Percy Boggis always comes for Christmas Day. He'll be here for breakfast. He's a nice boy.'

When Tolly came back he was properly dressed and carried a very small parcel in his hand.

'It's for you,' he said, 'for when you used to play with the doll's house. It's ALIVE.'

'What good ideas you have!' she said as she unwrapped the tiny rose tree. 'I always wished so much that there could be such a thing. I never guessed I should ever really have one.'

'It's alive,' he said again. 'It will have leaves no

192

bigger than bird-seed, and flowers like tiny wild strawberries. It will make a doll's-house room smell of roses.'

'Thank you very much for a perfect present. I will water it with my fountain pen filler, and put a salt-spoonful of compost on it in the spring. As for my present to you, you must Wait and See. I think I hear Percy.'

She went out into the hall to meet him, where there was some whispering before she brought him in.

He was a tough little boy with a shining, apple-cheeked face and hardy blue eyes. When Tolly shyly said 'Hullo', he made no reply, but stared around him like a lion. Mrs Oldknow made them sit down and gave them two eggs each.

'I expect you've both been awake since dawn,' she said. 'How did the breakfast party go off under the tree, Tolly?'

'I think everything is eaten up and everybody came. Hedge-prickles squeaked and grunted when he ate the truffles. He liked them very much. The peacock was quite nice to the partridges, like Miss Spudd with new boys. I brought one of the mice to tame. It's here in my pocket. I'll show you.'

He felt in his pocket while the other two watched him, but all he could find was his handkerchief with something hard in it. He brought it out to see what it could be and put it on the table. It was his own ebony mouse. Percy gave a loud country guffaw, and Tolly felt as if he had unwillingly done a conjuring trick. After a minute he began to laugh too, and so did Mrs Oldknow.

'It won't be hard to tame,' said Percy, and that was his only remark during the meal. He ate a great deal and looked quite at home.

Tolly sat, as usual, opposite the family portrait. He looked from the children to Percy and from Percy to the children again. Percy was so real. You couldn't imagine him vanishing. Tolly felt sure Linnet would have liked him. There ought, he thought, to have been a Boggis somewhere in the picture, if only in the garden that you can see through the window at the back. Or perhaps he was standing beside the painter, watching how he did it, and it was someone like Percy that Linnet was really laughing at, and with; not the artist at all.

Breakfast was over. Tolly's eyes, still smiling from what he imagined in the picture, came down and met

Percy Boggis's bold blue gaze, and was answered with a wide grin.

'I went to the circus,' said Percy briefly, as he left the table. 'They did this.'

He did two back-hand springs in quick succession and stood up panting and flushed, and hiccoughed. 'Too soon after breakfast,' he said, and did two forward ones, remaining on the same square of carpet. Tolly stood lost in wonder and ambition to do the same.

'Bravo, Percy!' said Mrs Oldknow. 'I see how you and Tolly are going to spend the day. But wait a moment. We have something to do first. You know what.'

'Aw, aye,' said Percy, disappearing from the room without more explanation.

'Tolly, shut your eyes and hold out both your arms. Come in, Percy. You can give it to him.'

Tolly stood there with his eyes shut, remembering the soft nose in the stables and the bump of the apple against his thigh, when suddenly his waiting arms were weighed down by a bundle of electrical activity so twisting and squirming that it was all he could do to hold it.

'It's Orlando!' he called out, opening his eyes. 'It's a real Orlando! Is he mine?'

'He's yours from now on.' Orlando was tugging at Tolly's sleeve, showing a great deal of white of eye. Tolly could not so much as speak to anyone else without getting his fingers nipped with pin teeth to recall his wandering attention. Puppy barks in a voice not yet broken made all conversation impossible. The two boys and Orlando let off all their surplus energy for half an hour. Then Percy said, 'In the circus they made them jump through hoops.'

'I know where there's a hoop,' said Tolly, 'hanging on a nail in Boggis's wood loft.'

'My old hoop!' said Mrs Oldknow. 'Tolly, your eyes really do see everything. Go off both of you and get it.'

Percy went down the garden in a series of cartwheels. Tolly was learning too, but Orlando was always barking either at his hands or his feet; and if he fell, the penalty was to be nibbled alive with pin teeth down the back of his neck and under his chin, or worst of all, on the bare back of his knees.

There is no need to describe the rest of Christmas Day – the turkey stuffed with chestnuts, the plum pudding that Tolly lit and Percy carried to the table in a circle of forget-me-not blue flames; the crystallized fruits, the crackers after tea, from which Mrs Oldknow drew a white paper bonnet that made her look more like the grandmother in the picture than ever. Tolly and Percy were luckier; their crackers dropped tiny metal aeroplanes and Snakes' Eggs.

Orlando shared everything. He even pulled a cracker with Tolly. Out of it he got a rolled-up paper tongue that, when Tolly blew, shot out suddenly to a stiff arm's length and flipped him on the nose, always slipping back into its roll before he could bite it.

When at last Mrs Oldknow came up to say good night, Tolly and Orlando were quite worn out. Orlando, curled up on the bed, would not open an eye however much Tolly nudged him. Tolly's eyes wandered sleepily over his room, acknowledging all his treasures, and their shadows that he loved perhaps almost more.

'Must I go to school next term?' he asked.

Mrs Oldknow kissed him good night.

'I can't waste your singing on Miss Spudd any more,' she said. 'You are going to the choir school at Greatchurch. I think they may let you sing in the choir. How Alexander would have envied you! And of course all your holidays will be here.

'And your father has written that he wants you to learn to ride.'

The River at
Green Knowe

'WHEN DO THE CHILDREN COME?' asked Dr Maud Biggin without looking up, as she licked her thumb and flicked over the pages of one of the many books open before her. The room was full of tables, collected from all over the house, and every table was piled with books, stores, photographs and boxes, which spread and spilled over on to the floor. Dr Maud was a short-sighted woman who never straightened her back, but moved about at the right height for consulting other books wherever she had laid them. If not reading, her attention was on the ground as if expecting that something very interesting might catch her eye there. She had spent much of her life digging up old cities and graves in deserts and shaly hillsides, and had got into the habit of searching the ground for fragments. She could not bear a vacuum cleaner because it left her nothing to look at. Her shambling way of walking made her look rather like a monkey, and if a chimpanzee were let loose in a shop to choose its own clothes it would choose much the same as she was wearing. When she needed more books, she brought out a little motorcycle with a large basket on the carrier and set out for the library. And very funny she looked in her crash helmet.

'Ah! The dear children!' replied her old friend Miss Sybilla Bun. 'They arrive at tea-time. I have made a three-tiered strawberry cream sponge for them. I hope they have healthy appetites. I am looking forward to seeing them eat.' Miss Sybilla's only remaining passion in life was food. She liked a lot of people to cook for, because that meant she could be ordering and cooking and seeing around her much more food, heaps of food. She loved to see it going into mouths. In that respect the children were likely to have a wonderful time if their digestions were good enough. Sybilla Bun, needless to say was very plump. She was not unlike a hen in many ways, especially on the rare occasions when she ran, for instance after the bus. She chortled over her food and sometimes bowed gravely to it several times, looking at it first with one eye and then with the other before she ate. Her clothes were all fuss and flummery, weighted down with mixed necklaces of every kind from golden sovereigns on a gipsy chain to ivory and ebony rosaries and even melon seeds dipped in silver paint.

These two ladies had rented for the summer a house called Green Knowe in the country beside a broad, slow-flowing river. Maud Biggin had chosen this remote and ancient place because she was writing a book. (She was one of a group of scientists who believed there had been prehistoric giant men as well as giant animals.) When she had settled in at Green Knowe and had taken in its Grimm's fairy-tale quality and felt how much room there was to spare, she threw off one of her ideas. She often launched an airy plan into action and then returned to her books and left the plan to work itself out as best it could. 'We will send to the S.P.S.H.D.C. for some children,' she said.

'The what, my dear?'

'The Society for the Promotion of Summer Holidays for Displaced Children. We will have two sent, and I will invite my great-niece Ida to take them off our hands.'

'What if they can't speak English? I know you can speak German, Spanish, Russian, Latin, Greek,

Hebrew, Arabic and the most important words in a dozen more languages, but Ida can't. And I can't ask them if they like grilled kidneys in Hebrew.'

'Don't fuss. I want to get on with my writing. I'll say they must speak English.'

'But my dear Maud – is it wise? What are they going to do? Because after all there's always spare time in between meals. We've no toys, no playroom. What will they play?'

'You can't stop children playing. They'll play all right. There's the river, isn't there? And a house you can hardly believe in when you see it. What more can a child want? Just turn them out. So long as they don't interfere with the Ogru.' (This referred to Dr Biggin's book, which was to be called *A Reconstruction of the Habits and Diet of the Ogru. A summary of recent discoveries.*)

'But will it be safe?' Miss Bun persisted. 'Supposing they can't swim?'

Maud Biggin tossed across the letter she had just typed.

'For heaven's sake! How you fuss! Put a PS. that they must be able to swim. And now please let me get on with my work.'

Miss Bun took the typewritten note and added in

204

her fat round writing – 'PS. It's imperative that the children shall be able to swim. The river here is *very* dangerous.'

The Society had replied that they would be happy to send two children.

'AH, HERE'S THE TAXI! Here they are!' cried Sybilla Bun.

'And ready for their tea I hope. Come in, children, come in.'

They stood shyly in a row. Ida was eleven, trim, grey-eyed and reliant, but so small her age was almost unbelievable. Next to her stood Oskar, also eleven, leggy and head in air with an obstinate thrust in his lips and chin. He clicked his heels together and introduced himself.

'Oskar Stanislawsky.'

Lastly there was a slim nine-year-old with an Asiatic face.

'What's your name, dear boy?' Miss Sybilla bent down to bring her nose level with his, so that her beads fell forward and the melon seeds hung like a skipping rope between them.

The boy gave a gurgling sigh.

'Come, tell Auntie Sybilla your name, love.'

He replied with exactly the same sound.

'Doesn't he speak English?' Miss Sybilla asked Ida. 'We said they were all to speak English. What is his name?'

Ida, though so small, was clearly the head of the group and had established her position on the journey.

'That is his name, that he said. It is spelt HSU and it can't be said in English. So we shall call him Ping. He speaks English very well, only he hardly ever speaks.'

Ping had black velvety eyes and a delicious smile.

'I thank you for your very kind invitation,' he said softly, with a little bow over his folded hands.

Maud Biggin coming to the door of her study, looked out.

'How d'y' do, Midget,' she said. 'You don't grow much.'

Ida came forward and after a moment's hesitation, because her great-aunt's bent position brought her cheek within range, gave her a dutiful kiss.

'I'm not a kissy person,' said Dr Biggin, 'but I'm glad to see you. Hullo boys. I hope you won't be any trouble. Enjoy yourselves. Be off now with Miss Bun. I'm busy.' She firmly closed the study door between them.

'Come children with Auntie Sybilla and see your room.'

As they wound their way upstairs after her the children were wide-eyed with surprise. 'Is it a Buddhist monastery?' asked Ping. 'It could just as well be a Crusader's castle,' said Oskar.

'I wish I had hair long enough to let down out of the windows for you two to climb up,' said Ida, shaking her two little pigtails, properly so called, for they were no longer.

They were to share a large attic room at the top of the house. It had windows on three sides, out of which they could see the river as if on a map. It was a beautiful river, flowing through meadows or under trees. As seen now, on a summer evening it looked smooth, sleepy and timeless. But it was a wilful river, ready to overflow its banks after any heavy rain even in summer, for which reason there were neither factories nor houses along this part of its winding course to the sea. If after several years of low rainfall people began to forget the past and put out plans for building housing estates on the meadows, or factories on the banks, the river would suddenly wake up, turn over in its bed, and pour deep lakes of water over half the country. However, the island on which Green Knowe stood was slightly humped, just enough to keep it clear of the floods, and that is how there came to be such an old house on it.

'What a lot of islands the river makes,' said Ida. 'We are on one, and I can see at least three others. We must go exploring and sail round them all. Perhaps we shall find one where nobody has ever set foot. It looks beautifully wild.' The boys leant out at her elbows. A hundred yards upstream there was a water gate controlling the flow into a branch that went off at right angles. The tumbling of the water over the bar filled the bedroom with its day-long, night-long sound. The main stream, undisturbed by the loss of half its volume, flowed quietly past Green Knowe, throwing out as it went, in its careless liberality, a loop of water that encircled the garden, and returned beside one wall of the house.

'Look at this house reflected in the water,' said Ping, calling the others to look out of the side window. 'Isn't it still. I can see us all looking out of the window, but our faces wiggle as if we were eating toffee.' They ran from window to window, eager to see all there was.

'The sky is so blue I wonder why it doesn't reflect the river just as the river reflects it, like barber's mirrors reflecting backward and forward for ever.'

'Before it could reflect it would have to have something dark behind it like the bottom of the river. That's why.'

'Well, outer space is behind the sky,' said Oskar, 'and that's dark, I suppose.'

'Then I don't know why it doesn't reflect,' said Ping. 'But once is enough really. Look at the fish rising.'

'Your eyes reflect,' said Ida. 'I can see a tiny pink sunset cloud and a tiny green pin-point earth. No colour photo was ever so *minute*.'

'I see them huge, though,' said Ping. 'The cloud is so

big that if it was a mountain you never could possibly climb to the top, and the earth stretches all the way to where the sky begins. Miles and miles and miles with woods and rushes and waterfalls and water-wheels and nightingales and bells and singing fishes.'

'I shall like that,' said Ida. 'We'll have to go quietly by starlight to hear singing fishes. Do you *know* there are some, Ping, or are you just thinking it?'

'My father used to say,' said Oskar, gazing far away at the sun which was shooting out rays like cartwheel spokes, 'that there isn't anything real except thoughts. Nothing is there at all unless somebody's thinking it. He said thoughts were more real than guns. He got shot by the Russians for saying that. But the thought wasn't shot, because I'm thinking it now. So if Ping has singing fishes, let's try and hear some. Why not?'

'I'm in a hurry to begin,' said Ida. 'I *want* the river. I could eat it. Let's go down to tea. Bags I this bed in the corner.' She threw her case on it. 'Come on!'

THE CHILDREN WERE told they were to make their own beds and keep their room tidy, but as nobody ever came up to inspect, it soon became a lively and special place. Oskar had a photo of his father that he pinned up, and Ping had a Chinese picture off the side of a tea-box. If Ping wanted to burn smelly sausages made of rolled clay and twigs, and call them joss sticks, or Oskar to shape candle-ends into little images of Kruschev and stick pins into them, or Ida to keep newts and water-lilies in the wash basin, it was nobody's business to know. The two old ladies fortunately seemed to think that children were as well able to take care of themselves as cats. You only needed to feed them and turn them out.

THE FIRST MORNING was fine and windless. Ida, Oskar and Ping went off after breakfast. At the bottom of the garden there was a wooden boat-house, its four corner posts planted in a marshy piece on the bend of the river. They ran across the unsteady gangway and opened the boat-house door. Inside it was half dark. There was a smell of concentrated river water. The roof and walls were greened with perpetual damp and wriggly with elastic water patterns. Low down, level with their feet, a canoe lay fretting and tugging gently on its mooring. It was painted blue and brown, and the water that reflected it received it as part of itself. The canoe was lightly built and beautifully balanced, and it would comfortably hold three children. When Ida put the weight of one foot into it, it was like treading on the water itself. It yielded so far that she feared it was sinking under her, but then the water resisted, and she sat down feeling like a water-lily on its leaf. The boys followed her in. Ping sat in front and Oskar in the stern. They parted the willow strands that hung like a net across the opening, and the river was theirs.

The sun had not yet pierced the haze of morning. The water was like a looking-glass with a faint mist of breath drying off it. The children felt it so bewitching that without even a discussion they turned downstream, drifting silently along, willing to become part of the river if they could. Along the edge of the water ran a ribbon of miniature cliff, the top edge undulating like the cliffs of Dover, the vertical sides pierced with holes the size of a golf ball. Sometimes the cliff was high enough to show seams of gravel or strata of different soils. Above it willow-herb or loosestrife or giant dock heavy with seed rose against the sky, and reflected themselves in the

water with an effect like 'skeleton' writing. The canoe seemed to hover between two skies. The banks of the river were richly alive. Moorhens hurried from side to side trailing a widening V, fish leapt along the surface, water rats swam underwater, their V trailing from the end of their projecting noses. Or they peeped out from holes, or it might be mice, or martins, or a kingfisher.

The rushes ticked like clocks, meadowsweet suddenly bowed down from above almost to the children's noses as a bumble bee landed on it; or a rush waved desperately as something attacked it out of sight at the bottom.

They drifted happily along, a twist of the paddle now and again being enough to keep them on a straight course. Presently the sun came out and beautifully warmed them in the shell of the canoe, and with the sun appeared another host of living things, butterflies, dragonflies, water boatmen, brightly coloured beetles and lizards; and high up in the sky a weaving of swallows. The canoe drifted to a standstill.

Ping's eyes were fixed on a small spider that was descending from the branch of a tree, playing out its rope as it came, its many feet all busy. It landed on the point of the prow, made its rope fast and immediately swarmed up again.

'We're tethered,' Ping said, smiling indulgently. 'Are there no big things in English rivers – no water buffaloes, no tigers in the bamboo, no crocodiles or hippopotamuses?' As he spoke there was a sound of a large body being jerked up out of the mud, and a shadow-flecked bullock on the edge of the bank that had escaped Ping's notice snorted in his ear. He fell over backward into Ida's lap, while the other two laughed and the bullock squared its forelegs and lowered its head. Ping stared up at it from underneath.

'I can see all of us in its eyes,' he said, 'reflected quite clearly. But you can see it means nothing to him. They are awfully stupid eyes. He isn't quite sure that we aren't a dog or a motor-car.' Ping stuck one leg straight up in the air. 'I don't believe he knows it isn't a stick.' The bullock stared a long time and other bullocks came and stared too. Then it lifted its nose and began a tremendous bellow which suddenly tailed off into a foolish query, mild and puzzled. Ping put his leg down again and the bullock sighed deeply in relief.

'Let's shut our eyes,' said Ida, 'and say everything we can hear.'

They all began together so that their voices sounded like a cluster of ducks or any other young things that might be sunning themselves on the river. Ida, however, said they must take it in turns so that they wouldn't count anything twice.

Water under the canoe's ribs, whirlpool round my paddle, drip off the end of Ping's paddle, bird flying off tree, larks singing, rooks circling, swallows diving, rustling in grass, grasshoppers, honeybees, flies, frogs, bubbles rising, a weir somewhere, tails swishing, cow patting, aeroplanes, a fishing rod playing out; zizz, buzz, trill, crick, whizz, plop, flutter, splash; and all the time everywhere whisper, whisper, whisper, lap, chuckle and sigh. If someone moved in the canoe, a moment later on the far side of the river all the rushes nudged each other and whispered about the ripple that had arrived.

'Everything's trying to say something,' said Ping. 'Fishes poke up round mouths as if they were stammering.'

'Do you think,' said Ida out of a silence, 'that the sound I can hear now might be singing fish!'

They all listened. There was a new sound coming from farther downstream, round the next bend, a musical bubbling, warbling whistle.

With one accord all three paddles went in and the canoe shot off. They were very vigorous after so much drifting and listening. The whistling grew louder every minute, and then appeared a huge white swan, sailing menacingly, a warship at action stations. Behind him came seven small grey cygnets, whose infant chatter was the noise that had brought the children, and behind them the mother swan guarding the rear. She now hurried forward tossing on the water with the violence of her foot strokes, and both parents bore down on the canoe, clapping their terrible wooden sounding wings, shooting out necks like snakes and hissing in the children's faces. Their open beaks were rough-edged mincers. Fortunately the canoe had enough momentum to be swerved at speed to a safer distance. The mother swan turned back to her brood and the cob contented himself with patrolling up and down between them and the fleeing canoe, keeping his implacable eye sideways to the intruders. As soon as the children felt safe they paused to watch.

'Look, there is one tiny cygnet quite left out. It's only half the size of the others.'

While the 'alert' had been on there had indeed been seven cygnets in a cluster. The smallest having succeeded in joining them while the parents' attention was elsewhere. Now, however, the mother swan had headed it off, and it swam with great agitation alone, uttering heart-rending peeps. Its only and persistent wish was to join the others, but this was not allowed. Whenever it thought it had, by sneaking round behind, achieved its aim, a long white snake would descend, and a beak used like a spoon flip it away.

'Why is she so horrid to it? The littlest ought to be her favourite,' said Ida in distress. 'She won't let it eat anything.' But when the cob saw the poor little thing trying to get round behind him, he hissed, and closing his wicked mincers on its back held it under water.

This was too much for Ida, who leapt to her feet, nearly upsetting the canoe, and hurled her paddle. The attack and the noise – for the two boys shouted at Ida as the canoe rocked – brought the cob back to his duties. He wheeled to rap with his beak on the paddle that was now floating beside him. The poor dazed cygnet came to the surface and paddled away for dear life, straight into Ida's hands. As she had now no paddle she cradled it tenderly in her lap while the boys worked to get out of range of the angry parent. They were not pursued. The six remaining cygnets cuddled up together and whistled contentedly. The mother swan up-ended herself and searched the river bottom for food. After a decent interval to cool his temper, the cob did so too.

'Their feet remind me of umbrellas blown inside out,' said Ping.

The little cygnet continued to make the most mournful squeaking.

'Ours must be an orphan,' said Oskar. 'It's a Displaced Cygnet.'

'We'll keep it and bring it up, and have a tame swan swimming beside us wherever we go,' said Ida. 'I wonder if swans fight? Suppose it's a he-swan and there are fights whenever we go out. A sparrow fight is bad enough. Imagine a swan fight! Think of the noise their wings make taking off. Like a paddle steamer.'

'I don't think they fight like dogs,' said Ping. 'I think they wrestle, each holding the other's right wing in his beak. I would like to see it.'

'It won't even be grown up by the end of the holiday,' said Oskar. 'It will still be a baby. And what are we going to do with it then? And where will it sleep?'

'I'll make it a nest in a box. In the cupboard there is an old eiderdown with a hole in the corner. We'll shake out a lot of feathers and make it feel at home.'

But the grief of the cygnet was very hard to bear. It went on and on. The children could hardly talk because of it. It never stopped to take breath. It made the river journey one long execution party. The children got quite miserable.

'It will go on squeaking till it dies,' said Ida.

At this point they came to a mill and a lock. The lock-keeper happened to be on the bridge, so they paddled straight into the narrow stone passage and the gate was closed behind them. As the water sank, it was like going down in a lift. The walls rose and rose till it was frightening to believe that the river anywhere in its course was as deep as that. The plug gurgling of this giant's bath sucked and tugged. The cygnet's cries, magnified in the enclosing slimy walls, filled Oskar's ears like anguish in a prison. At last the gate was lifted, and after a final rush and babble of conflicting waters the new level was established and the canoe could be paddled out into the mill pool. This was as big as a lake and as wild as a marsh. Near the mill it was overhung with trees, but its distant edge was fringed with tall rushes in which were openings where smaller streams flowed into the pool.

Just below the lock two more swans were sailing. They had none of the majesty and organization of the family upstream. They were restless, nervous and appeared to be looking for something, thrusting their long necks at water-level into the rushes, or turning round and round in one spot with necks stretched up into watch-towers.

When the canoe breasted the pool and carried the squealing cygnet into earshot, the two swans heard at once. They sailed along wing to wing turning their heads sideways to the canoe while they circled round it. As they drew nearer their bearing stiffened and grew fiercer, while the cygnet, now quite hoarse, yelled and fought in Ida's hands. The swans came so close they could have overturned the canoe, their unwinking eyes level with the children's.

'What shall I do now?' Ida cried, shrinking away.

'Let it go,' said Oskar, 'I think these are its proper parents.'

Ida opened her hands, and the cygnet wildly scrambling on its elbowy little black legs and flapping wings hardly stronger than a butterfly's, left the canoe for its mother's back. She fluffed up her wing feathers to hold it there, and both swans paddled off at full speed into the distant rushes.

'Whew! What a relief!' said Ida, but Oskar was following the course of the swans with happy eyes, his jaw thrust out.

'I suppose it got trapped in the lock the last time somebody went through in the other direction. Look, Ida, it's off her back now and they are both showing it how to nibble water.'

While they were watching, the canoe drifted into a grass bank and Ping put his arm round a post that stood there.

'Here's a good place for mooring. Let's have a bathe.' They all scrambled out on to the bank, and soon had dived in like three frogs.

'I'm going to practise up-ending like the swans, and see what I can find on the bottom,' said Ida. 'Let's see who can find the most interesting thing on the bottom.' She vanished leaving only her little feet and ankles on the surface. When she came up for breath she saw Oskar's long shanks waving madly about, and Ping's neat gilded legs cool like fish. At the first attempt nobody found anything. The bottom felt unpleasant to the hands. It was deep slime with here and there the rusty edge of a tin, or things that did not feel quite alive and yet moved.

'There must be all kinds of things,' Ida persisted, looking with her wet plastered hair and chattering teeth very determined, like a hunting otter. 'People always drop things getting in and out of boats. I expect this has been a mooring place ever since boats were invented. We might find Hereward the Wake's dagger.'

Up came all their feet again; and again. The third time was lucky. Ida came panting to the surface with a bent piece of iron, and Ping with a live eel held firmly in both hands. When he had shown it to the others he hurled it up into the sky where it shone silver for a moment before entering the water again with no splash at all, like a needle entering silk. Ping seemed supremely satisfied, his almond eyes lifted at the corners making the same kind of smile as his mouth.

'What's this that I've got?' said Ida. 'It's like a starting handle. It was awfully heavy to swim with. It would be useful if we had a motor boat.'

'It's a lock key,' said Oskar. 'Much more useful. Now we can go anywhere we want quite by ourselves.'

'What a lucky find! Because this pool seems the centre point for exploring lots of islands. I can see five or six waterways from here. We shall be always coming and going. What have you found, Oskar?'

'I don't know what it is – some kind of metal bowl. But it is such an odd shape – as if it really was for something special. It might be silver. Do you suppose this is all of it? It wouldn't stand steadily on this knob thing underneath. Perhaps it's the lid of something.' He turned it the other way up.

'It's a helmet!' screeched Ida.

'A head lid,' said Ping. 'An Oskar lid.'

Oskar put it on. It fitted him perfectly. As his hands passed over it, the raised part on top that he had thought was the pedestal, became obviously the socket for his plumes.

They picked flowering rushes and tied the stalks into a firm base to fit the socket, and there was Oskar looking like King Arthur himself, at least to Ida's eyes. And because the helmet seemed to demand it of its wearer, Oskar stood up in the canoe all the way home – an art requiring much practice if the canoe was not to be overturned, and leaving all the work to the other two. But it looked magnificent.

T
HEY WERE ALL VERY hungry when they got back to the house, their first morning on the river in retrospect seemed like days. Miss Sybilla was delighted as she looked round the table from plate to plate, even from face to face, and saw large helpings of lovely food going down. But alas, Ping had only eaten half his first plateful when he put his knife and fork tidily down and turning his black almond eyes first to one hostess and then the other said:

'Excuse me, please. I beg your pardon for my rudeness, but I cannot eat any more. Already it hurts. Excuse me, please.'

'Nonsense, Ping,' said Miss Sybilla, 'I don't cook just to have it left.' She piled second helpings on Ida's and Oskar's plates, which they received with willingness. 'Come along, Ping. Don't disappoint me.'

'Leave him alone, Sybilla,' said Dr Biggin looking up from the book she read during meals. 'Remember he's an Oriental. They can live on a few grains of rice. Look at his slight bones. You can't expect him to eat like a Teuton.'

'Thank you,' said Ping, holding his stomach with both hands.

For this reason Ping could never be a favourite with Miss Bun. No one in fact could compete with Oskar at table. The two ladies had not asked any questions about the morning's outing, nor did they throughout the holidays. Perhaps they thought children's occupations too foolish to interest grown-ups. Not a word was said about the lock key or the helmet. The latter was carefully cleaned by Oskar and hung up beside his father's picture as an offering.

IN THE AFTERNOON the children set off again, this time going upstream. 'We will make a map of the river,' Ida proposed, 'and put in it every island that we have been right round, and all the weirs and locks. It will be in colours, with little pictures of the important things. We will paint it on a roll of white wall-paper, because I expect we shall go a long way up and down. Green Knowe will be in the middle.'

Hardly out of sight of Green Knowe they paddled round a small island only a few yards across in any direction, on which the swan family had their nest. The six cygnets were having an afternoon nap under their mother's feathers. She sat erect and alert, but the cob was off duty, lazily cruising around. The first island on the children's map was therefore to be Swan Island. They passed under a wooden railway bridge that was built low over the water, and were lucky enough to get the thundery rumble of a train going over just above their ears. It was a train suitable to deep country, a ridiculous unlikely toy engine with goods trucks, and the only train in the day. Its squawky whistle and the drone of aeroplanes so high up as to look like gnats were the only sounds they heard that were not made by the river, as it were under its breath, or the wild inhabitants of its banks and pools. It seemed as though all the noise was in the sky, and at earth-level nothing but sighs of contentment and midsummer dreaming. They were not a talkative trio. Ida and Oskar were firm friends almost at sight, and they both loved Ping. Ida's laugh was like a bird's flutter, Oskar's more like a puppy's woof. Ping seldom laughed out loud himself, but his smile was often a reason why the others did. Generally they paddled silently like Indians. They made their way all round a narrow island completely and thickly covered with brambles and nettles and thorny sloes that leaned out over the water. They christened it Tangle Island, and this was the first one about which they felt certain that no human being had set foot on it for as long as they could imagine. There simply wasn't room for a foot even at the very edge. Beyond this, the river divided into two. Both ways looked promising, so they went a little way up each, far enough to find that both arms divided again. It was a labyrinth of waters waiting to be explored, but it was time to turn home again. The only rule of any kind that was imposed on the children by their hostesses was that they must be in time for meals. To have been late would have caused Miss Bun real distress. Though Oskar had no sense of time whatever and Ida when she was set on one of her ideas could think of nothing else, Ping could not bear the idea of rudeness to a hostess. He felt so strongly about this that Ida and Oskar never challenged it. Miss Bun however gave him no credit for the good manners of all three. Ping was no eater.

THE NEXT MORNING they strolled up the village street to buy a roll of white lining paper and some drawing pins. (Ida had brought poster paint and brushes with her for wet days.) They pinned the middle of the roll to the middle of their bedroom floor, so that, with Green Knowe as the centre, they could unroll as much as they wanted both for up stream and down. They pencilled in as much as they could remember of what they had explored already, just to make a start. Then they set off again. Each day they took a different arm of the stream, and always the best part was out of reach. Then, overnight, the holiday season began in earnest. The river was crowded with boating parties, some of whom had never been in a boat before. They shouted instructions in voices of hysteria, they went bungling from bank to bank, lost their tempers when the boat rocked under their staggers and fell over-board amid jeers. Dogs stood in the bows and barked incessantly, outboard motors drummed and snorted past, bearing ladies who spoke shrilly to be heard above the noise. Bathers leapt from the banks dog-wise, and the impact of their bodies on the water sent waves that rocked every boat and added to the din. It was no longer the mysterious river on which the children had been so entranced. True it was winding, sparkling and cool, the water lip-lapped under the ribs of the canoe and the clouds had all the sky from horizon to horizon to move across. But the river had become ordinary, a playground for humans. Every creature whose real home it was had gone into hiding. It had no more private life than a swimming bath or fun fair.

Ida as usual made a decision.

'All these people spoil everything. Our river is different. If we want to see it again we shall have to come out at dawn. We'll get up every day when it is just getting light, then we can do our exploring before breakfast and spend the daytime sleeping in the sun. We'll tell Aunt Sybilla we are going out before breakfast – we needn't tell her how early – and ask her for a thermos and some biscuits. She'll be awfully pleased when she sees how much breakfast we eat when the time comes. And if we get up really early we'll have time to go twice as far.'

VERY EARLY NEXT MORNING, creeping down through a curtained house, they came out into a world that Ida hardly recognized. It felt tilted, with the moon in the unexpected side of the sky, because it was setting, and the growing light of dawn was farther east than she had ever seen it before, as if the points of the compass had been displaced. The bullocks were asleep, so were the swans. No smoke came from any cottage chimney, no birds moved. A vivid red fox cantered across the field with a moorhen in his mouth. Only the water was loud. The fall at the watergates shouted carelessly to the dawn as if certain no one was listening.

The children loosed the canoe and set off, paddling expertly and swiftly because they were half afraid of such an empty world. They operated the lock for the first time, rather anxiously, with their own lock key. Both boys were eager to turn it while Ida sat in the canoe and hoped they would not do it too suddenly so that she would be sucked down and under. She need not have feared, for it took both of them to turn it at all. They puffed and panted and stopped several times to rest. When they were all in the canoe again, they launched out across the mill pool and were caught up and whirled along in the mill race. The current pounded on the bottom of the canoe like hammers so that it bucked and tossed. The children sat helpless and apprehensive under the unfamiliar setting moon, but were carried safely into the lower reaches.

It was a dawn without sun or wind. The sky was not crowded with cloud shapes, it was just pale, the water like tarnished quicksilver and the leafy distances like something forgotten. The canoe moved in a close circle of silence so that everything that was near enough to come within the magic circle was singled out for the imagination to play with. Such were the twisted pollard willows striking attitudes along the bank, many of them old and bent like old men, or more correctly like old men's coats, for they gaped open and were quite hollow inside, looking, as Ping remarked, ready for demons, who could step in and wear the tree like a coat at night. Ping was a great believer in demons but the thought of them did not seem to disturb him. They were just what he would expect.

The river grew steadily wider, flowing handsomely over a clean weedless bottom. Large trees crowded down a low hill to the edge of the water, their branches hung with hop and wild clematis. Here and there an overloaded trunk leant out over the water at such an angle that it seemed impossible the roots could take the strain any longer. At the top of one such tree a bright yellow cat lay along the trunk, not too high above the canoe to have leapt on someone's shoulder as they passed underneath. It looked down on them with the defiant glare of hostile cats, and the tip of its tail twitched.

'It might have been a tiger,' said Ping, with that gleam of pleasure in his slit eyes that thoughts of danger seemed to bring.

The light broadened, the orange East turned to unbearable dazzle, and the water flicked off little reflections of fire. The children's eyes were screwed up against the fearful inquisitiveness of the rising sun at eye-level. Ahead of them on the river's edge stood a derelict building. The walls rose up out of the water, their stones green and yellow with slime. In its welcome shadow the water too was green and yellow, but each paddle as it dipped was surrounded by a sky-coloured ring. The place had so long been abandoned that it was impossible to tell for what purpose it had been built, whether house, barn or warehouse. It had the remains of a balcony from which iron steps led down to the water, but the ivy, which once perhaps was planted to take off the newness, had for generations been allowed to grow as it pleased. Nobody cared any more if the walls were wrapped around in a vast embrace, the windows covered, the gutters blocked, the slates lifted by prying ivy fingers. So unhampered and vigorous was the ivy that having covered the house its stringy growth, waving in the wind and feeling for support like caterpillars at the top of a stalk, had caught on neighbouring trees and wrapped them round too in its cocoon, as if the building had towers. Two windows still showed above the balcony. The sashes fell sideways, some panes were missing and the rest heavily curtained with layer upon layer of grey cobweb. As a last humiliation for the house, there was an ash sapling growing out of the chimney.

The children took hold of the iron rails of the steps and tied up the canoe.

'This must be where Ping's demons hide in the daytime,' said Ida.

'Displaced demons,' said Oskar dreamily.

'Let us visit them,' said Ping.

One by one they climbed out, their rubber shoes silent on the iron, and mounted to the balcony.

Having got there, it was impossible not to turn and lean out over the river to admire the view. The wide perennial pastures had the serenity of land that is never tended except by the refreshing floods. This expanse was the true river bed, once a marsh extending all the way to the sea. The far side was wooded along the skyline. It was easy to imagine forest coming to the edge of the marsh.

'I don't wonder they built a house here,' Ida said. 'But whatever possessed them to leave it? It seems mean, to the house.'

There were double doors on to the balcony now barred with ivy stems as thick as men's arms and much hairier. Ping and Oskar were peering between them and fumbling for a door-knob. Oskar found it, but when he turned it and pushed, the whole lock-box came away from the rotten socket and his wrist went through with it. The three children pushed on the door where they could reach it. It hung askew on its hinges and the bottom edge bound on the floor so that they were only able to force it open a little way.

'Ping and I can get in,' said Ida inserting herself between the ivy arms and wiggling through the door. 'Oskar's too big. Ooh, it's a tight squeeze.

Perhaps we can open a window for you, Oskar, when we are inside.'

But it was wonderful what Oskar could do. The only part of him that gave trouble was his head that was too wide from ear to ear. And the head can't be drawn in like the stomach.

'Of course I can do it,' he said sharply to Ida who was still talking about windows. And do it he did, his profile streamlined along his shoulder as in Egyptian pictures, while Ping watched the impossible with approving eyes.

They found themselves in what had once been a fine room. There were high windows on three sides, letting in a bottle green light through the ivy blinds. The handsome plaster ceiling was still further decorated by small patches of twinkling watered silk where the river managed to play its flashing mirrors through gaps in the leaves. Opposite the balcony had been another pair of double doors, now missing, as were the fireplaces and all the doors in the house, so that on going through to the wide stair-well and its banistered landings, one had the impression of a continuous but much alcoved room from ground floor to roof. Cobwebs hung everywhere as if the owners had left muslin curtains to moulder away through the years. Dead leaves and straws littered the floors, shiny snail tracks climbed the walls. The children crept around apprehensively, greatly oppressed by that feeling in empty houses that if you think nobody lives there *you are wrong*. Dust and silence, and boards that creaked, not when you trod on them, but minutes afterwards behind you. Ida's heart began to feel tight. She was looking across the stairs into an open doorway where a shadow was moving on the wall, when she felt a sharp rap on the back of her hand, as if someone had thrown a pebble. Something thudded on the floor. Ida clutched Oskar and they bent down to look.

'It's an owl pellet,' said Oskar laughing. 'There must be an owl here and he spat at us.'

High above them on a cornice that surrounded the base of a lantern window a kingly white owl sat, making himself in his indignation as tall and thin as a spectre. When he saw them looking up at him, in a swooping and tyrannical gesture he dropped his head beyond his feet, and in that position glared at them, afterwards turning his face upside down on his neck to glare at them the other way up.

Not having frightened them away by that trick, he resumed his normal position, swaying his head from side to side and rocking on his feet.

'I believe it's his house, his very own, all of it, and he didn't invite us,' said Ping. 'I feel rude.'

The owl in a movement more soundless and flowing than wind or water, opened its wings and was upon them, zooming at the last moment of its dive with savage claws turned up and spread like fingers. It seemed nearly as big as Ida, its eyes far bigger than hers. It swept at them again and again, its approach absolutely unhearable and its curving flight unpredictable. They ran for the door. Ping and Ida went through like cats. Oskar had to do his conjuring trick again, Egyptian-wise, so that when his body was half-way through and helpless, his eyes and nose were still inside turned to the owl. In this vulnerable position he saw it fly a triumphant, slow patrol over its premises and return to rest.

The children crossed over to the opposite bank and sat there considering the Owl's Palace, as Ida called it.

'The ivy should be full of thousands of sparrows, but I expect the owl has eaten them all. And all the mice too.'

'Oskar,' said Ping. 'Can you make your face long and thin by *thinking* it?' Ida and Ping stared at Oskar in hopeful and co-operative silence while he tried.

'Did it?' he asked after a while.

'No,' said Ida truthfully. Oskar felt ashamed.

Ida in sympathy changed the conversation.

'Let's see if the house is on an island. If it is we can put Owl Palace Island on our map.'

'If it's an island it must have a bridge.'

They paddled on. Sure enough there was a shallow stream, silted up and overgrown, that led round the back. There was a bridge too, rickety and rotten, barred with a tangle of barbed wire. As they went along, the channel, though fairly wide, became more and more clogged with weeds till the canoe could hardly move forward. The paddles dug into floating greenstuff that had to be pushed along like yards of sodden flannel. Obviously no boats came this way for picnics though the big trees and the slope of the hill behind them made it a sheltered and enticing spot. With determination the children toiled at the paddles until the thought of fighting their way back again was unbearable – there was no alternative but to go on. At last the way was blocked by a submerged tree-trunk, leafless, black and slimy. It was this that broke the flow of the water and concentrated the weeds into a stagnant mass. On its far side the water was nearly clear. The children scrambled on to the bank, and using the trunk as a roller – the thick slime was nearly as good as grease – they shoved and tugged the canoe over it. In the process Ida slipped in on the weedy side and came out as green as a mermaid, and Oskar from the other side came out wearing tights of black mud. Ping remained clean and golden. It was warm enough and nobody minded being wet. The obstacle had been surmounted, and now they paddled swiftly and quietly through a tunnel of overarching elms, delighted to be back in real lip-lapping water.

Suddenly Ping, sitting as usual in the prow, made a startled sign to the others as he caught hold of a branch to bring the canoe to a standstill. Ahead of them sitting on the bank, his bare feet dangling in the water, was a strange figure. He had a brown mane over his shoulders and all that could be seen of his face uncovered by beard or hair was the fine bridge of his nose with curving nostrils and bright eyes in skull-like sockets. He was naked except for a piece of sacking round his hips, and was as lean as a greyhound.

'It's a man-lion,' said Ida.

The man was intent on his line and float and had not noticed the canoe beneath the trees. What had most startled the children was his expression, unlike any they had seen before. It was the expression of a man alone in the universe, though they could not know that.

'It's a he-witch,' said Ping softly.

The man pulled in his line and sang under his breath:

> *Tum túm tee úmptity úmpty eye*
> *Tum túm titi úmptity éye.*

'That's not witch-music,' said Oskar. 'He's a displaced person that's escaped.'

'Shall we go and say good morning to him? It would be polite.'

They climbed out of the canoe and walked along the bank.

'Good morning,' said Ping, bowing. 'May we visit you on your island?'

The man looked round slowly as if he didn't believe he had heard anything, but all the same, perhaps? He cleared his throat and looked away again as if he had seen nothing, then looked back and cleared his throat a second time.

'Who may you be?' he asked a little croakily.

'We are displaced persons too,' said Oskar. 'We thought you wouldn't mind.'

'Have a toffee,' said Ida, politely holding out a paper bag.

'Toffee?' the man repeated dreamily. 'I had forgotten there was such a word. Toffee!' He put his hand to take one, but stopped to look furtively all round as if a multitude might be closing in on him. He put the toffee in his mouth and shut his eyes while he savoured it. Then opening them and jerking his teeth free from the stick-jaw he said:

'It takes me back, that does.' After a while he added: 'Steak and Kidney pie! Bacon and eggs for breakfast! Was there really – bacon? That's a thought.'

Oskar understood at once, but Ida was at a loss.

'Have you run out of bacon?' she asked.

'Have I run out of bacon?' The man began to laugh, but his laughter was out of running order. It began and stopped, it blew up and skidded into choking ha! ha!s. He wiped his eyes with the back of his hand.

'Where have you nippers come from – if you're

real? One's a chinaman,' he added doubtfully, talking to himself.

'That's me.' Ping bowed and smiled.

The man frowned.

'I've not seen a living soul for so long I don't know what to think. But a chinaman's not likely.'

'It's all right,' said Oskar. 'It's us, and we won't tell anybody at all. Do you live here?'

'I've lived here alone for more years than I can count. I haven't kept count. What's the use? Who wants to know? I don't. Maybe I'm an old man, maybe not yet. Would you say, now, that I'm an old man?'

'Your face is rather skinny,' said Ida, anxious to give him the truth, 'but your hair is quite brown and there's heaps of it. So you can't be *old* old, can you? I think you're not having enough to eat. Couldn't you get some bacon in the shop?'

'Shop!' he repeated contemptuously. She might just as well have said from the herdsmen of ancient Troy. 'Is that racket still going on? Shops want money.'

'Haven't you got any money?'

'I haven't, and I don't want any. I came here because I was sick of hearing about it. Everybody working all their lives just to get it, and everybody all the time, day in and day out, saying they hadn't enough of it. And the shopkeepers telling you what they had to pay for what you've got to pay them for. I got sick of it, I tell you. It seems funny to be talking to someone about it. I never have done all this time. Sometimes I don't know whether something I remember wasn't a dream. I used to be a London bus driver. I got so that I couldn't bear all those people, all along every pavement waiting for me in pushing crowds, always running in front of my wheels and closing in behind me, skidding in ahead of me in cars and puffing out stink. And the whole way along every road posters of people larger than life killing each other or kissing each other. I got so that I couldn't stand it. Then one day I found myself here, because it was a Bank Holiday and this was the only place I could find where there wasn't somebody already. I had to wade through bog up to my knees to get here. And nobody's been here from that day to this and I haven't missed them.'

'I hope you don't mind us,' said Ping. Ida was inquisitive, so she was less polite.

'It wasn't so very difficult to get to. What's on the other side?'

'The bog I told you of, running to the edge of a wood. There's courting couples in the wood most nights, but a marsh is no use to them. Well, I got here. And I sat down and took off my coat and shirt and lay in the sun. And the sun up in all that blue sky was my own, just for me; and the sound of the water and the leaves, rustling and stopping and rustling again. I can hear it now as if it was yesterday. I just stayed. I didn't know it was going to be for always, only when I thought of going back I never could stand the idea. I had a bit of money in my pocket and I went and bought an axe and some nails, to build a tree house, just to pretend.'

'Do you live in a tree house?' All the children spoke together, turning every way to look for it. The man looked sly.

'You see, if I had built it on the ground, some nosey parker some day might have come asking for the rent. I wasn't to know nobody would ever come but a parcel of fairy-tale kids. It's better too for the floods. I can sit up there, above miles of flood water, watching the hayricks and planks sail by. That's a wealth of solitude.'

'What did you eat?' asked Oskar, thinking of Miss Bun.

'I fished from my front door instead of from the bank.'

'How do you cook in a tree house? I'd be afraid of it catching fire.'

'I don't cook. I eat it raw. You needn't shudder, young lady. Have you never seen a sea-lion in the zoo eating raw fish, and clapping his flippers because it's so good? I just cut it into strips and let them slide down, same as he does. You see, right at the start I decided I couldn't have a fire, because smoke can be seen from everywhere. I'd have had to keep it going always because of having no matches. Sooner or later somebody would have noticed there was always smoke in the same place, and have come looking for trouble.'

Ida and Oskar were aghast. No fire ever, no hot soup, no cocoa, no warmth in winter, no dry clothes! But Ping said: 'Lots and lots of lovely things don't want fires. Birds and donkeys and horses and cows, and badgers and hares and hedgehogs and mice and moles.'

'Exactly. Just what I thought. I watched the others, and anything that they could eat so could I. In spring and summer we all live like lords. I never could fancy insects, though some find them delicious. And a man's teeth aren't really made for eating grass, not with any pleasure. Listening to sheep and horses cropping it, it sounds good, but it's a poor mouthful. But almost any new twig with a bud on it makes good chewing. Most trees have buds all winter. Elm – when you crunch you feel you're getting something. Wild rose is like apples. Every schoolboy knows young hawthorn leaves. There's wild carrot and wild spinach, and oats and clover and watercress and eggs and mushrooms and beechnuts and hazel and elderberry and blackberry. But I don't mind telling you the first winter was real hard. When everything's frozen it's no use looking. Unless you've made a store there isn't anything at all. And I hadn't made a store. So I did, because I had to, what bears and hedgehogs and bees do by sense. I decided to sleep it out. If they can, I thought, why can't I?'

Oskar's eyes were brilliant and big with interest. 'And did you?'

'Well, young long-legs, it's difficult to say. I haven't no calendars here, nor anybody to wake me up and say: 'Hi, you, it's tomorrow week.' I curled up in my house and went to sleep. And when I woke up the frost had gone. I can't tell you more than that. But when I woke up and crawled to my door I saw what you might call visions. They say starving people see visions. I saw things that shouldn't by right have been there. Stags and wild boar. Often see queer things when I hibernate.'

'May we please, if it isn't intruding, see your house?'

'With pleasure. *With pleasure*, ha! ha! that's what they used to say, isn't it?' He led the way, and Ping saw it first. It was in a yew tree close against the bole, thatched with yew sprigs that drooped round the walls. The door was also the window, opening half-way up the woven walls like the entrance to a tit's nest. There was no ladder. It was reached by climbing the tree.

'Ladies first,' said the owner scratching his head and laughing as he triumphantly remembered this phrase out of his far-off incredible childhood. Ida was only too keen, and might even have pushed if manners had not been established. She hopped in like a tit.

'Isn't it lovely! How clean you keep it.'

'No need to live like a pig.'

The house was not meant for four people. Before the others could even get in, Ida had to sit on the bed. This was a neat platform of rushes tied in flat bundles, on which lay two big sacks loosely stuffed like eiderdowns. The pillow was a smaller one. The three children got into the bed together to try it.

'You see I've made myself quite comfortable. It took quite a time to collect enough wool off the hedges to fill those. There was a field of sheep on the other side of the wood. I used to cross the bog by a way of my own to get there. Bulrush fluff helped, mixed in with it. And then I had a piece of luck. Two swans took to living on this bit. In the moulting season they sit preening their feathers and leave bags-full on the ground. I've been very lucky. I only brought with me my knife and my fishing line, and look what I've got now.' He looked round with pride. On the floor stood a tin mug, a gaily painted tin jug, a turnip chopper, a dipper full of moorhen's eggs, a bucketful of grass seeds (as if for a horse, thought Ida), a sackful of beechnuts. In one corner hung dangling a very old pair of trousers, a just recognizable busman's leather jacket, and what looked like Robinson Crusoe's coat. Oskar fingered it admiringly.

'Have you got a gun?'

'No, of course I haven't got a gun. And I wouldn't have shot the owner of that coat. That was a real nice little dog, that was. Must have got lost in the bog while his owner was courting. Got proper stuck in it and nearly drowned. So I brought him home with me, and he had a nice supper of fish, and while I was scratching him behind his ears because he was company, I noticed his coat was just ready for stripping. Just ripe and pulling out nicely. So I filled myself a bagful and turned him out lovely – long moustachios, gaiters and riding breeches, all ready for a show. Next morning I took him across the bog and off he went home to surprise them. Because you see, I had had an idea. I made myself a hook out of a spindle tree, the sort of thing my sister used for making rugs for her posh little never-never house. And I took my aertex vest and I pulled tufts of fox-terrier hair through the holes in knots. And there you are! Keep warm in any weather and wash as easy as the dog itself. The chopper I found in a dry ditch. That was luck too – couldn't have cut reeds without it. Everything that you see came out of the river. It's wonderful what a little flood will bring down – wood with nails in it, sacks with bits of string – always useful, those two. You may have been wondering, little miss, how I sew. So did I till I thought of persuading a horse to let me have some of his tail hairs. I don't take anything without asking.

251

I'm beholden to nobody. The great thing is, not to be noticed. What isn't noticed isn't there.'

'You mean,' said Oskar, 'nobody's thinking of you. Except us. And we won't tell, ever. We are displaced persons too.'

'Tell us about your visions that you saw when you were starving,' said Ping.

'It all looked much bigger. I could hardly see across the river, and the rushes were twice as high. It was alive with duck. Their quacking was like a headache, so that it all seemed unreal. There were big animals wallowing somewhere in the mud and the forest seemed to rustle and almost to talk. Then I saw a canoe nosed into the bank, empty. And I thought "they've got me". But they weren't after me. They were wild long-haired men . . .' He paused, forgetting his audience.

'Like you are now,' prompted Ida.

'Eh? What?' The lion-man stared unbelievingly at her. Then he put up a hand and felt his hair and looked at his thin brown legs as if for the first time, and began to laugh.

'So that's how it is! Do you know, I still thought I was a busman! There's my coat hanging up . . .

But they had the advantage over me. *They* hadn't escaped. Nobody was coming after them with cards and papers to fill up. They were free. And they lit a fire under my tree, and a smell of roast pork came up so that I cried like a baby. The place was teeming with animals, they could take as many as they liked. Even if I could, I wouldn't kill the few poor wild things that are left, peeping out here and there when it's quiet, the hedgehog and moorhens and herons that treat me as one of themselves. We're all that's left. Precious few fish left either. Some days I only catch one. Better go and look at my line.'

They all scrambled down, the man in a couple of agile swings. Sure enough the line was taut and pulsating. There was a biggish fish on it.

'There's my dinner for today. I'll come along with you and give you a hand over the wire upstream. You'll have left your paddle-marks in those weeds where you came up. I bet you have.' His voice was suddenly furious. Feeling themselves dismissed in disgrace, the children got into their canoe and paddled upstream while the man moved like a shadow in and out of the trees along the bank. They came at last to a fence of wire mesh across the mouth of the stream where it joined the larger waterway.

'Don't know what that was put there for, but it's useful to me,' the man commented in a less hostile voice. 'No end of things coming downstream catch on there. Push that bit of wood along to me with your paddles, will you? See, it's got nails in it. Good ones. Got to keep my eyes open. We must carry the canoe over the bank. Careful – don't want no marks. There you are. Make off now. And don't come back.'

The children looked so crestfallen that the lion-man considered them for a moment with the ghost of his busman's humanity.

'I've never met three nicer behaved kids,' he said. 'But where one boat's been others will follow. Let be. I've dreamt you and you've dreamt me, see?'

In the canoe Ida waved, Ping bowed and Oskar stood up long-legged as any savage. The man stared after them for a while, then bent down over his plank, which was enriched with a good piece of wire twisted round one of its nails.

'I was thinking,' said Ida after they had paddled unhappily in silence for some time, 'we would go back and take him some lovely food. But I filled one of his tins with toffee when he wasn't looking.'

'I put a Mars under his pillow,' said Ping.

'I put an envelope of fishing gut in the pocket of his busman's coat,' said Oskar. After that they all felt better.

For breakfast that day Miss Bun had cooked the most wonderful, the most mouth-watering bacon and scrambled eggs and mushrooms and fried bread. Ida opened her mouth to say something, but Oskar, thought-reading, kicked her under the table, and Ping drew a finger across his throat.

'What were you going to say, Ida love?'

'Only that I'm hungry,' Ida said sadly.

I T WAS TURNING INTO a hot day. In the little village street there was still no one about and smells of bacon came from the cottages. But Ida, Oskar and Ping had had a day full already and could hardly keep awake. They had only enough energy left to find the quietest sunny bank and go to sleep there curled up like mice. Sometimes Ida spoke into her arm, to say something like: 'Are you asleep?' And Ping or Oskar would answer: 'Yes.'

They spent the hot afternoon bathing in a deep

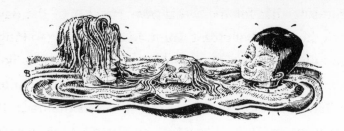

pool above the water-gates. They plopped in like frogs, they bobbed like corks. Ping's face swimming looked as smooth as a sea-lion pup, his velvety eyes blinking in the glitter off the ripples. Oskar's hair was always in his eyes. He reminded Ida of a wet sheep. She laughed till she forgot to treadle and the water came into the corners of her mouth and her grinning teeth. They came out to rest, to let their bodies steam and toast in the sun and ripen for the luxury of the cool swill of river water receiving their limbs again.

Other holiday-makers thronged the river in sun and shadow. Punts passed slowly and travelled far upstream with the tall figure poling at the stern dwindling to a matchstick. Girls lolled and dozed trailing their fingers in the water ribboned with weeds while young men feathered them along. Cabined cruisers chuffed majestically from distance to distance and casual eyes looked down on three sprightly children, never guessing that for them this busy summit of the day was the hour that didn't count. Ida was saying to Ping and Oskar: 'I've slept so much today I don't feel like going to bed tonight. Let's be out all night. Quite different sorts of things must happen in the dark. If we want to come out when all these people aren't there, so must other things. River things.'

'Giant water snakes,' said Ping. 'Far more majestic than cabin cruisers. They would ride like swans pulling a whole train of their own curves behind them with all the fishes dancing ahead of them in terror. And perhaps two king water snakes will meet and have a battle. Or we could ride on their necks like elephant-tamers.'

'Let us spend the night on the big island opposite the house,' Ida suggested. 'It has notice-boards everywhere saying "Landing Forbidden", I can't think why. And for some reason nobody ever does land. Aren't people obedient! But I'm sure whatever comes out at night takes no notice of boards. We won't. I think it ought to be a good place because it, whatever it is, will be used to having it to itself.'

During tea the children were quiet, saving up their energy and excitement for the night. Dr Biggin was deep in thought, studying her tea-leaves or pushing the crumbs round on her plate as if she expected to find bits of the Ogru there. Miss Sybilla Bun was cooing to her food, turning the cake dishes round to look at them from all sides, bowing to congratulate the cakes for having risen perfectly. When she was icing them in the kitchen, patting and putting the last touches, the silver sweets or the borders of up-ended almonds, you would have thought she was dressing a child for a party, she talked so lovingly to them. When she came to cut them it was the same again. Her knife hesitated in the air, and always as she was going to cut she widened the slice a little and laughed merrily. So now, if biscuits and rock buns slipped into pockets in provision for the night hours, it was not noticed except that Miss Bun would say with pleased surprise: 'Oh! the plates *are* emptying fast! Are you ready for the Praline and Coffee Sponge?'

After tea the children began their map. Ida said they were not to paint any part till they were sure it was right. Then they would put in pictures to show what each island was famous for. They had marked Green Knowe in the middle and continued to extend the river on each side as far as they had gone, marking the boat-houses, the weirs, water-gates and locks. They were able to name Swan Nest Island, Tangle Island, Owl Palace Island, Hermit Island and mark out others that they knew but had not been on. One of these was the large island opposite Green Knowe, where they were going to spend the night, which as yet had no name.

A T MIDNIGHT, WHEN Ida woke the two boys, a dusty curtained blackness filled the house, and the cold windowpanes were all that separated them from the void outside. They put on their warmest clothes and crept silently downstairs. Although nobody had told them they were not to go out at midnight, they knew enough of grown-ups to expect to be sent back to bed if they were caught. Creaking floors and old obstinate doors and steep uncarpeted stairs had to be passed, the flashlight travelling from banister to banister till they were down on the brick floor of the hall, where all the scents of the day before were settling as mud settles in still water.

Outside it was less dark, though there was no moon nor any star showing. After a moment or two the earth could just be distinguished from the unbroken cloud of the sky. It was recognizable as a huge dim mass. As the children moved uncertainly along – for Ida would not allow the flashlight because it was cheating – they could not even see the avenue of shaped bushes along the path, though they knew when they were near one because of a looming feeling in the darkness, and a yew smell. The river, however, had a just perceptible glimmer of its own, though where it was reflected from was a mystery. In the boathouse the dark was absolute and the smell of water and rotting wood as powerful as in a forest. The familiar fidgeting of the canoe came to their ears, but they had to feel for its rim with their hands.

It seemed a long way as they paddled across the river in darkness towards a bank they could not see. The sound of the water-gate was magnified to an ominous fall, much too near. It was a relief when the prow of the canoe grounded on the bank. Ida had brought her groundsheet.

'We'll sit beside the water-gate,' she said, 'and then if we want to talk it will drown our voices. We shan't be heard.'

Their eyes were getting used to the darkness. They

could see the line of foam below the fall, and the bars of the water-gate showed hard and black against the soft sooty ceiling of cloud. They could not see each other except as densities. As they sat and waited they gradually acquired a feeling of the position in space of open ground or trees, and the different kind of openness that was the course of the river.

They huddled together, overcome by the immense solitude. Or perhaps it was not solitude, thought Ida, but rather that the three of them were the only ones who ought not to be there.

'I am glad we are on this side of the water-gate,' she said. 'If Ping's water snake comes, the gate will keep it on the other side.'

'You don't know my water snake,' said Ping. 'It will rear up and look over the top bar, and slide its body over length after length, slippery like a water spout, and –'

'Shut up about your water snake,' said Oskar. 'You'll make it come real.'

'All right,' said Ping. 'Would you rather have a spider as big as a haymaking machine, with curved springy legs coming up one after another, crossing the island *now*?'

'Don't!' said Ida. 'That's worse. Can't you think of something nice, like your singing fishes?'

'If it weren't so cloudy,' said Oskar, 'we might see two stars come from outer space and have a collision and make a blaze and falling sparks like a Roman Candle. I don't know what we expect in this darkness. Even if there were a parliament of badgers we shouldn't see it. We'd only hear the barks and squeaks. The thing is to listen. We might hear a Litany of worms. Their noses would be as thin as blades of grass and they would sway from side to side in supplication. We shouldn't see them, of course.'

'What do you imagine worms would sound like?'

'Like wind through a keyhole.'

'Thou knowest that we are but dust,' said Ida. 'I wouldn't like to miss the worms. If we stay here we can't hear anything but the waterfall. Let's move to the quietest place, so that if anything comes we shall hear it.'

They walked along the grass till they came to a quiet reach on the far side of the island with a gently sloping bank. There they sat down.

'What a lovely smell there is everywhere. What can it be? I have smelled it all the time, since we landed here. And when I strain my eyes there is a sort of whitish look in the air.' Ida put up her hand to brush something away from her hair, then caught it and drew it down to her nose. 'It's meadowsweet. This side of the island must be covered with it. How comforting! I am sure only nice things live in meadowsweet.'

They sat and listened. Quiet water sighing; now and then a rustle in the reeds; in the near distance the known weirs and faster currents of the encircling water, in the far distance the screech of young owls among the trees in the churchyard.

Presently Ping said: 'I can hear something coming.'

They all held their breath. They heard, from a little way off, very slow footfalls, one step at a time with long pauses in between. Ping breathed: 'This is it.' Then they saw above the gleam of meadowsweet a crowd of white blurs that moved dreamily up and down.

'Can it be will-o'-the-wisps?'

'With footsteps?'

For a while there was nothing but their heart-beats banging in their ears, then suddenly, close at hand, crisp short tugs, here, there and everywhere.

'Horses!' said Ida laughing. 'Hundreds of them!

The will-o'-the-wisps are the stars on their foreheads. I never saw them here in the day-time; did you, Ping? This island's always empty.'

The sky was very slowly growing less dark, as if the cloud ceiling was going up higher leaving less shadow and more space over the featureless earth. Against this space could vaguely be seen the outline of horses' backs and necks, a big herd moving along together, cropping clover and meadowsweet as they went.

'Let's try them with our apples.' The three children went out to meet the horses, but the herd, without hurrying, without even seeming to notice them, turned aside and could not be met face to face. Running, stalking, cajoling were all in vain. The indifferent creatures kept just out of reach.

Tired, Ping and Oskar threw themselves down on the river bank. 'Perhaps they'll come down to drink,' Oskar said. 'What we want now is a Word of Power.'

'Shut up!' said Ping. 'I'm listening to the river and doing magic.'

Ida remained standing, her eyes straining after the horses. She caught her breath and seemed to herself to become nothing but a wire for a current of electric attention. Above the line of a horse's back *something* had flapped up and blocked out the sky for a minute. And another. And again. And there was a sound to match it.

'Ping!' she cried. 'What have you done? They are winged.'

And now in the glimmer of the night the horses as if all moved by the same inclination, one after another put up their wings, pointed like yacht sails, and still browsing moved majestically on.

'Oskar! Ping! Oh, Ping!'

Ping answered, scrambling up from the position where he had been leaning over the river. 'I asked the river to give me a Word of Power, and it answered over and over again, my own name, HSU.' As he said it, the leading horse lifted its head in his direction and gave a docile whinny – taken up by all the herd as they too raised their heads and drew forward. Ida remembered the sound for months, trying to describe what it was like. The nearest she could get was the excitement of an orchestra tuning up, with flutes and oboes running up and down above the buzz.

The horses all holding their wings in the same ceremonial position, advanced, the quickened pace of their walking hooves thudding on the grass. They put

out their noses with wide flaring nostrils to Ping, who murmured his name to each in turn, and received a reply very like it.

After this they accepted all the children. They let themselves be handled. They nibbled themselves under their wings. They had immensely long manes and tails and their ears twitched like mouse whiskers. As the darkness shifted into less than dark, the children saw each other's faces and hardly recognized them. Ping stood leaning his head against the leading horse's neck and its black mane fell round his face so that he looked like a witch girl, his teeth showing white as he smiled with great joy. Oskar looked like a lean prophet absolutely believing the impossible. He was nearly crying. Ida's grey eyes were black because they were all pupil. She was curled up between the legs of a winged foal that lay on the ground. She looked like a cat that was its stable companion. The musky smell of horse was all round them. The foal smelled young, like a puppy.

At this happy moment the wail of a distant fire siren tore the long silence of the night. Up and down, far and wide, vibrating like panic, it ripped up the space of dreams.

The horses wheeled away from the children and were off, galloping to a flying start, their wings clapping till the air was bruised. When they were airborne, the sound had the pulse and drumming of an express train fading far away – a sound the children had often heard from their beds.

Ida wanted to say that the foal had flown with its long legs hanging down like a mosquito. But none of them dared to speak at all.

It was not until they were back in their own beds and Ida, waking up at normal breakfast time, had stretched her arms and legs and relaxed again into comfort and laziness, that she dared to say:

'Ping! What did you do with your apple last night?'

'The horse ate it,' he replied sitting up in bed golden and slit-eyed. Ida smiled. 'Mine too,' she said.

'Mine too,' said Oskar into his pillow. So nothing more needed to be said. But when they were dressed, Ping knelt on the floor by the map, and in beautiful strokes with a paint brush he wrote the Chinese for Flying Horse Island.

At breakfast Sybilla Bun remarked: 'I don't suppose you children heard the Fire Alarm last night. It gave me quite a fright. I got out of bed to look.'

The children's eyes all turned to fix her with a questioning gaze.

'Did you see anything?' Ping ventured.

'No. Anyway, the milkman told me it was only a

飛馬島

haystack somewhere.'

Dr Biggin had received a letter from somebody called Old Harry, who, as the children already knew, was her chief partner in the excavations they had done in Abyssinia, where tools that seemed to have been made for giants had been found, and a queer bone. Old Harry wanted her to hold a meeting for their Committee at Green Knowe, at which he and she would both read papers. He was also pleased to be able to tell her that, as requested, a bag containing a sample of the much discussed grass, *Paradurra megalocephala abyssiniensis* Var. Andrewsii would be delivered separately. 'And here it is,' said Dr Biggin, picking up and shaking a parcel. 'My dear,' she went on, speaking to Sybilla Bun, 'this is the seed that Old Harry considers the main cereal food of the giants. We think they ate it as a sort of porridge. In quantities, of course. I often wonder if Scotland might not yield some surprises if we dug there. I think if you make a little porridge every day and give it to Ida, we can measure her before and after and see if it adds anything to her stature.'

'Would it not be better,' Sybilla said tactlessly, 'if we gave it to Oskar, as he is growing so much anyway.

You would get much more interesting results.'

Dr Biggin was deeply affronted.

'You have no idea of scientific investigation at all, Sybilla. I specially chose Ida because she is *not* growing. For one thing, if she does grow it will be as near proof as we could get. For another thing she is much too small so we can afford to experiment with her. It would be an improvement. Whereas the effect on Oskar might be disastrous. He might shoot into a giant before the end of the holidays.'

The children were not sure if this was one of Dr Biggin's jokes or not, but they could not help laughing. Ping put his hand above his eyes as if gazing up into the sky expecting Oskar's face to appear there.

Miss Bun was a little hurt too. She lifted the lid off the coffee-pot and inhaled the aroma with closed eyes to restore herself. Then she said: 'Well, that means that dear Oskar can have some nice real porridge. I don't imagine,' she added, twitching her shoulders so that her beads rattled, 'that the Ogru were *good* cooks.'

'The latest theory is that they lived like gods. But I admit we are a long way from having access to any of their recipes. We can guess at some. But where can you get meat on the spit now except in the most expensive restaurants? And then it is only over gas. No flavour of burnt cedar in it. Gas! Pooh! But of course you have never eaten kid cooked under the stars.'

'Do the stars make it taste?' asked Ping gravely.

'Eh? And why not, I should like to know! Now don't get upset, Sybilla. Nobody in England does better with our wretched modern substitutes. After all, Old Harry has suggested bringing the Committee here for your cooking as much as for anything else.'

Miss Bun was mollified. Smoked salmon, chicken Maryland with dry Hock, crêpes Suzette, melon and ginger ice . . .

'It would be nice,' said Maud Biggin openly winking at the children, 'if you could make us a kidney risotto with *Paradurra megalocephala abyssiniensis*. They would be interested.'

Miss Bun grew crimson.

'I shall do no such thing, Maud. The most I shall do with your miserable grass seeds is a gruel for Ida. It is the domain of medicine, not of good eating. Good eating is an Art.'

After breakfast Ida was solemnly measured, lying

on the wooden floor so that she could not cheat by stretching. After that the children were free.

THEY STILL FELT that after meeting the winged horses they had had enough excitement for some time. Also, in order to cherish this secret memory and keep it from being rubbed out or discredited by the presence of hum-drum holiday crowds, they decided not to go on the river at all, but simply to cross over the moat into the orchard belonging to Green Knowe, and to spend the day there. Sybilla Bun had even excused them from lunch, giving them a picnic basket, because she wanted to go shopping in preparation for the Committee's luncheon party.

The orchard itself was an island, connected with the garden by a rickety willow-pattern bridge. It was derelict, the trees were old and leaning. Under them the uncut grass was bulgy and soft like an eiderdown. It was bordered by a thick hedge of hazel and hawthorn and was quite hidden from the river.

The sky was cloudless and the sun beat down with a heat that hushed both birds and humans. Oars squeaked going up the river but the people in the boats were silent, flopping back and saving their energy. The three children lay in the grass and watched the activity taking place there. In this shady world of criss-crossed stalks the heat brought everybody out. Ants, beetles, spiders, grasshoppers, butterflies, bees, caterpillars and the rest were all as busy in the crowded space as city dwellers. Some of the caterpillars were so stupid it was maddening to watch them, but the spiders and bees knew exactly what they were doing and wasted no time about it. The butterflies and big sealskin-coated bumble bees were bent on pleasure only and showed that they knew it. Over all, the birds swung and peered and picked off the fattest. The grass grew high round the children's flattened bed.

'There's a little road here,' said Oskar, gazing into the stalks near his face. 'It looks as though it might be a mouse road. Yes, it is. There's one running along it now. It's his garden path leading to the nest. He's climbed up the stalks and gone in.'

The children all watched. The harvest mouse took as little notice of them as if they had been calves or foals. The nest was woven round three strong stalks of wild barley. It was hardly as big as a tennis ball and the mouse itself not much bigger than the sealskin-coated bumble bee. He looked all head, tail and hands, and was adorably pretty. He seemed to be collecting stores of grain to take to his mate, who now and again put her head out at the door to wait for him. Inside they could be heard talking in squeaks no louder than you could make with a pair of scissors.

'Let's see who can make the best mouse nest,' said Ida, after they had watched for some time.

They all set to work. Ida had done basket work at school, but all the same she found it difficult and fiddling and very slow. It was not beyond any of them to make the initial platform that bound the three tall stalks together, or to continue as far as an egg-cup shape, but when it came to leaving a hole half-way up for the door and then closing in the roof, they were all beaten. No harvest mouse would have recognized their clumsy efforts as intended nests. Ping's was made from strong broad green grasses and looked like something a cow had dropped out of its mouth. Ida's was of straw, hard and spiky like a doll's linen basket. It was also big enough for a rook.

Oskar was frowning with concentration, his long fingers delicately manipulating fine dead grass, but in vain.

'My hands are too big,' he said. 'Anyway, they do it from inside.'

'Let's have our sandwiches,' said Ida, 'then afterwards we can climb trees.' She and Ping began to unpack the picnic basket, but Oskar was in one of his obstinate moods and would not stop.

'I am going to do it properly,' he said. 'From inside.'

Ping and Ida laughed. 'It will be big enough for a bear.'

Oskar took no notice. He began tearing up big swaths of grass which he wrapped round himself till he was hidden. He then turned round and round inside like a dog determined to lie down just right.

The other two were setting out the meal and joyfully drinking home-made lemonade out of bottles with straws, closing their eyes to enjoy it more. When they looked round again at Oskar, the swaths of grass were tightening up round him into a passably firm ball, from inside which, through a hole that his hands were fashioning, they could see his face looking out.

'Doesn't he look small,' said Ping. 'It must be the hole working like the wrong end of a telescope.'

Oskar's eyes were immensely big and bright and his

nose sharp as he continued to work inside his nest, tightening it ever closer round him.

'Don't you want any sandwiches, Oskar? They are lovely. And there is melon too.'

'Not yet.' Oskar's voice from inside sounded faint. He grunted with effort as he turned round and round in the rustling grass ball where every moment the space grew less.

Ping and Ida ate, putting aside Oskar's share. The melon was most delicious, and as the pips that they had emptied out dried in the sun, they were thrilled to see the harvest mouse come and take some away. Afterwards they watched the two mice at the opening of their nest, holding melon pips with their hands and wiggling their whiskers as they ate.

'Oskar! Do come and look. Oskar!' There was no answer. 'Hush!' said Ping. 'Don't speak to him. *He's really doing it.*' The grass ball had tightened up till it seemed impossible Oskar could be inside. And it was growing smaller every minute.

It was very hot. The midday siesta was on. The birds had vanished, the butterflies lay with wide-open wings fearing no attack. The harvest mice went in to sleep. Smaller things crept under leaves. Ida and Ping were drowsy too. Looking at tiny things closely for a long time makes one sleepy. They lay back in the grass and snoozed.

Something made Ida wake with a start. A ginger cat was sitting in the grass staring with its purposeful eyes at a little ball of hay that was rocking slightly on the ground. For one second Ida's heart stood still, then she made the most tigerish sound she could and threw the vacuum flask at the cat. It fled, pursued by Ida and Ping with every stick or stone they could lay their hands on.

When they came back, Oskar was standing beside his nest. He was perfectly recognizable, two inches tall. His tiny voice came up to them. He did not seem to have noticed anything wrong.

'I've made the nest all right. It is beautiful inside. I just didn't know how to make it up on the stalks. But I see now. It's quite easy really. I'll have to begin again. I'll make one next door to the mice. Get your big feet out of the way, Ping.'

'Do be careful not to tread on him,' said Ida. 'Isn't he *sweet*?'

'Idiot!' said Oskar. He was obviously shouting, but it was the littlest voice in the world.

They watched him make his way along, tacking and working out how to get round obstacles exactly as all the other grass dwellers do. The ants to him were as big as dogs, the grasshoppers like kangaroos. Before long he picked up a pole as big as a match to use in self-defence. When he came face to face with a stag beetle he gave it a whack as if it were a bullock, and it veered off. He came at last after a lot of scrambling and sprawling, to the mouse road where the going was easier.

Ping and Ida on all fours watched spellbound. Ping's face had his happiest golden moon look, but Ida looked like a fox terrier whose dearly-loved owner is behaving incomprehensibly.

Oskar stood at the foot of some grass stalks swaying them to see if they were stable enough. He chose three good ones and began his second nest. To save him many laborious journeys Ping and Ida from the immense range of their arms picked and handed him the fine dead grasses he needed. His pink hands, no bigger than mouse hands but still recognizably Oskar's, came out through the hole and took what was offered them. Sometimes he rejected them and asked for softer ones, and finally for moss. And now a second nest was swaying on its three poles next door to the mice, whose anxious faces peeped out with twitching noses. Clearly they didn't at all want a neighbour.

Oskar looked out of his door, laughing with teeth like pinheads.

'I'm hungry after all that. What is there for lunch?'

Ida felt peculiar. She broke off a corner of egg-and-salad sandwich and offered it on a wild-rose leaf. 'Oskar!' she pleaded, '*please* don't grow wiggly whiskers! He can't drink lemonade out of the bottle, Ping – he might slip in down the neck and drown.'

'I've got an acorn-cup in my pocket. Fill that.'

Oskar took it between his mouse hands. It was like drinking out of the salad bowl, but he was very thirsty.

'You can't think how cool and nice it is in this moss,' he said. 'I must just curl up and have a sleep. It was awfully hard work.' His head withdrew into the nest, and Ping and Ida were left out.

'We'll have to sit and keep watch,' said Ida, 'because of that cat. What do you think will happen next, Ping?'

'I don't know! But I wish I had thought it too.'

'Could you have done, Ping?'

'Well, I knew what he was doing. I could think it for him but not for myself.'

'I can't think it at all. I'm frightened because of that hateful cat. And maybe the beetle was a blood-sucking one. Oh Ping! There's a woolly bear going up Oskar's stalk. It's as tall as he is. Just imagine those baggy suction legs walking over you.'

Ping picked it off and immediately it curled up into a ring in his palm.

'You see, he'd only have to give it a poke in its soft underneath and it would curl up like a hedgehog.'

'I hope hedgehogs don't eat mice.'

'They eat beetles, I think. But it would be horrid if one rolled on you by accident.'

They sat on, anxious and puzzled. And after a while bored.

'I wish he'd wake up,' said Ping. 'I want to see him walking along the high road.'

'No. He might get run over. Besides, think how slow he would be. Like going for a walk with a woolly bear.'

Presently, however, Oskar put his head out and said: 'I'm hungry again. What is there?'

'Apple pie, Melon and Chocolate.'

'I think I'll go and call on my neighbours. Break off a piece of pastry, Ida, and give it me when I get to their door.'

He shinned down his stalk and began to climb up to the harvest mice. As their stalk swayed under his weight, the mice looked out in wonder and alarm. When he was at nest-level, Ida with her huge fingers handed him a fraction of pastry which he clutched to his chest as he went in.

There was agitation and squeaking inside the nest as it swung from side to side, but after a while all was still.

'Do mice bite visitor mice, do you think, Ping? It is terribly quiet.'

To Ida's great relief Oskar's face appeared.

'They are nice. They eat out of my palm like ponies. Their eyes are as big as hand mirrors and their tickly whiskers reach across the nest. It's like being in a room full of aerials. You have to be careful not to step backwards through them. But I've combed their coats with my pocket comb and they loved it. They lie on their backs to have their stomachs done.'

In fact, Oskar was so delighted with his new view of the world that when it was tea-time he wouldn't come in with the others. 'You go. Just say you don't know where I've got to. It's too nice here and too exciting. I'm going to stay. I want to explore the forest

again to see woodlice like armadillos and earwigs like crocodiles. Besides, I'm going to sleep here in the moonlight.'

'Yes,' said Ping. 'I do feel stupid being this size. Perhaps in the night a death's-head moth might look in at your door.'

'Oskar,' said Ida, 'I won't budge unless you come with me, and that's flat. I'm bigger than you and you've got to do what I say. If you go in the grass you could get lost, and we might tread on you while we were looking for you. Or a cat might get you and bring you in and play at killing you on the floor. Or an owl might eat you and spit your bones out in a pellet. You come with me or I'll break your nest open and catch you.'

'I wish you'd go away. You talk like an ogress.'

'Come with me,' said Ping. 'I promise to bring you back again. You can sleep in your nest, only we must be there on guard.'

'What a lot of fuss about nothing,' said Oskar, stepping out on to Ping's hand.

'Besides,' said Ping, looking lovingly at the little person on his palm, 'think how exciting the house will look. No cathedral was ever anything like so big.

The biggest cathedral imaginable would go under the table, spires and all.'

Ida was miserable because Ping had got Oskar, and because she had nagged just like any grown-up woman. When they reached the house Ping put Oskar in his pocket and they went in to wash for tea. As they stood side by side at the basin, Ida could bear it no longer. 'Let me have Oskar in my pocket, please, Ping.'

Ping amiably fished him out. 'He kicks like anything,' he said, standing him on the glass shelf.

'My legs have been nearly broken by your pocket-knife,' said Oskar buzzing and squeaking with annoyance. 'And why do you want to fill your pocket with fossils and shells. They nearly crushed me.'

'There's nothing in mine, and it's a patch pocket. You can hold on to the edge and look out. I would like to see Aunt Sybilla persuading herself she wasn't seeing you.'

'I wish I was back in my nest. This is just tiresome. I'm not going to be in anybody's pocket. Put me down, Ping. I'm going upstairs by the mouse route. I'll meet you there after tea. Bring me something to eat.'

Ping put him down on the floor, and they watched him make his way round the side of the bath to the hole where the pipes went through the floor.

'Be sure you make plenty of noise, so that we can hear where you are,' said Ida, as he lowered himself into the hole. 'Promise!' she called urgently to the tiny fingers clutching the edge of the floorboard, which was the last she could see of him. The only answer was the faint scraping of his buttons as he slid down the lead pipe.

Tea was to be in the garden because of the heat. It was a blow to Ida, who would not be able to hear Oskar's progress behind the wainscot. She hated lying, but it is no use saying what nobody will believe, so she made the best of it and carelessly announced, as she sat down to tea:

'Oskar said please excuse him tonight. He met a thatcher and stopped to learn how it is done. And he was very good at it and he has stayed for tea with the thatcher.'

'Oh dear! And I have made chocolate eclairs for a treat. Who is the thatcher? Not a gipsy I hope.'

'I know him,' said Dr Biggin. 'A decent sort of man. I had a talk with him the other day. It's a trade that goes back further than any other, probably, that and wattle-making for the walls. Paleolithic man must have thatched where there were no caves. Very interesting survival. Surprised you two were not more interested.'

'We were,' said Ida. 'We were terribly interested, but we were no good at it.'

'Too small, I suppose. Sybilla, have you made that gruel for Ida?'

'I made a sort of girdle cake of it, Maud. It seemed more appetizing for the poor child.'

'Aunt Maud!' said Ida, suddenly brightening up. 'May I keep it till bedtime? I read once that we only grow in our sleep so surely it will work better then?'

'It's never been tried before, so one experiment is as good as another. But promise me that you will eat it.'

'Yes, Aunt Maud.'

While they were having tea, sudden banks of cloud reared up high and toppling, one on each horizon as if threatening each other. The air had gone copper-green and electric. The wind blew first from one side and then from the other, urging the opposing storms towards each other. The leaves shuddered and showed their pale undersides, the birds hid – all except the swallows who continued cutting figures of eight at ground level till it was as dark as in an eclipse. Then the first lightning flicked like a whip and Miss Bun cried out: 'Here it comes! Hurry, children, before the cake gets wet.'

They ran indoors carrying plates and finished the meal in the dining-room. Nobody talked much because of the oppression of the hush that precedes the real downpour. From time to time above the ceiling unusual slitherings and scatterings occurred, not convincingly mouse-like to Ida and Ping. But Miss Sybilla cocked her head and said: 'I wonder if mice come indoors away from the lightning. I never heard so many. I must set some traps.'

'OH, NO!'

Miss Bun and Dr Biggin looked at Ida in surprise.

'I love mice,' she said lamely. 'Besides, you might catch the wrong thing. Such as . . . a robin.'

'Or a butterfly,' said Ping helpfully.

'Please don't put traps, Aunt Sybilla.'

'Schoolgirl sentimentality,' said Dr Biggin with her mouth full.

It had grown quite dark. Miss Sybilla was turning on the lights, but Ida and Ping went up to the attic where they were right in the middle of the storm and could watch it out of three windows and see the lightning reflected in the river.

'Oskar's missing this,' said Ida. But at that moment they heard a little fluttering noise behind the cupboard door. A clap of thunder made them jump, but when it had finished tearing and crashing, there was the impossibly small noise again, as if a fox-terrier as little as a harvest mouse was waiting to be let in. They opened the door, and Oskar ridiculously walked in. He was covered with cobwebs. 'Beastly stuff,' he said. 'It's sticky and elastic and I can't get it off. I'd hate to be a fly.'

'Could you see the lightning?' asked Ping.

'Of course I could, through every crack. There were long corridors under the floors between the joists. In the flashes they looked endless and awfully ghostly. Sometimes I had to climb over beams with sides as high as a cliff. It wasn't too difficult, because fumbling about in the half-dark I could always find worm-holes big enough to put my fingers and toes into. Then the lightning would come and show me myself hanging on high up, and that was frightening. Mice must be very good alpinists. I gave up the stairs and came by the slanting waterpipes, but the hot ones were terribly hot and when they cooled down and clanked they bucked me like a horse. What have I missed? I heard you shouting that I was missing something.'

'I wasn't shouting. I was just talking. I meant the storm. Come and stand on the window-frame.' She lifted him up. They were still three special and equal friends, but the friendship had a most uncomfortable, lopsided feeling. They counted the seconds between the flashes and the thunder, the interval getting less and less until both happened together and the house rattled its window-frames. Then the rain hurled down and they could see nothing more.

Ping believed that a promise is a promise however small the person to whom it was made.

'Do you still want to go back to your nest, Oskar? Because I promised I would take you. It would certainly be exciting in the orchard with apples flying like cannon balls and trees being struck, and the nest rocking under the gale. But the two outside the nest would get very wet.'

Oskar magnanimously agreed to wait till early morning. 'I'm hungry again,' he said.

'I read that field mice have to eat every twenty minutes

or they die.' Ida gave him some of her medicinal girdle cake. It had a pleasant ship's biscuit taste.

The rain continued to sluice down the windows and gurgle like brooks in the gutters. The thunder circled round the outside of the sky and the lightning lit up the room every few seconds but seemed to have no further connection with any detonations.

The children were tired. Things had become more complicated than they had expected. Other adventures had not left them with a problem like Oskar's aberration. The storm had sucked up and dashed away all their energy.

Ida punched a dent in Oskar's pillow and laid him in it, with enough girdle cake by him to last for the night.

'Don't play dolls with Oskar,' said Ping. 'It's horrid.'

'I'm not playing dolls.'

'You are. You're nearly as silly as Aunt Sybilla,' said Oskar. 'I'm fed up with your big hands.'

This was the nearest to a quarrel that they had ever had.

They lay lonely and angry in their beds. And the rain teemed down and battered on the roof.

Ida had bad dreams. Out of Oskar's nest a huge

hornet was crawling, its triangular face evil and satisfied. Then the lightning was the glint of cats' claws striking and striking. She fought her way out of the sheets to a sitting position. She could hear Ping tossing in his bed, but not a sound from Oskar's. She felt for the switch and turned on the shaded lamp. Oskar was lying in bed, his hands under the back of his head, his long legs making a ridge down the middle and his feet lifting up the blankets at the end. He turned his big grey eyes to Ida and smiled.

'I've just woken up too,' he said. 'Such a funny dream. Parts of it were lovely. But I got bored with it in the end, so I unthought it. Don't let's get up yet. I could do with hours more.'

Ida stared at his blissful ordinariness.

'Wiggle your toes, Oskar.'

'Idiot! Whatever for?' he answered, wiggling them.

'I just wanted to be sure.' She put out the light with a deep sigh and turned back into dreamless sleep.

B Y MORNING THE sky had emptied itself and the river had filled to the brim and over. The children ran out after breakfast, determined to be first on the river and to get far away before the crowds came. Miss Bun had given them a picnic again, because the proposed visit of the Committee had so filled her with hospitable ideas that her head was in a whirl. The day's outing therefore could be a long one and the children could go far afield.

When they reached the boat-shed, the gangway was submerged and the canoe, held by too short a mooring, was shipping water at the prow.

On windy days the surface of the river is raised in little pyramids streaked like the criss-cross fork patterns on mashed potatoes. The children knew already that even a little wind can make a canoe tiresome to manage. Today, however, there was no wind. The surface seemed just off the boil. Inverted bowls of smooth water travelled along it with a suggestion of waltzing and the grasses at the edge had no power to play at equal tug-of-war with the stream as they do on dawdling days. The children, however, were not experienced enough to know these as danger signs, and if there were no other boats out, they just thought they were successfully early. They held the canoe to the side, laughing as they mopped it dry because it tugged so impetuously. Then they got in and pushed off. Away it went downstream broadside on. The children enjoyed the sensation of easy speed, thinking that the first lock would bring their joy ride to a safe temporary stop. They managed after a struggle to keep the canoe straight, as was only proper. They might, Ida suggested, enjoying the adventurous thought, have to shoot a rapid. However, they kept well away from the weir, where the rapids were only too lifelike. They wanted to go as far down the main stream as possible.

When they came in sight of the lock, they were surprised to find both sides open and a heaped-up and purposeful swoop of water going straight through. They had no alternative but to swoop through also, holding their breath as the canoe struck the rough water on the other side. It shuddered and the water battered under it as if it would stave in the bottom, whirling it sideways in a hopping motion, but the momentum carried it over. Almost before they realized they were safe they were travelling rapidly down the lower reach.

'Isn't this fun!' said Ida. 'We must be travelling faster than salmon. Would you think there could possibly have been so much water in the sky. I expect by this afternoon it will all be gone out to sea, and when we come back the river will be just ordinary.'

She underestimated the amount of water there can be in the sky. After a cloudburst the river goes on rising for many hours as the high ground nearer its source drains into it. Nor did she guess that, to prevent a flood, all the locks all the way to the sea were standing open to get the water away. Laughing and exhilarated the three of them rushed along in their cockle-shell.

Soon they had passed the island that hid Hermit Island. They thought of him fishing from his front door. They passed Owl Palace Island and were going farther than their farthest trip while the water stretched wider and wider on either side. None of the usual anglers were on the banks, for the reason that the banks had disappeared. They would have been fishing in the fields. For the same reason no one was out walking, or working. The swans, the wild duck and the herons had the landscape to themselves. Where the current was swiftest the children rode along. The sun was now mercilessly out, the sides of the canoe burnt their hands and knees. They passed through lock after lock, by small villages where cabin cruisers were moored fore and aft to the quays. A woman popped her head out of a cabin and shouted: 'Are you all right?'

'Yes, of course,' they replied waving.

'Look out for the bridge!' cried a man. 'Look out!'

Just in time the children lay back flat in the canoe as it went under a stone bridge with no head-room. The flickering underwater-coloured arch passed close over their faces, so that their eyes were obliged to focus on the grain of the stone, the cracks and the lichen and the moss. It had a cold secret smell, soothing on a hot day. On the far side of the bridge the land was less absolutely flat, with occasional patches of wood. They went through a long stretch with no houses at all, till they saw on a slope ahead of them, beyond a spread of flood water, a disused windmill. The proper course of the river took a right-angled bend in front of it.

'My arms are getting tired with trying to keep the canoe straight,' said Ida. 'I don't want to wait till we get to the sea before I have lunch. Let's make for that windmill, straight over the bend.'

It took the last ounce of their united strength to get out of the main current even though it went close to the bend, but they made it, and there was enough water to float them, digging their paddles into the earth, over the bank and on to the quiet overspill.

It was a relief to be able to pause. Over the meadow the water was barely nine inches deep and the current negligible. They paddled softly towards the windmill, and now that the excitement was over they chattered and laughed, and together with the quacker of the ducks that they disturbed their voices were carried by the water to the far banks.

Ida was watching the butterflies that were travelling across all this water where there was no place to land – except on her up-ended paddle where two stopped to rest. Ping's eyes were shut. He was sunning, smiling and thinking his thoughts.

Oskar spoke in a tense voice:

'Look, you two. I haven't gone small again, have I?'

Ida and Ping turned their heads. 'Not unless we have too,' Ping answered.

'Then look in front. There, on the bank.'

Ida looked towards the windmill. She had been facing it all the time, but had been more interested in what was round her – water rats swimming in search of land, earwigs troubled at finding themselves afloat on sticks. Now she searched the hillock where the windmill stood for something unusual. She saw nothing except a dead tree lying uprooted near the water's edge. Its roots had been broken off, all but two which were bent back under one of those fuzzy knobs that the boles of elm trees often have, which, if the tree had been a piece of sculpture, would have been the head of a reclining figure. There were only two branches left, and they were crossed one over the other like legs. Quite an ordinary thing to see, really. Only while she was looking at it the branches moved and crossed the other leg over. And the foot swung contentedly in the lazy noon air.

Ping paddled the canoe nearer with all the strength of his silky melon-coloured back, and as the three voices sharpened into exclamations, the swinging foot froze into immobility.

They grounded the boat and walked abreast through the shallow water, silent now except for the splash of their feet.

It did not move again, but Ida taking her eyes off it for a split second to look towards the windmill, saw behind the broken window-pane a watching eye as big and blood-shot as a bull's.

Another eye as big, but clear, bright and inquisitive, now opened in what Ida had once stupidly taken for a knob of a tree.

'Good morning, Giant,' said Ping, bowing.

The giant sat up. He was brown and tousled, but except for his size they would have supposed him to be about fifteen years old.

'You weren't taken in, then,' he said amiably.

'It was Oskar,' said Ida. 'This is Oskar. I would have walked past you without thinking. And this is Ping.'

'It's good to be noticed, for a change. I sometimes wonder whether people aren't going blind, or perhaps can't see anything bigger than themselves, like ants. I see them rushing about, but they never seem to look higher than their own shoulders. Except boys. Boys are always best.' (Ida was ashamed.) 'Babies, of course. They gaze up out of their prams with round eyes, willing to see anything that comes. I can even poke them and make them gurgle, but nobody takes any notice of what babies are looking at. Otherwise cats are the only things I have to talk to. They don't seem to notice any difference. Dogs always bark at me. They are a nuisance when I'm out foraging. But I manage. There's everything you could want in sheds and yards. They lock the gates but I just reach over the top or put my arm through the skylight.'

'Do you just take what you want?'

'What else could I do? Mother keeps saying I'll get caught and put in a cage, but it doesn't make sense. Anyway, if there's a commotion because somebody's missed a pig or a sack of potatoes, I just lean against a wall with a poster and everybody thinks I'm an advertisement. Or I lie down by the side of the road and they think I'm a new watermain lagged with sacking. Or I go on all fours behind a hedge and they think my backside is a horse. It's easy. Once I accidentally put my hand into some porridgy stuff that builders were using, and left a print there. It was a very convenient place where I had taken a lot of different things. Afterwards I watched them holding a council round the print of my hand. The constable was there and he got very angry about it. So did all the others. It wasn't a hand, he said, because it couldn't be, and he was not going to report it. What did they take him for? And all the time I was being part of a chestnut tree and he had propped his bicycle against my legs.'

'That's what the Hermit said,' said Oskar. 'What you don't notice isn't there.'

'My mother won't believe me when I say people don't see me. It wasn't like that when she was young, she says. You should hear her.'

'TERAK!'

From the windmill came a voice like a cow's cracked with too much mooing.

'Terak! You will be the death of me. Didn't I tell you to come in.'

'That's Mother.'

She came out, dropping to all fours in order to squeeze out at the double door. Her body was about as big as an elephant's and as shapeless and sloppy. She lumbered erect on to her legs, helping herself up by pushing with her hands on her knees. The many creases of her huge bony face showed a lifelong discontent. There was not among them a line to show that she had ever smiled.

'Oh, my lumbago! What have you gone and done now, you good-for-nothing boy. They'll be after us. We'll have to move along again. And where will we go now, I'd like to know? In this miserable country we show up like pyramids. There's never a forest or a hill one can walk behind. Hardly as much as a haystack. All flat enough to break your heart. And the farther east we go the worse it is. And just when we were settled in this nice windmill you've got to go and be seen.'

'Why have you got to move? We won't tell anyone.' Oskar was always the first to promise silence.

'Because I won't have my boy laughed at, that's why,' she said with sudden ferocity. 'I won't have it. He's like his father, growing as big as he can just to be annoying. But he's my boy and I won't have him laughed at. Dratted children! They're like water and lovers, get in anywhere. And their tongues will wag. Why didn't you do as you were told,' she went on, aiming a cuff at Terak who easily dodged it. 'You'll come to a bad end like your poor father. The same one. I'm warning you. Now keep an eye on those children and don't let them escape. I don't know what I couldn't do to you for this. When I've put our things together you can stow them in the canoe and pull it after you. The children will just have to stay here till the water goes down, and by then we'll have got clear.' She heaved a sigh that scattered the straw on the ground like the flap of a blanket. 'I wish I could lay my old bones down in my family cave. Blue and amber stony mountains they are there, with our own goats cropping and bleating among the boulders. But your poor silly father must want to be a great King! And his son's as silly as himself. Ah me, the bigger the woman the bigger the burden laid on her. Watch those children now, Terak, or they'll be off like mice!'

She trundled away, dropping to all fours again to squeeze back into the mill. With amazement the children watched the bulk of her seat and the soles of her feet in the last heave before she disappeared. Across the back of her coarse blanket skirt the words BRITISH RAILWAYS were stencilled in white.

Terak sat crestfallen and dejected, all the animation of his face had drained away, and it looked as lifeless as a water-butt.

Ida, Oskar and Ping stood round him sympathetically not knowing what to say. It was clear they had brought on a real calamity. For themselves, it was going to be difficult at home to explain the loss of the canoe, but it would be easier to get back without it, since they couldn't hope to paddle against the current. They would have to find a road and hitch-hike in any case. For the moment they were only troubled by the fabulous gloom of Terak's expression.

The silence lasted unhappily, until it seemed that no one would ever speak again. Terak sat unmoving like a great sad lump of tree. Then from inside the windmill came a gusty sound that was like a mixture of rookery, pigsty and donkey farm. It snuffled and groaned and squealed and brayed in a long monody.

Terak came to life. He winked lovingly at Ping and uncovered his teeth in a smile. They were as big as matchboxes and whiter than the whites of his eyes. He nudged with his head in the direction of the mill.

'That's Mother playing her bagpipes. She always does that when she's upset. When she has used up all her puff she'll go to sleep. So we have plenty of time to talk.'

The three children sat down in a ring in front of him.

'What happened to your father?' was Oskar's first question.

'Where were the blue and amber mountains with caves and goats?' was Ida's.

'If your father wanted to be a king, was there a horse big enough for him to ride on?'

All three questions happened together, while Terak cupped both his ears with his hands. There was a silence after this traffic jam, then Ida began again.

'How old are you, Terak?'

'Mother thinks about a hundred and fifty. She notches the years on her walking stick, but some of the notches have worn off. You needn't look so unbelieving. Giants live longer than you do. Mother thinks she is five hundred, but she says she is very old for her age. She says she's worn out with trouble. She's melancholy company.'

'Tell us all about everything, from the beginning.'

'I don't know the beginning, except what Mother has told me. I don't remember my father. But mother talks all the time, sometimes to herself, sometimes to me. She can't stop. Perhaps if she wasn't talking she wouldn't believe in herself. I don't know where the mountains were. Somewhere to the East. They were very high, with such cliffs all round that nobody could get up or down. The giants lived on top. They had big caves with carved doorways along the side of a valley with a little stream. They kept goats and wove cloth and read the stars and worshipped the moon. They made music by hitting tall stones with wooden hammers. That was religious music for full moon. The bagpipes were only woman's music for funerals and sickness.

'One day, after an earthquake, my father found a place where rocks had fallen, where he could scramble down to the lowlands. He took my mother with him because they were courting and he wanted to show off. They went a long way for the pleasure of exploring. There were things they had never seen before, forests and flowers and animals, and a great river. All the time my mother kept on saying "We ought to go back now," but my father would not. Then coming out of a forest on a hillside they startled some shepherds. These were the first little men they had seen, and of course my father was very interested and spoke kindly to them. But they ran away, leaving their sheep behind. So my father and mother became shepherds, and stayed there because it was spring and a lovely hillside. My father heaved up rocks and made a house, but my mother was homesick because she had left all her crocks and blankets in the cave. So he made her the bagpipes.

'One day when my father was watching the sheep and looking down over the valley, he saw a procession of little men on horseback, leading pack animals laden with bundles, and a long covered wagon drawn by eight horses. The little shepherds were with them, pointing up the hillside to him where he sat. Six of the riders came up the hill towards him. Some of them were fair haired with faces coloured like sandstone, but most were dark like the shepherds. When they came near enough they shouted wonderful words, and bowed down, and waved flags. My father did not understand their language, but he sat still and made them a sign to come on. My mother was a good way off, in the house, playing the bagpipes because she wanted to go home.

'The men came near. They had brought presents which they laid on the ground, an embroidered cloak, a turban with a peacock's feather sticking up at the front, a box of big blue beads, a dish of dates and figs and another of sweetmeats, and a bottle which the white man offered with a long speech and a specially low bow.

'When they saw that my father did not understand them, nor their interpreters either, they began to act in dumb show. Two of them placed the cloak and the turban on my father. They could reach because he was still sitting on the ground, leaning on one elbow to watch their antics. He liked the turban and the peacock feather, and when they started beating their foreheads on the ground and then waving their hands towards the waiting horsemen below in the valley, he understood that they wanted him to come and be their King. He let out a bellow for my mother, and it made the men turn and run. They couldn't help themselves. But the white man called them back. When they saw my mother – she was in her prime then with a face and figure like the Sphinx, so she says – coming down the hill, the men sat down plonk, like so many babies bumping on their bottoms.

'"What's that tomfoolery?" she asked my father, pointing at his turban. He told her they wanted him to be King.

'"King of that miserable little lot?" she said. "Don't be such a fool." But she sat down and tried the sweetmeats, and my father out of curiosity tried the bottle. It made him sneeze, but he liked it and came back for more. And my mother put on the blue beads. She wanted the turban then, but my father wouldn't let her have it. In the end they went with the men, who were very polite, bowing and scraping and flattering, and serving up more and more food and drink, making signs that it was proper kings and queens should be fat.

'But of course it was all a cruel hoax. They kept on luring my father towards his Kingdom. He liked them less the more he saw of them and my mother soon saw through it. They crossed the sea in a miserable ship with horses, elephants, tigers, lions and monkeys, and arrived in the end at a place called Bristol. By that time my parents were learning English. My mother was very quick. Soon she could understand what they said to each other as well as what they said to her. My father was a simple, easy man. He believed everything he was told. When they explained to him what he was to wear and do to be a proper King at his public acclamation, he learned it all very carefully. It was to take place in a very big green and yellow tent. They told him the ceremony had to take place for seven nights in every city of his Kingdom. My father walked about very proudly, wearing his turban and peacock's feather, bowing and blowing kisses as he had been taught. He promised my mother they would go home again when it was all over, because kings and queens could do whatever they liked.'

Terak paused for effect.

'But it was a Circus, and they laughed at him.'

He looked at Ida, Oskar and Ping to see the result of this pronouncement. Their faces were keen and polite, but not struck wild-eyed with horror.

'My mother says it is the cruellest thing there is. He died of their laughter.' Again he looked from one to the other, expecting groans.

'How?' asked Ping simply.

'It was this way. On the first night when everybody was screeching and laughing, and the circus master had come on in his smart tight trousers and scarlet riding coat and cocked hat, and his whip, my father lost his temper. He snatched the circus master up and put him across his knees and walloped him till the stool he was sitting on gave way. Then he chased the midget clowns with the whip, and they ran in every direction, tripping up and bolting between his legs. And the one he wanted most to beat ran up the ladder to the tight-rope and took refuge on that. But he trod on the sausages dangling out of his pocket and slipped, hanging on to the rope with hands and knees.

Then my father swarmed up the main tent-pole and started along the tight-rope too angry to think, and everybody shrieked with laughter still. And the rope broke and my father fell and broke his neck. But the clown clung to his end of the rope and swung down safely, and it looked as if he was climbing down his sausages. But when my poor mother ran in with her bagpipes under her arm – for she was afraid of losing them – and saw that he was dead, she was so heart-broken, she sat down in the middle and played the bagpipes most desolately. And the crowds laughed more and more. Then clowns ran back and cleared everything away, including the carpet and Father, and the next thing was the lions and lion-tamer. While they were in the ring, my mother took me and ran away. She crossed the river at low tide and went and hid in the green mountains, where there were sheep. We lived there in a real cave. We have been hiding ever since; because it is a very dreadful thing to be laughed at. Very dreadful indeed. Sometimes I try to imagine it when Mother has been scolding me. But I can't imagine it dreadful enough.'

'What did your father have to do in the ring that made him suddenly so angry?' asked Ping.

'He came in blowing kisses to the people, and called for the royal barber to shave him for his coronation. Crowds of midget clowns ran before him and after him, getting under his feet, spreading red carpets for him that they pulled away just as he stepped on them, and doing a great many rude things that only happen in circuses. For instance, a midget clown came in pulling a giant chamber-pot along after him by a rope. That was very rude. But they called him Majesty all the time, and when at last he was seated on his throne, the barber came. He was the smallest of the clowns and the one my father hated most. He wore a white apron and had his hair curled like a baby's top-knot, with a comb stuck in it. He had a pair of hedge clippers to cut my father's hair. Of course he couldn't reach so he went trotting off on his busy little legs to fetch a step-ladder, but that was still not high enough. It only came to my father's chest. So the clown could not reach his head, but he cut the hair on my father's chest instead, like someone clipping grass.'

At this point Ping opened his mouth and let out a charming sound rather like the notes of a chaffinch.

Terak looked at him in astonishment. 'What was that?' he said. 'What were you doing?'

The children were frightened and sorry. They all wanted to laugh, but held tight and said nothing.

'It was nice,' said Terak. 'Do it again, Ping.' He grinned in expectation.

Then Ping laughed again, and the others could not help it. They laughed too. Terak gave a couple of hicks like someone who does not know what comes next.

'I'm afraid we're laughing,' said Ida, wiping her eyes. 'I'm awfully sorry.'

'Laughing? But it didn't hurt me at all. It was nice.'

'Yes,' said Oskar, wiping his eyes too.

'Laughing! Is that all it is?' And Terak began to laugh too, wildly, with more breath than he had got. 'Oh! Oh!' he cried, clutching his ribs. 'It hurts now. Oh! Oh! I shall die of it. Ooooh.' He sat up at last and fetched out a handkerchief to wipe his eyes.

'Well I never,' he said. 'Fancy that. Let's do it again.'

'Something has to be funny first,' said Ping. Terak looked at him with adoration.

'I think I'd like to be a clown,' he said.

Ida picked something up out of the grass.

'This rolled out of your pocket when you pulled out your handkerchief. What is it? It looks like an ivory carving of four women.'

'Oh that! It's my tooth. I had toothache and Mother pulled it out. She tied it by a string to the lowest sail of the windmill, then she took hold of the highest sail and jerked that down. It was easy. Would you like it for a keepsake, Ping?'

Ping accepted it with proper courtesy, but before he had finished his sentence, Terak, who was kneeling, bent forward and hid his face and hands in the grass, turning himself into a mere mound that could be sacks of carrots, or compost, or whatever one expects to see in the country. And the reason for this manoeuvre came into sight. A large and businesslike launch painted with official letters and numbers came down the middle of the stream. Several men were on board looking very alert with field-glasses and a megaphone and a lifebuoy tied to coils of rope. They spotted the canoe first with great excitement, and then the children. The skipper bawled 'Hullo there!' through the megaphone, a magnified intrusion most unwelcome to the children.

'Hullo there! Are you all right?'

'Yes, thank you.' Their voices sounded as squeaky as young swallows by contrast, and they waved out of politeness.

'Is the canoe damaged?'

'No, thank you.'

But already two men were climbing overboard in thigh waders and splashing across the flooded field.

'I suppose you're the lot we're looking for,' one of them said as they drew nearer. 'Three kids in a canoe who shot under the bridge at Wigglesoke at about twelve o'clock? We're the search party,' he added with a grin. 'Lucky you didn't get out into the Wash. Tide's running out strongly there. What a trio of innocents! Didn't you know any better than that? However, it looks as though we shan't need you, Doctor,' he said to his companion. 'Unless it's to certify them as idiots. Come on now. We'll give you a lift home and tow the canoe. Where do you come from?'

'Green Knowe, near Penny Sokey.'

'It'll take us longer to get back than it took you to come. We'll telephone from the first pub and tell your people what we think of you.'

The children were in a confusion of mixed feelings, they were abashed at being thought so silly, they were delighted at the prospect of the launch, and unwilling to leave Terak, especially without saying good-bye. Ping solved this difficulty by running over Terak's back from collar to seat and jumping down over his heels, as any child does to any challenging mound or boulder. Ida and Oskar followed, and the two men saw nothing but children behaving like children.

'Get in,' they said; and towed the canoe by its mooring rope to the great humiliation of the three sitting in it. 'Don't want you carried off downstream again.' As they neared the launch which was moored to a tree by the main channel, the children looked back for a last glimpse of Terak. There he was, boldly visible, cupping his hands round his mouth to shout: 'I'm going to be a clown.'

'Listen to that cow,' said the Skipper. 'In the worst flood I've known them get stuck in trees. But judging by the noise I should think that one's only separated from its herd. They're like women – can't bear to be alone.'

When the children were pulled on board the launch, they thought of nothing but the glory and power of the return journey, perched up on the top deck and moving, with all the vigour of the engine beneath them, steadily upstream. They bit into their sandwiches with happy teeth, and the men made them hot cocoa and teased them about their reckless canoemanship in a way that left them feeling they were not too bad.

They took a much longer route because the launch could not pass under the stone bridge at Wigglesoke. When they arrived home Miss Sybilla was certainly flustered, but it was difficult to tell whether it was because it had been given out on the one o'clock news that three children were at large on the flood, or whether it was because for some reason the cream would not whip up. Maud Biggin was not upset at all.

'Hullo, Ham, Shem and Japhet!' was all she said, and thanked the rescue party politely but casually, as if they had brought back the cat.

'Children have nine lives,' she said, 'and if Ida takes after her aunt she's got ten.' Even when the men told her that she would receive a bill later for the expenses of the rescue party, she only said: 'Well, all experience has to be paid for, and a triple funeral would have cost much more.'

'Maud! How can you say such things!' Miss Sybilla twisted the string of her melon beads round her hands so that it broke and all the pips shot down inside her clothes. 'Oh!' she said, hurrying out of the room.

Dr Maud grinned at Ida. 'I hope your voyage of

discovery discovered something. They don't always, you know.'

Ida felt at that moment particularly fond of her aunt. It was dreadful not to be able to tell her that they had discovered what would interest her more than anything on earth. She opened her mouth and shut it again tightly. Oskar had promised silence for all of them.

'Come on, don't look so miserable, all of you,' Dr Maud went on. 'I should have thought you'd had a first-class adventure and nobody any the worse.'

U P IN THE ATTIC the children faced each other guiltily.

'It does seem a shame not to tell her. I'm sure she dreams about giants every night,' said Ida. 'If the Committee gave her some money she could take Terak's mother back to her mountains and be shown the caves and the giants still living in them.'

'I promised,' said Oskar. 'And a promise to a Displaced Person is the most solemn promise of all.'

'But Terak's mother wants to go back.'

'You don't understand,' said Ping. 'They don't send

Displaced Persons home. They put them in camps. They might even put them in the Zoo.'

'Without telling Aunt Maud anything about Terak, couldn't we show her the tooth? It would prove one giant.'

'She'd enjoy it much more if she found it herself,' said Ping. 'And we wouldn't have to tell any lies. Where could we put it for her to find?'

'On the gravel path where she always walks up and down thinking out her book.'

'Yes! Since the new gravel was spread there she can't take her eyes off it. She is always hoping, I don't know what for. She must find the tooth before the meeting tomorrow, then she can tell them all.'

Three pairs of sand shoes pattered and skipped down the steep wooden staircase, only noticed by Dr Biggin as a sound of gaiety and by Sybilla Bun as a sound of healthy appetites.

The children crossed the garden as if they were going to mark the fall of the floods. They drew a deep line in blue pencil on the bark of an ash tree at water-level. Anybody could see their only interest was the river. On the way back along the gravel path, Ping stooped to pick up a woolly bear, and the tooth was planted. Anybody could see that he had found something that interested three naturalists. They withdrew to their attic, and there, two went on with the map while the other kept watch at the window. The full length of the roll of lining paper was not enough for their day's travel. They could only put an arrow with the direction: 'To Terak's Windmill.'

'Is she there yet?' the artists on their knees on the floor asked from time to time.

'No, not yet. She ought to have a lot to think about for tomorrow. Why doesn't she come? Bother, here's a caller. What shall we do if someone else picks it up first?'

The caller, however, went along the path looking

only at the house, noticing its ark-like shape and the cluster of heads like the monkeys usually painted on the attic windows of Noah's Arks. At the window of the second storey a giraffe's face should have been seen. He asked for Mrs Oldknow, to whom the house belonged, but she of course was away. Very soon the children saw him retrace his steps looking to left and right, but never on the ground. The iron gate clicked as he latched it and his footfalls along the river path made a kind of clock, to tick-tock away at least five minutes of the children's suspense. Soon the gate clicked again. Seldom, they thought, had the little gravel path had so much traffic. This time it was a neighbour come to ask if the children who had been lost were all right. With anguish they saw her stop half-way down the path and stoop to the ground. It was only to retie a shoe lace, and on she went, thinking perhaps of washing machines.

'She pushed it with her toe,' said Ping. 'After all, it's big. I can see it from here.'

'Perhaps it's too big to be seen,' said Oskar, 'like Terak himself. Perhaps you should have buried it so that only one prong stuck out.'

'Too late now. Here she comes.'

320

Dr Maud Biggin came out to take the air. As usual, she walked along the gravel path, bending forward, her hands clasped behind her, humming a tuneless sound and shuffling the loose surface absent-mindedly as she paused to undo a knot of thought. Sometimes she even, surprisingly for a woman of her age, dribbled one of the rounder stones in little kicks before her for the length of the path. After passing over the tooth no less than six times while the children held their breath and tried to will her to see it, Dr Maud at the seventh time kicked it sharply. It did not roll, but sprang and turned somersaults as if determined with its four molar legs to attract her attention with odd acrobatics. She merely followed it up and kicked it again.

Ida groaned. 'She must be thinking horribly hard. Suppose she kicks it into the river.'

But at the gate Dr Maud turned, as usual, and still spasmodically sending the tooth before her, advanced towards the house. The children, forgetting that they must not seem to expect anything, stood at the open window above her. Ping's face was inscrutable. Ida was trembling, and Oskar had his fiercest will-power stare. Dr Maud suffered a sort of spasm of thought.

She unlocked her hands from behind her, slapped at the midges on her arms and legs, and as if something was now quite clear in her mind set off at twice the pace towards the house and her desk. And she came to the tooth lying where she had kicked it, she as good as passed it – stopped dead, frozen into the bent position that was habitual to her, and stared at it.

'Eh! What! No!' she ejaculated picking it up and turning it over. She wiped her spectacles and looked at it again. Her hand trembled. 'No!' The children had the reward of seeing her look as surprised as people are supposed to look on arriving in heaven.

A little later, when they and Miss Sybilla were ready for supper, Dr Maud came in wearing the crash helmet that sat so incongruously on her studious head. She looked purposeful and secretive, almost guilty.

'Maud! It's supper time. Where are you going?'

'Sorry, Sybilla. Something has turned up – yes – umhum – umhum, has come to my notice, that I must have Dr Odmolar's advice about before tomorrow. Very odd. Very odd indeed. Very interesting. I wish there was more time before the meeting to examine the situation. No time for supper.' Off she went hurrying as if she had nearly tripped up and had to catch up with her balance. The silent supper party heard her motor-cycle kicked into action and pop-popping away down the drive.

A T BREAKFAST NEXT morning, which was the day of the great meeting, Dr Maud was almost unrecognizable with excitement. Her eyes darted here and there and she looked ready to defy the world. So distant were her thoughts that she ate as people eat alone, with a bulging cheek and uninhibited swallowing noises, until Miss Sybilla said:

'Maud! Maud, dear! What are you thinking of today. You are not yourself.'

'Ten times myself today, Sybilla. Today I'm going to make archaeological history. Today I'm going to throw a bomb that will rock the Society.' She pushed away her unfinished plate.

'Maud, dear! Eat your grilled tomatoes while they are hot. They cool in a minute.'

'Grilled tomatoes! Is that all you can think about? Look at the children.' She looked from one to the other and met three pairs of eyes fixed on her with brilliant expectation and sympathy. 'Look at the children

– even they realize that some things are important. Ida! Are you taking your paradurra abyssiniensis regularly?'

'Yes, Aunt Maud.'

'Good girl. Now help Sybilla to carry the chairs and get things ready, and then make yourselves scarce.'

THE RIVER HAD GONE down better than could have been expected in one night. It was back within its banks, running strongly but without those wanton waltzing dimples that the children knew now as danger signals. The canoe had been left at a boatbuilder's on the way home yesterday, because it had sprung a leak in dragging across a submerged strand of barbed wire at the edge of Terak's meadow. The boatbuilder had hired them a punt until the canoe could be repaired. After the light balance of the canoe it seemed as steady as a liner.

HOLIDAY-MAKERS IN launches were venturing out again. The river bank was thick with people carrying picnic baskets and wireless sets. The children decided to go to the millpool and from there to explore a mere crack of a waterway that could only float a boat when the water was high. They found the punt cumbersome to manage, but it had the advantage that one could lie down in it to sunbathe, or sit facing one another to talk and eat, and move freely fore and aft.

The little tributary seeped between an avenue of bulrushes, whose handsome chocolate maces bowed to them as the ripple that the punt pushed before it reached their stalks and set them in motion. Ping said he felt like a mandarin approaching his palace. But it was not a palace that they came upon, but a second and totally secluded pool on whose circumference three little weirs tinkled like musical boxes. Their waters lost themselves in the bulrushes which quickly hushed them, leaving the central expanse still.

The delighted children stopped paddling and every crease faded off the surface. The punt lay as if on a mirror which itself lay in empty space, for above and beyond the frame of bulrushes they could see nothing at all. There were white clouds above them and white clouds below, floating in a complete orb of hyacinth blue. When the swallows dipped, they disputed each fly with the swallow that came up to meet them from below.

The flies themselves in alighting on the surface met foot to foot with their doubles. Even an ice-cream carton alone in the blue space had a twin soul leaning towards it with the same enticing words in pink written upside down. And all the doubles were mysterious, both more shadowy and more brilliant than the originals because of an azure varnish that alone distinguished them. Ping lay over the end of the punt with his arms in the water up to the elbow and considered the black and golden Ping that considered him. Ida was twiddling above the surface with her fingers as if they were mosquito legs, to watch the precision with which the other fingers came to touch them. Oskar was standing, tall and sunburnt, and the other Oskar stuck down into the water exact and beautiful.

'It makes me wonder which is you,' said Ida.

'This one and I are sharing arms,' said Ping. 'He's got me up to the elbow and I've got him, like Siamese twins.'

Oskar said: 'It's only if we stay above the water that there are two. If I were to dive in I should slip right inside him and there would only be one. Doesn't that prove that the one underneath is the real one, and I'm only a sort of water ghost? I'm going to try.'

He neatly dived in, and Ida saw the two Oskars meet and fuse till there was only one swimming away underwater. She was surprised how wretched she felt. 'I wish he would come up again,' she said looking anxiously all round. Oskar's head bobbed up some distance away.

'There he is,' said Ping. 'Unless it's only a water ghost coming up to climb in the punt with us.'

'Let's all be water ghosts then, in case,' said Ida, and in they flashed.

When after struggling up over the side with elbows bent up like grasshoppers' legs, they were all in the punt again and getting their breath, Oskar said: 'I was right, you see. That was the real one.'

'Which one are you now, then?'

'I still feel the real one.'

'Then what's the one that's in the water now, underneath you?'

'Oh, I expect that's just the one that thought he was me.'

'We shall get horribly mixed up,' said Ida, diving in again. When she came up, she turned on her back and floated among the reflected clouds. The sun beat on her eyelids which looked to her crimson like pieces of stained glass.

They never had a more delicious day. There was no sound except the splash of their dives and the drip off their hair and elbows as they sat in the punt, and their own happy nonsense. The pool was a world as much their own as their most private thoughts. Ida's nicest dreams for a long time afterwards were ringed with a palisade of swinging bulrushes.

Towards the end of the afternoon she saw Oskar, who had gone exploring, standing among the bulrushes with something in his arms. 'Bring the punt,' he shouted. 'I've got something here I don't want to drop.' Ida paddled across to him and he climbed in with his treasure. 'I found it bedded in the rushes.' He was hugging a green glass bottle. It was thick and balloon-shaped with a long neck and a rim at the mouth. It had a cork tied with wire and covered with sealing wax. It was not heavy enough to be full, but it had something inside.

'It was bedded in the rushes and all grown over. I trod on it by mistake and it went right down in the mud. I expect it came down once in a flood and was left in the rushes when the water went down. Isn't it a splendid shape.' Nobody had a corkscrew to open it. They must wait till they got home.

As they approached Green Knowe, they saw crowds of people stopping to look over the garden wall with amused curiosity. The drive was full of cars belonging to the archaeologists attending Dr Biggin's meeting, which was taking place indoors behind wide open windows. Miss Sybilla Bun was standing outside with an expression of deep but muddled distress, lacing her fingers into her beads as if trying to tell half a dozen rosaries at once. She was eavesdropping, if it can be called that when people have forgotten everything but their desire to make themselves heard. For the meeting was in an uproar. The sounds that came across the garden were surprising in the extreme, as if only the most preposterous voices could force their way out from the angry buzz inside.

Ida, Oskar and Ping were less squeamish than Miss Sybilla. They dropped their picnic baskets and ran to the open windows to satisfy their curiosity.

Nearly all the guests were standing up, very red in the face. The chairman was shouting: 'Order! Order!' and banging the table with one hand while with the other he pushed his white hair on end, leaving his spectacles mislaid and useless on top. Some members were shouting at him, some at each other, some simply into the air which was already so full of noise it couldn't absorb any more. 'I protest!' 'Shame!' 'Sit down!' 'Outrage to the dignity of . . .' 'Impudent fake!' 'A plastic advertisement for the forthcoming Dental Conference!' 'All the more shocking because of the previous honourable record . . .' 'An insult to our revered chairman.' One gentleman lifting his hand in a gesture of deep shock, accidentally knocked off the pincenez of another, and for a moment or two they snarled at each other like a couple of fox-terriers. Another crumpling his sheaf of papers into a ball hurled it down in front of the chairman, shouting: 'I resign!' and elbowed his way out of the room.

All this time Dr Maud Biggin stood her ground and continued to make herself heard when she could. 'This most startling piece of evidence . . . bewildering and stimulating lines of thought . . . no time as yet to submit laboratory tests . . . The necessity of an immediate charter to explore the gravel fields . . . probable proof on our own doorstep . . . duty of facing up to truth however unlikely . . .' and so on. She was sorrowful but undaunted, and perfectly even-tempered under abuse. When however somebody pushed up opposite her and bawled: 'I accuse Dr Maud Biggin of fraud,' she replied almost casually: 'You're a silly old fool!' and sat down.

The three children applauded vigorously from the window-sill. The Committee appeared to notice them for the first time and even to see themselves as others saw them. The noise died down while the Chairman announced sternly that the meeting was adjourned indefinitely. He then made his way out, stopping to apologize to Dr Biggin for his inability to keep order. 'Scientific passion ran very high, dear lady, very high indeed.' The others put themselves and their papers in order and followed him out. Some marched past their hostess with a harsh inclination of the head, some shook hands and apologized for 'bad behaviour in some quarters' as if their own had been any better. Old Harry put a wax-white hand on her shoulder and after moving his thin wolfish lips in and out, said:

'I would like it, Maud. I would like it very much. But it won't do. Pity. It's just a little ahead of the evidence.'

'Evidence! This is the evidence,' she retorted, angry at last, shaking Terak's tooth under his nose. '*It's a giant's tooth*. All we need now is to find the gravel bed that it came out of and fix the date. Admittedly I don't understand its almost perfect preservation, but analysis of the site will perhaps explain that.'

Old Harry shook his head and patted her shoulder again. 'A pity, Maud. A great pity. But you took it very well.'

Dr Maud turned to the three children who were looking on all this time with profound sympathy and indignation. She winked at them.

'Ever heard the proverb: "There's none so blind as those that won't see"? Anyway, I called one of them a silly old fool, didn't I? There's no pleasure like letting rip.'

Meanwhile the departing guests, ashamed of their behaviour to one hostess, were thanking Miss Sybilla with extra warmth for her kindness and the most delicious luncheon. Really exquisite. They smiled, 'we shall never forget it'. So Miss Sybilla came in and said: 'There! After all, Maud, it went off very well, I think. I think they all enjoyed it. Perhaps just a little indigestion in the afternoon. The lobster was very rich. But it passed off.'

T HE GREEN BOTTLE was taken upstairs to be opened in private.

'It has been thrown out of a ship in the middle of the ocean, I expect,' said Ida, 'with a farewell message inside from the last survivor. But I can't think how it got here. The tide couldn't bring it up so far from the coast.'

'Perhaps it could sail upstream before a strong east wind.'

'It would have to go through hundreds of locks.' Ida jerked the word 'locks' very loud, because at that moment the cork came free. 'It is a message. I knew it would be.' She pulled out a roll of parchment, kneeling on the floor to spread it out. It had been rolled up so long that it shot back like a roller blind. It took all three of them to hold it flat. It was closely written in a difficult handwriting. The paper was headed with an ink drawing and a title. The picture showed the silhouette of a tall house in a clearing among big trees. A full moon appeared to rest on the point of the roof. The title read: 'The Island of the Throning Moon'.

They all read it aloud with different degrees of excitement and disbelief in their voices.

'He was marooned on an island,' said Ida. But Ping pointed with his slim finger.

'I think that house is this house.' And so it could have been.

After a gasping moment Ida's brain began to work again.

'One of these islands round here must be called the Island of the Throning Moon. And it must be somewhere opposite this house so that when the moon is full it looks like that, from there.'

'We'll have to go by moonlight, then,' said Oskar.

'A Yellow Chinese moon, like a lantern,' said Ping lovingly.

'Now let's try to read what it says.'

'THIS IS THE CONFESSION of Piers Madeley Vicar of the Parish of Penny Sokey, written in the year of Our Lord 1647. It has been my Misfortune to undergo an Experience so far outside the Logic that should rule civilized Thought, that the whole Fabric of my Mind is suffering Strain therefrom. Inasmuch as I cannot disburthen myself of this Matter to any living Soul, neither to my Lord Bishop nor to any of my Parishioners learned or simple, for fear that they, being unable to believe me, should impute to me either Witchcraft or a Lunatic humour, Yet because of the Need that afflicts me to confide to some Human Being concerning that which I have seen, and been present at, I have devised to set it down in writing enclosed in a Bottle, entrusting it to the fearful Floods that now overwhelm the Land, that they may carry my Confession away from here, and haply after many

Days it may come into his Hands who will give it Credence. And lest it fall into the Hands of ignorant or malicious Persons, during my Lifetime (which if such Trails continue cannot be long) I have writ it in Latin. Of which, though the Language may be faulty, for I have ever found Latin a difficult Tongue, being but an indifferent Scholar, yet every Word is true. And this I swear before the Almighty's awful Throne.'

'Oh, Blow!' said Ida. 'All that and we can't read it.'

'We can go and find out,' said Ping in his little remote voice.

'It's obviously something pretty awful.'

'Demons,' Ping smiled deliciously, 'by Moonlight.'

Ida was still thinking aloud. 'Flying Horse Island is exactly opposite here. Surely he can't have been so frightened by *them*. I know they aren't supposed to be here, but wouldn't anybody think it a lovely secret to have? There's an island beyond that. Perhaps we could see the house from there. We will have to go anyway. The moon will be full tomorrow. We will watch what time it rises tonight, and tomorrow it will be forty minutes later.'

The next day, very early in the morning, when the moon was setting and queer enough for anything, they set off for the island lying north of Flying Horse, to find out whether Green Knowe could be seen from there. To their surprise it could not. It sank back into a belt of trees among which even the yews could not be distinguished. It was hard to believe that a house, which, when you were near it, cut into the sky so proudly and dominated the surroundings with the assurance of its stone-built corners, could from half a mile away efface itself completely. The children looked for it in vain.

'We are on the wrong track,' said Ida. 'If we can't see it by daylight we certainly couldn't at night. But just *in case* the drawing is of Green Knowe, we will come out tonight and watch to see if the moon really does pass exactly over the gable point. Perhaps it doesn't at all. I can't imagine fearful things happening near Green Knowe. I know it is very old, but it feels like a refuge, something to be trusted.'

'Green Knowe hasn't been there always,' said Oskar. 'Perhaps whatever frightened poor Piers Madeley was older than the house. Something so old that it didn't make sense, like the worst things in dreams.'

They calculated that the moon should rise at eleven and might be over the house by midnight. There was a light in Maud Biggin's room when the children crept out. 'She's still thinking about the tooth. She won't hear us.'

Outside, had there been street lights or headlights you would have thought it was dark. There were massed shadows on the earth, but the sky was aware of the moon just under the horizon, and was catching a reflection of its light and relaying it to the river. Seen from the punt, the world was a symmetrical but unfamiliar pattern of bulky blacknesses jutting on to quicksilver. The daylight line between reality and reflection was gone. All the shapes were equally black, equally dense, and hung like clouds whose position in space is unknown, so that it was only if the punt passed through it, instead of bumping on it, that a reflected shadow could be known as such. The water, that is, as much of its surface as could be seen, wound among looming masses which at one moment, if one put out a hand to ward them off, were found not to be there, at another would be lowering, smothering and catching on one's hair. The course of the river that they thought they knew so well was as mysterious as a foreign language. They had to keep touching the surface with their paddles to reassure themselves that it was there, that they were on it, that it was the river they knew.

When at last the moon, heralded by a coppery haze, appeared above the flat earth and rolled behind the cottages like an immense orange beach ball, the enchantment was complete. Moonlight alone was a breathtaking adventure. The Amazon could not have bettered it.

At its first coming the moon seemed almost to bounce up, its movements could be watched. But once properly in the sky it hung like time. The children were so much under its spell that anything which might happen in its wild and ancient light could only seem in keeping. They were afraid only of missing the magic moment when the moon should sit throning on the point of their bedroom roof. They paddled up and down the home stretch, passing repeatedly.

'Of course!' said Ida suddenly. 'Green Knowe itself is on an island! *It happens here.*'

They moored the punt in their boathouse, and stole back hesitantly on to the lawns, for once hand in hand. There was no denying that it looked very strange. When the sun is in the sky every eye turns away to escape the blaze, but the moon compels sight and thought to follow its course up towards the zenith, with the result that by contrast the height of trees and buildings seems dwarfed. Green Knowe seemed smaller, but at the same time charged with awe. It had changed its friendly old fairy-tale quality for something far older and terrifyingly different. The house drew and held their attention so that the transformation of the moonlight-flattened garden went unnoticed. The bone-white walls were streaked with shadow patterns of leaves that were rhythmic and interlacing like patterns left by the ebb tide on sands. It had a curious look of wickerwork, which the rippling unevenness of the roof repeated. By daylight Green Knowe looked planted on the earth deliberately for all time, but now the glimmering outline before them looked as if it grew out of the earth, lightly springing up. No windows showed, but the house had a kind of dim glow. If Ida allowed herself to think of the walls as woven of rushes, instead of stone-built three feet thick, then the hollow interior was so much the bigger, and having no upper floors must be imagined, by the marvel of its being constructed at all, as a sort of cathedral.

'Doesn't it look queer,' said Ping. 'Almost as if the moon shone through it!'

'It's built of rushes,' said Oskar as though that were

not a matter for disbelief.

The moon was going up like a kite. She had cleared the trees and was moving above the slant of the roof, just short of the finial. A drift of silky cloud was moving along to meet her ascent. The children approached the apex of the shadow of the building where it lay across the ground. Quite suddenly the cold brilliance above and the darkness into which they were walking filled them with a sense of fear as limitless as the night. They all had the same thought – while their eyes had been mesmerized by the moon *they had forgotten to watch out*. In that moment they became aware of a figure just in front of them, standing immobile at the point of the shadow and gazing up at the point of the house as they themselves had done a second before. The dark form was tall and roughly cloaked. It seemed to have a stag's head with antlers, and long naked human legs. The children dropped to the ground and backed into the nearest clump of bushes, from which they looked out like foxes. In the unnatural silence they could hear each other's teeth chattering. It sounded loud enough to give them away but they could not control it. It grew, as if in a nightmare the volume had been turned up. It seemed to shake the shadows and fill the open spaces, to materialize in figures that had not been there and now were. They grew out of the milky darkness and showed as silhouettes with deer's horns, with skins flapping over their shoulders as they moved. Each carried a spear which he shook high as he leaped repeatedly in salute to the moon, a wild homage which took place in absolute silence except for the unexplained rattling which increased as the leaping grew more furious. It had grown out of the chattering of their own teeth but was now something quite outside themselves and very threatening. Meanwhile the leader, wearing the stag's antlers, remained motionless like an inspired sorcerer proud with power.

As the moon moved to her appointed throne and shone there resplendent and worshipable, the leader gave a long wolf howl and broke into a pantomime of dreadful activity. The horned crowd opened out into a ritual dance, stamping round him to the accompaniment of a rhythmic rattling that was continuous and unnerving. It suggested rudimentary instruments such as tambourines and 'the bones.' It suggested also pursuit and death and the rattle of dry reed beds. The movements and gestures of the dancers

were only less frightful than those of the leader, who was a genius in horror. They had a dramatic but inexplicable compulsion. The white-faced children felt that their limbs twitched and stamped of their own accord, that they could not keep out of it. This lasted until the moon had passed over, and was reigning, gloriously independent, in her sky. Then the dancers slipped the deerskin off their heads, wearing them like capes, and whirling round they charged – as it seemed to the children – straight at them, as if they had only waited for the end of their ritual to take vengeance on the intruders. They came within a spear's length – but passed straight on, making for the river bank. In that dreadful moment the children saw at close quarters the savage faces painted in black and white stripes, the hands painted red. They saw too, glinting in the cold light, the cause of that skeletal rattling, for every hunter wore round his neck strings of tusks, or horns, or teeth which knocked together as they swung to his movements. It was not a sound that could travel far, but the chatter of dead teeth must have come as the first warning of danger to nervous ears waking out of sleep in the marshlands.

The hunters streamed by the children, almost

jostling them, but as the leaders had passed them unnoticed, sō did all the rest, like a herd of animals. They boarded canoes that from the sound of it were hidden in the rushes near at hand. Their rapid paddle strokes drove through the water, where the moorhens fled with loud midnight cries, and the wild duck wheeled into flight with half-breathed clucks of alarm.

The children cautiously parted the leaves and crept out from their hiding-place. They looked down the river hoping to see the craft with its standing crew. But the moon had now met the shoal of cloud and passed behind it, so that from one moment to the next everything became dim and shadowy. A cold shudder of wind blew on the backs of their necks and ears, and rustled the balancing surface of blade and leaf along the river's edge and across the wide meadows. They were standing at midnight, alone, under a sky that was there before either earth or moon had been, and would be there long after. In this agonizing second of revelation that *all* passes, the bark of a disturbed heron caused them to clutch each other, and jerked loose their tongues.

'Where can we go?' asked Ida. 'Where is there for us to go to, now?'

'I suppose we could just *look* in that – that wattle . . . place,' said Ping, for once hesitant.

'We've got the busman hermit for company. He's been wherever this is, once,' said Oskar. 'I mean *whenever* this is. But I don't want to go on the river. It's too much. We are *really* displaced now.' Yet they turned instinctively towards the house – 'that wattle place', as Ping called it. Because where else? Above its obscure silhouette the cloud was outlined with silver on its upper edge, where suddenly a dazzling diamond white segment appeared, and the moon came out. She dropped the cloud from about her, and round and brilliant as a singing note she hung in the centre of the sky.

Under her lovely light Green Knowe was revealed again, gentle, heavy and dreaming, with its carefully spaced bushes and trees standing in their known positions enriched with moonlight on their heads and shadows like the folds of Cinderella's ball dress behind them.

The children gasped with joy and relief, and slowly, taking in, holding, and keeping what they saw, they moved towards home. They all three slept in one bed that night. Because, as Oskar had said, it was too much. As Ping wriggled himself into the little space allotted to him between Ida and Oskar, his last words were: 'They had as many beads as Miss Sybilla.' And he laughed to himself.

'AUNT MAUD,' said Ida (by arrangement with the others), as she helped herself to cereals, 'have there ever been wickerwork cathedrals? I mean, in the Stone Age.' She spoke casually, as one might ask: 'Did they eat honey?'

Dr Biggin put a spoonful in her mouth while she turned over a page, and then answered rather mouthily: 'There are some still, in places like Borneo and the Persian Gulf. Or were till the other day. Nowadays civilization moves so fast you can't travel fast enough to keep up with it. The only thing anyone can say for certain is, it was there yesterday, if they haven't pulled it down since.'

'Oh! Might they be as big as this house?'

'They couldn't be as big, but they might look it, because of being so much bigger than anything else around. They *look* the biggest house you can think of. And they are, because you couldn't possibly make anything bigger out of the material.'

'Oh!' said Ida again meekly. 'Thank you.'

'Do Stone Age people worship the moon?' she ventured again a little later on.

'Eh? How should I know! Very probably. Goddess of the Chase and patroness of fishes.'

Miss Sybilla burst unexpectedly into the discussion. Rattling her beads with excitement and looking rather pink, she recited:

> *Queen and huntress, chaste and fair,*
> *Now the sun has gone to sleep,*
> *Seated on thy silver chair*
> *State in wonted splendour keep.*

She smacked her lips.

Oskar and Ping looked at her as at an oracle.

'*Seated on thy silver chair,*' repeated Ping softly. And Oskar continued: '*State in wonted splendour keep.*'

Miss Sybilla blushed crimson at their appreciation. 'Don't you know that poem, Ida?'

'Yes, Aunt Sybilla. It goes on about *Goddess excellently bright.* I like it. Excellently bright sounds sharp, like scissors. As if the Moon was cutting the sky.'

'You've all been sleeping with the moon on your

pillows,' said Dr Biggin. 'You too, Sybilla. I never knew you were poetical.'

'It was so romantic last night. It made me feel quite ...What shall I say? Quite *wild*. I wanted to dance on the lawns.'

Dr Maud, for want of any other woman to wink at, winked at Ida. But the children were not laughing. They looked at fat Sybilla Bun and her beads, with eyes full of questioning astonishment.

IT IS NOT TO BE expected that every day of the holidays will be filled with such adventures. Ida, Oskar and Ping were never at a loss and never bored. Many pleasant ordinary things can be done a second time, though they are never twice alike. The really extraordinary things can never be repeated.

One day, near the end of their time, Ping came back from the village where he had been with Miss Sybilla to carry her basket for her to the bus stop. He had been away a long time, while Ida and Oskar had been kicking their heels waiting to start out until he should come back. He was very excited and could not get his news told.

349

'What an age you have been,' said Ida.

'I know. I've done a lot in the time. There's going to be a Circus at Penny Sokey.'

'Well, we shan't be here to go to it. Hurry up, it's our last day on the river.'

Ping began again, refusing to budge even when pushed.

'I saw the posters in the shop. It begins tonight, so we could go. The posters say – Ida! You are not listening.'

'You can tell us on the way,' said Ida walking off with Oskar full tilt towards the boathouse.

Ping caught up and danced along backward ahead of them to make them listen.

'It's exciting. It's important. The poster says:

GREAT NEW STAR TURN
TERAK THE GIANT.'

'What!' Ida and Oskar plonked everything they were carrying and stood stock still.

'He's done it,' said Ping. 'He's a clown. We must take Dr Biggin and let her see him. I have been helping at the shop, unloading a van full of boxes. That's why

350

I was so long. I have got some money. They say they are short-handed, so if we all go back and help we can make enough to invite Dr Biggin to the circus as a Thank You. Then she will have to come.'

Ping was quite right in his understanding of Dr Biggin's mind. She was not very interested in circuses except as survivals – very degenerate of course – of circuses and games long past. But she appreciated gratitude, and as the children had invited her she accepted. She was, besides, in a high good humour. Ida had been measured for the last time and had grown three-quarters of an inch. Miss Sybilla, of course, had said it was nothing to do with those silly old grass seeds. It was the Good Food the child had had and plenty of fresh air. The two ladies had wrangled and back-bitten on the subject, with the result that Miss Sybilla had refused to come to the circus, giving as her reason that she couldn't bear to see a horrid man bullying the poor helpless tigers. Which was a funny way of looking at it but quite true. Oskar understood. The tigers stood for his fearless father, overpowered, imprisoned and angry.

They hired a second canoe to take Dr Biggin and Ida. She proved to be a powerful canoeist. As she paddled, she made wild noises, which she said she had heard savages do to keep the beat, on her voyages of exploration. Only, she said, they stood up to paddle. Oskar and Ping had been sitting in their canoe, because they thought it was to be a sedate grown-up excursion. They now accepted the challenge and stood to paddle, for of course Ping had been practising this too. Dr Biggin urged them on with short barking shouts and the two canoes raced neck and neck. It was a wonder Oskar and Ping did not take a double header into the water. Dr Biggin did not care whether they did or not, which is probably why it did not happen. They began to wish she had been with them on the river all the time. It was stimulating to be with someone who was always thinking of jungles or marshes, who when she shouted: 'Paddle, boys!' might be addressing pigmies or South American Indians. They felt guiltily that they had underrated her company. Ping remembered the yellow cat that had been lying along a branch over their heads and that reminded him of a tiger. He felt that if Dr Biggin had been with them, it would have been a real one.

However, after a while she roared out: 'Take it easy, boys. I'm an old woman,' and got out her cigarettes.

Ida and the boys paddled along till they came to the wide water-meadows. At the far end they could see the roof of the Big Top, surrounded by swings, tractors, trucks and caravans of every sort.

Dr Biggin, between puffs, said she liked tents. 'I have no doubt tents go back nearly as far as wattle. As far behind my civilized giants as they are behind us. And that's a thought! Right back. And funny men too. As soon as there were three men, one of them was a funny man.'

'Why are funny men always little?' said Ida, who couldn't keep her mouth shut any longer. 'What if one of them was a Giant?' Three pairs of eyes met in an electric flicker of excitement, for Maud Biggin had as yet no idea what she was to see. She merely grunted at Ida's childishness, too foolish to need an answer. The children, however, were as pleased as if she had exclaimed: 'I would give my eyes to see a giant just once.' They knew she would soon grunt to a different tune.

As they drew nearer to the Circus, a noise as savage and primitive as anyone could imagine travelled to meet them along the water. Several steam organs were playing different tunes of giant loudness. The din seemed to tear one ear away from the other. It was painful but intensely

353

exciting. Mixed in with the strident clashing tunes, and the babel of men yelling the attractions of their swings or coconut shies, were occasional angry jungle roars and sinister cat-fight snarls. Quietly detached from all this, walking in single file towards them across the meadow was a man leading three elephants. The children thought they were coming for a drink and were delighted at getting a preview at close quarters. They paddled nearer to the elephants, but the keeper shouted and waved his arms, and Dr Biggin rapped out: 'Lay in to the far bank!' There they held on to the willow branches and watched while the elephants, squealing like pigs, took to the water, making as they submerged their great bodies, waves that would have capsized the canoes. This, of course, was the best jungle scene the children had ever had, and their imaginations were so fired they almost managed not to hear the din from the circus ground. The elephants lolled and rolled slowly about in the water all ways up. Sometimes nothing showed but the big rounds of their feet, sometimes the pointed domes of their foreheads or backs stuck up like rocks washed with muddy ripples, and disappeared again. Or the great island of their barrel sides divided the stream with water running off it all round as if off a hillside. Once quite near the canoe a snorkel trunk-end came up near Ida, tumbling in the air like a laughing mouth without a face, followed later by a flat wrinkled drift of sideface, out of which a small humorous eye opened, saw her, winked and submerged again, while the canoe rocked with the backwash of huge but soft displacement of water. When the keeper called, the elephants like children who obey but only just, slowly drew to the bank, squirting their backs as they waded out, then rolling in the mud again so that they had to have a second wash. They set off then in single file back to their job, frisking their comic tails and vigorously swinging their trunks. By this time crowds of children were running up from the circus ground, some luckier than others with buns to offer, which the elephants took from their hands in passing with no sign of gratitude except the smile they sucked in with the bun.

In the distance a drum began booming while a man yelled into a megaphone: 'Walk up! Walk up!'

They hurried downstream towards the mooring place, passing the caravans and trailers, among which Oskar noticed a truck with a hooped roof of new canvas, extra high.

'Look!' he said, pointing. Ida and Ping, who in the

excitement of the elephants and the circus in general had momentarily forgotten what they had come specially to see, gasped with a sudden rush of joy. 'That must be HIS!' From this moment they were all agog. They moored the canoe and leapt out, urging Dr Biggin to hurry. She looked at them quizzically as if to say she didn't know they were such babies. But all she actually said, bringing out a tin from her pocket, was: 'Have a bull's-eye. They calm the nerves.'

They had good seats by the ring, and sat there listening to the creaking ropes and the flapping of the ornamental scallops round the tiers of the roof, and the hubbub of people coming in, until the band began to play inside and drowned everything else.

When the show opened with an inrush of clowns the children were positively sparking with excitement. One after another the clowns cart-wheeled or somersaulted in, yelling 'Hola!' and tripping up on their trousers. But they were all midgets or little men, and before they had run out the horses were there, plumed, reined-in, with round eyes and flaring nostrils, manoeuvring without riders, scattering sawdust and foam as they tossed and pirouetted. Next, at a steamroller's pace, the elephants came on. They struck Ida as noble, wise, gentle and merry – intelligent enough to do anything. But all that their trainers had been able to think of was to make them stand on their heads on low wooden stools. It was a sad thing to see. Afterwards the biggest one was covered with a cloth painted like a bus. It stopped by a toy bus stop, and all the clowns clambered or sprang on to its back, clutching each other by the seat of the trousers or the ears or neckties till all were on somehow. The last, before leaping on, pulled the elephant's tail on which was a bell, to set it in motion. It lumbered out holding a motor horn in its trunk and tooting as it went. These and other amusements, though they made the children laugh with everyone else, were not enough to quieten their fierce impatience for Terak. Ida who had done theatricals at school knew that he couldn't have had more than a few days to rehearse in. Perhaps he would only be a side show – 5p to see the Giant. And they had no money left. It was a thought that spoiled several turns for her, including some Chinese acrobats who were sending Ping into a trance of approval as they flew through the air and landed as lightly as birds on each other's shoulders. The horses came in again, and then the lions. Turn after turn and still no

Terak. There was the man who stands on a rolling ball, balances a chair by one leg on his forehead and invites his lady friend in tights to climb up him and sit in it. It was all done so slowly and so carefully the children were mad with impatience.

At last the clowns ran in chattering like monkeys that are frightened, and pointing backwards to the entrance passage. The children saw Terak first, leaping to their feet, waving and shouting: 'There he is!' Their voices were drowned in the general clamour of surprise.

Terak was dressed in tartan trews *and* a kilt, and a velvet jacket. His mother's bagpipes were under his arm. He was disguised with a red beard and hair and false eyebrows. His boots were four times as large as his feet and his sporran was as big as a bear cub. It was a shock to Ida that he did not look like himself. But there was no mistaking his eyes, nor himself when he got going. It was an effort to take her attention off him even for a second, but she had to look to see how her Aunt Maud was taking it. Dr Biggin was sitting at the very edge of the ring. With her round back, her arms crossed and hugging herself, and her nice wrinkled monkey face, she looked as if she might be one of the performers. She was watching with black shifting eyes, but not showing more interest than she had done in the other items. She was steadily sucking bull's-eyes.

Terak had the gift of stage presence, quite apart from his size, although at his first appearance it was this which had made everybody gasp. But oddly enough, though he had spent his life in unwilling invisibility, now that people saw him they could not look at anything else. He had a genius for making any silly little action both funny and lovable. The public took to him at sight and roared applause, which he acknowledged by blowing kisses and shaking himself by the hand, his incredible eyes creased up with joy at so much company. His own huge pleasure was in itself both ridiculous and infectious, it was a gathering snowball of success. The clowns meanwhile fooled around, shaking hands with each other, getting under his feet, and scattering with squawks when he shoo'd them, only to return. At last he cunningly caught them one by one, buzzing like flies, and after various attempts to get rid of them he hung them up by their trousers or the back of their coats to hooks on the main tent-poles. There they hung as if on a fly-paper. His great wish, it seemed, was to make music, for which he had his bagpipes, which he dusted and caressed. But something was wrong. He could not get them to play. He blew and pumped, but either no sound came or the wrong one – a moaning fog-horn, or a dreadful hee-haw just behind his ear, or a police whistle. At this last a clown with a blue helmet and a formidable rubber truncheon cycled in looking for trouble but quite unable to see Terak, against whose legs he leaned his bicycle. Both he and it were lifted up and hung on a post, simply to leave the would-be musician in peace. After much tinkering and shaking Terak drew out of the mouthpiece of his instrument the inevitable string of sausages, and settled down to some soulful playing. Immediately, out of his pockets, his sleeves, the back of his coat collar, his sporran, came half a dozen wriggling dachshunds, howling their hearts out to the music. He pushed them all back again and again. He bribed them with sausages, but it was no good. In the end they all made music together in their own fashion, the clowns hanging up on the poles joining in with mouth-organs, comb and paper, yodelling, whistles or any percussion that their position allowed them to make. The audience could not resist joining in too, till Terak, rising to his full height, roared in a voice that would have silenced lions:

He held in his hand a shrivelled balloon, which he began to inflate. Instantly there was dead silence. It was a giant-sized balloon which slowly, slowly grew bigger. When it was beginning to get tight, Terak tried scratching it with his finger. At the squawk, out popped the dachshunds again barking as if at a snake. They were silenced and treated one by one with puffs of air out of the balloon. Its diminished size was then inflated again to the same point and bigger. The tension and expectation were kept up so long that the audience became quite hysterical. The clowns hanging on the poles kicked and pleaded for mercy as the balloon grew fabulously, filling the space of the ring and bouncing and wobbling on its mouthpiece. Terak seemed frightened of it himself. He brought it to his mouth for another blow, then let a little out instead. He became madly brave, taking in a last huge lungful and addressing himself to the balloon with distended cheeks. It exploded with a bang so loud you could hardly hear it. Terak went over on his back. The hooked-up clowns whizzed down to earth (they were all on pulleys) and ran for their lives leaving their coats and trousers on the hooks. The dachshunds swarmed

out to lick Terak's face and by an unrehearsed accident two of them ran off to have a tug-of-war over his beard which had come off. And there was Terak sitting up with his own face exposed, blowing kisses to Ping, Oskar and Ida and tossing them spare balloons. Before they could do anything but grin back, the midget clowns rushed in again with a strawberry net which they threw over Terak's head and tied with ropes. Then an elephant was brought in to drag him away.

This was the end of the programme. The audience stood up to clap. They stamped and shouted: 'Terak! We want Terak!'

The children turned to each other. 'Isn't he having a wonderful time! Let's go and talk to him.' Then they remembered that this was a benefit appearance for Dr Biggin.

'What do you think of the Giant?' they asked, but at that moment 'God save the Queen' began and everybody had to stand up and be quiet. When it was over, they all began again. 'What did you think of the Giant? Were you surprised? That proves it, doesn't it? No one can say your tooth isn't real now.'

Dr Biggin smiled knowingly and condescendingly. 'I enjoyed him immensely. He was a really wonderful fake.'

'Fake!' cried the children, appalled. 'He was real, as real as anything. Didn't you see his face when the dogs pulled his beard off? Didn't you see his teeth, like your tooth?'

'The rest of him was just as false as his beard. They can fake anything nowadays. There aren't teeth like the one I found. That was the whole point of it. Probably this was a man on stilts, padded. It's an old trick.'

'But Aunt Maud! His eyes! They are as big as horses' eyes and all laughing. And he saw us.'

'Probably done with magnifying lenses. But it doesn't matter how it was done. We weren't meant to spot it.'

'Let's go and find him, and then you will see.'

'My dear children! I almost envy you your credulity! We won't go and find him, firstly because they would never allow us to see how it was done, and secondly, because if they did, it would be the first big disillusionment of your young lives. A heap of gadgets and an empty suit.'

'But we thought you believed in giants.'

'I believe there were giants once – 20,000 years ago. But not now. There aren't any now. Because if there were we should know, shouldn't we. They're not things you could overlook.'

'But . . .' said the children, but gave it up in despair.

As they were walking back to the canoes, each with a large ice-cream which Dr Biggin had fallen behind to pay for, Ida said: 'I'm sorry, Ping. One can't do anything for grown-ups. They're hopeless.'

Ping sighed. 'I can't understand, when it's the thing they want most in the world, and it's there before their eyes, why they won't see it.'

'They are often like that,' said Oskar wisely. 'They don't like *now*. If it's really interesting it has to be *then*.'

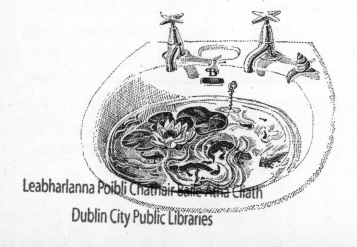